TOWERING

TOWERING

ALEX FLINN

An Imprint of HarperCollinsPublishers

HarperTeen is an imprint of HarperCollins Publishers.

Towering
Copyright © 2013 by Alex Flinn

Library of Congress Cataloging-in-Publication Data
Flinn, Alex.
   Towering / Alex Flinn. — First edition.
      pages   cm
   Summary: "A contemporary retelling of Rapunzel told from the alter-
nating perspectives of three teens whose fates unknowingly bind them
together to destroy a greater evil"— Provided by publisher.
   ISBN 978-0-06-202417-6 (hardback)
   ISBN 978-0-06-202418-3 (lib. bdg.)
   ISBN 978-0-06-227632-2 (international ed.)
   [1. Fairy tales. 2. Magic—Fiction. 3. Blessing and cursing—
Fiction. 4. Missing persons—Fiction. 5. Drug abuse—Fiction.] I. Title.
PZ8.F5778Tow   2013   2012051742
[Fic]—dc23   CIP
                                              AC

13 14 15 16 17   LP/RRDH   10 9 8 7 6 5 4 3 2 1
❖
First Edition

For my mother

1

Rachel

I had not been outside in years. I wasn't sure how many, exactly, because I didn't keep track from the beginning. I didn't realize I'd need to. But my dresses had been replaced many times, at least six or seven, and I could tell I'd become taller. The top of my head didn't reach the bottom of my window when I came here. I could see the sky, the sky and nothing else, blue sky some days, gray sky most. Then, I could see out only if I stood on my toes. But finally, at seventeen, I could see out easily. The birds, which are often below me, the clouds above, and the tall, green forest with miles and miles of trees.

But no one could see me. My window was high, high above the ground, and no one ever came this far, no one but Mama.

Mama wasn't my real mother. I knew that, but it felt better to call her Mama. My real mother was killed when I was a baby, murdered like the woman in white or Rebecca, people in books I'd read, and the person who killed her might come back for me. That was why Mama spirited me away in the night and brought me here. To protect me. Mama promised that when my real mother's killer was found, she would let me go out into the world, but only when I might go without fear.

That was also why she cut my hair.

When I was little, before I came here, I had beautiful, wavy, spun-gold princess hair. Mama would sit up every night, brushing it a hundred strokes, then braid it into two long, shiny braids that ran down my back like a train going nowhere. This was our nightly ritual, and I loved it. I knew that my hair was special, and that I was special because of it.

Sometimes, I'd wake in the early morning and find Mama there, pressing my braids against her wrinkled lips by moonlight, whispering, "Sleep, my lovely, my only lovely." And later, when I woke for good, she'd brush and braid it again. My hair grew fast, and once a week, Mama cut it, so that it would grow no longer than my waist.

Mama kept me out of sight even then. I didn't go to school but read at Mama's knee. Sometimes, I was allowed to go outside and play, on days that weren't too sunny, days when people weren't out. Mama watched me carefully, as if one of the hawks in the sky might take me in its talons and carry me off.

But, one day, I was playing and Mama was tending her garden, not paying much attention to me. I was digging my own hole. It was May, and I was planting carrots. We'd gotten this wonderful thing, a tape with carrot seeds on it, so that they could be planted exactly the right distance apart. I dug a little trench like Mama had taught me, and I was about to show it to her, so she would give me the tiny, golden carrot seeds when, all of a sudden, I saw a face at our gate.

A little girl! She was about my age, I thought, with curly, brown hair and spots on her face that people on television called freckles. I should have said something to Mama, but I didn't. I knew, with a child's instinct, that if I said something, she would pull me inside and I didn't want to go inside. I went to the gate.

"Hello," I said. "Who are you?"

"Are you Rachel?" Though her hair was drab brown, her eyes were a beautiful shade of blue, almost purple like the irises Mama grew.

"Yes," I said. "How did you know?"

"I knew by your hair. They said it would be yellow. It's so pretty. Can I touch it?"

I hesitated. I did not want this strange girl to touch my hair. It was mine. And yet, I wanted her to stay, to talk to me. I'd never met any other girls before.

"Please," she said. "You're just like a princess. I'd love to be friends with a princess like you."

I made my decision. I nodded okay and leaned forward so she could reach her hand out to touch my hair. I thought it would hurt. Only Mama touched my hair. But she was gentle, twirling the ends between her fingertips.

At least, at first. Then, she touched it higher up, nearer the roots, and held it tight.

"Stop that," I said, whispering at first so Mama wouldn't hear. "It hurts."

But she stroked harder, and finally, she gave a big yank, as if she was trying to separate my hair from my head.

I screamed. Oh, how I screamed, and Mama was there in an instant, shouting at the little girl to get away from me, and the little girl ran, shrieking, down the street. I knew not where.

"Come, Rachel." Mama motioned me toward the house.

"I'm sorry, Mama." I was crying, scared of the little girl who had pulled my hair but also scared of Mama's sudden anger. "It was just a little girl."

Mama didn't say anything, so I thought it was okay. But that night, she didn't brush my hair or braid it. She left it down, and I could barely go to sleep with my hair crawling around like ants and spiders. I knew that in the morning, it might be tangled into a thousand knots, and my head would be raw and bloody from trying to get them out.

But in the morning, my hair wasn't knotted. Instead, it was perfectly cropped to a uniform short length like a boy's. It wasn't jagged, as if Mama had shorn it herself. Rather, it looked perfectly neat.

And perfectly ugly.

Since that day, Mama never brushed my hair with her special brush. When I asked, she said it was lost. My hair grew back again, but not as fast as before. Mama locked me in the house for days, and the next week, we took a long journey on a train, hidden in a special car with our bed the whole time. Then, I was moved to this tower. At first, I loved it. It looked like the castles I'd seen in fairy-tale books, and I pretended that I was a princess, special, who needed to be protected from the world. But, as I grew older, I realized that the tower was not a palace but a prison. Here I stayed, all alone but for Mama's visits. I tried to prepare for the day I might leave. I didn't know when that would be. If it would ever be.

2

Wyatt

The train station outside was black, and the train window had frost on it. End of the line, or almost. I dug my fingernails into the seat. The wind howled in a way I wasn't used to, would never get used to, almost like a human voice. If I tried, I could probably decipher the shapes of things I'd seen on a childhood trip upstate. Back then, Mom had been with me, pointing things out: mountains, a cute farm-house. Now, I was alone, and outside the train there was nothing. Mom had suggested I come here. I didn't know why. Or I did know why, but I wasn't sure it made sense. For the past twenty miles or more, I had stared at my own reflection, my dark hair fading into the darker background of the wilderness.

It wasn't that I missed home. I hadn't been away long enough for that, just a few hours on the train. Or maybe I'd been away longer than I thought. "Emotional distance," the school psychologist would call it, had called it the three times I had been brought in to "discuss things." Maybe the rest of my life would be like this, a series of train stations, none more meaningful than the others. Maybe that would be better, to be disconnected from everyone, so no one could hurt me—or be hurt by me either.

But probably, any train station would be better than this. Slakkill, New York, sounded more like a crime than a town. Since leaving Penn Station, with its bright lights, Christmas music, and bustling tourists, the stations had become steadily bleaker until this one: unmanned, freezing, nothing but a platform in the middle of the grim, Adirondack wilderness.

My copy of *Wuthering Heights* (required reading for my online virtual school class) had fallen onto the floor when I'd dozed off. I scooped it into my backpack and pulled my duffel bag from the over-head bin. The only other people exiting at Slakkill were a mother with a little girl, staring straight ahead. No one was waiting for me on the snow-covered platform. I used my coat collar to protect my face against the bitter cold.

Suddenly, the little girl began to scream. "Mommy! Mommy!"

"Quiet!" the woman said.

"But I forgot my bunny! My bunny!"

"What? Then, it's gone. The train's leaving."

The little girl was crying. The door was still open, and I was closer to it. I dropped my duffel bag on the ground and ran inside the train, not even knowing why I was doing it. The bunny, frayed and more gray than white, was in the middle of the floor. I grabbed it and ran out, nearly slipping on the icy platform. The mother and daughter had already started to leave, though the little girl was struggling and bridging up the way toddlers do when they're angry. I ran after them. "Here." I shoved it into the girl's hands.

If I'd expected a thank-you, I got none. I said, "Hey, do you know if there's a pay phone?"

Maybe the woman didn't hear me, but I thought she did. In any case, she shielded her daughter's face with her hands and kept walking to the stairs. Nice. I could have been stuck on the train if the door had closed, stuck and bound for someplace even farther north and colder than Slakkill. At least the little girl had stopped crying.

I returned to my duffel bag and checked my phone. No bars. No surprise. Once we got out of the Catskills, reception had been patchy from a combination of too many mountains and trees, too few cell phone towers. The Adirondacks were worse. What kind of animals were these people? Occasionally, you could send a text, but I hadn't because there was no one I wanted to text. They'd all forgotten me, my friends. Maybe I hoped they would. Anyway, now, there were no bars at all.

But cell phones were a necessity of life, especially when someone was supposed to pick you up at the train station at midnight in the middle of nowhere. I had a name, Celeste Greenwood, the mother of my mom's childhood friend, and a phone number. Without a phone to call from, though, those facts were useless. Tomorrow's commuters (if there even were any) would be greeted by the pathetic sight of my preserved, frozen body when they arrived the next morning.

I tried the number anyway. Sure enough, the phone flashed, "No service."

The sound of the train's wheels echoed in my head, the lights getting smaller in the distance as it sped away, blending with the way too many stars, which would have been pretty if they hadn't been so lonely. There was nothing here, no lights or people, only darkness and stars and one train platform in the wilderness.

I shivered and looked for a pay phone.

"You Wyatt?" a voice asked.

I started. The guy—if it was a guy under all the layers of coats and scarves—had sneaked up on me, making me once again consider my mortality in this place. It was a campfire story waiting to happen. . . . *And then, the claw-handed man grabbed the teenager and he was never heard from again.*

I looked down at the stranger's hands. No claws. "What?" I said. Then, I didn't know why. My name was, in fact, Wyatt, a name that my mom, who'd been nineteen when I was born, had gotten from a soap opera. It was a Long Island name, a name that didn't belong to me anymore, as I didn't belong to Long Island anymore. "Yeah, I'm Wyatt."

The guy was tall, taller than me, even though I was six feet. He moved his scarf down a bit so I could see his face enough to tell he was about my age, about seventeen. "I'm Josh. That all you have?" He pointed to the duffel and the backpack that held what were now all my worldly possessions.

"I'll be fine," I said.

"Don't be sure. It gets cold here, much colder than Long Island." He said "Long Island" with the same kind of scorn people in Long Island used to talk about "the sticks."

As if on cue, I shivered again. "There's always online shopping." I cursed my teeth for chattering. I looked like a wuss.

"If Old Lady Greenwood even has the internet." He gestured for me to follow him. The platform was slippery, and I had to step carefully, so for a minute, we didn't talk.

"How old is she?" I finally asked.

Josh shrugged. "A hundred or so. I didn't know she even knew anyone. We live up the road from her, and my mom makes me check on her sometimes. She says it's to be neighborly, but really, I think it's to make sure she hasn't dropped dead. Around here, they might not notice for months." He laughed.

I laughed too, even though I didn't really think it was funny. A chill wind whistled down the tracks.

"Anyway, I've never seen anyone around there."

We reached the staircase. It was even icier than the platform, and I struggled to pull the duffel bag down it. I slid and grabbed the railing. Stupid. Josh could see I obviously didn't have much experience with the elements. He just waited, watching me, beside a beat-up red pickup. Walking to that was no easier, so we didn't speak again until I'd reached it—Josh had left it running—and until my teeth had stopped chattering.

"My mom was friends with her daughter," I said.

Silence. We pulled onto a road that was nothing but pine trees, no gas stations, nothing else in sight. Finally, Josh said, "I heard she had a daughter who disappeared."

My mother had said something similar, that Danielle had gone wild, apparently, after my mother's family had moved to Long Island. Then, she disappeared, probably ran away. "Yeah, my mother told me something about that. She didn't really know what happened."

Josh didn't answer, and the wind whipped through the trees. The night was moonless, black. Finally, he said, "Dunno. It happened a while ago. My dad says he doesn't remember much, except he said the police didn't look very hard when she disappeared. He figures the girl ran away. Lots of people do."

"That's understandable."

"How so?"

Awkward. "Well, I mean, it doesn't seem real exciting here. Maybe she wanted to go to the city or something."

"So you think all we do around here is hang out at Stewart's all weekend?"

I knew Stewart's was like a 7-Eleven, and if I'd thought about it, that would have been what I'd thought. But I said, "No, of course not."

He grinned. Now that it was warm, I could see his face, a sort of goofy face that suited the jock he obviously was. He looked like the type of guy I'd have hung with at home.

Home.

"Actually, that sort of is what we do on weekends. I was just messing with you."

I laughed. Nervously. "Oh, okay."

"You should come sometime. It might not be much, but it's all we've got."

I nodded. "Maybe so." I thought about what he'd said, *Lots of people do.* Do what? Run away? Or disappear? How many people was *lots*?

"Are you starting school here after vacation?" Josh asked.

"No. I'm taking these online classes, so I guess she'll have to get internet."

The questions hung between us. Why had I moved? Why here? Why wasn't I going to school? I huddled in my coat, willing my teeth to chatter, letting the cold serve as an excuse for why I wasn't volunteering the information. But Josh wasn't asking, and for that, I was glad. I wasn't sure whether I wanted to get involved with people here. New people I'd only disappoint. The creepy old lady and her missing daughter, who my mom said had probably ended up in a ditch—they sounded more my speed.

We drove in silence another mile or so. At one point, I checked Josh's speedometer. He was going ninety. No one noticed or cared. That seemed to describe a lot of things around here. Finally, he slowed at a mailbox with no name on it, just the number 18. He turned and drove down a private drive that was maybe another quarter mile long. At the end of it was a house, two stories high with dark windows. Even with just the porch light, I could see it was in disrepair, a shade of gray that was more neglect than paint. Josh took a key

10

from the cup holder. "She said let yourself in."

I stumbled from the car. The frigid wind hit me worse than before, and inside my gloves, my fingers felt like stiff wires, making it almost impossible to pull my bag from the bed of Josh's pickup. Finally, I wrested it out. I started to wave good-bye to Josh.

He rolled down the window. "Wyatt?"

"Yeah?" I stopped. The wind rolled under my hat and through my ears. I could only see his outline in the shadowy truck.

"Good luck, man."

3

Wyatt

I heard the roar of Josh's motor long after it would have disappeared at home. Then, nothing. I dragged the duffel bag up the path. Snow soaked through the tops of my sneakers. Above my head, something—a bird of prey or maybe a bat—shrieked. I looked for it but saw nothing. The trees did a skeleton dance in the December wind. I stumbled forward. The key, forgotten in my haste to climb the slippery path, slid from my frozen fingers, falling soundlessly into the snow. I knelt to fumble for it and felt the distinct sensation of being watched. I glanced up and saw a small, dark movement in the upstairs window. My imagination. I heard a rustling in the trees. Just squirrels. I returned to my fumbling and finally found the key, which had nearly turned to ice.

I rose and climbed the steps to the door. The key fought against the lock, as if it was not much used to working. Finally, it turned. I tugged the door open.

A scent met my nose, not one I associated with the elderly. I had expected mothballs or powdery perfume, but this was something different, some rare spice. The room was pitch black. I felt for the light switch, but when I flipped it, the bulb flashed bright then died instantly. In the moment it was on, I saw the staircase ahead of me. With still-frozen hands, I pulled my bag up and climbed the stairs, feeling along the wall as I walked, looking for another light. Finally, I found one as I reached the upstairs landing.

The hallway before me looked from another time. Old photos of long-dead people lined the walls of the staircase. A couple posed formally, the woman wearing a 1920s wedding dress; a little boy by a boat. The spicy scent strengthened. I didn't know which room was mine, but all the doors but one were closed. One was open barely a crack. I chose that one. The light there worked, and as I entered, I saw there were photos there too, all of a young girl with long, dark hair and an impish grin. Was this Danielle? My question was answered as I studied the room, finding more photos of the same girl. In a Girl Scout uniform. Dressed in an old-fashioned gown in a school play. And, finally, arm in arm with a blonde girl whose face I knew well. My mother. In the photo, my mother was laughing. Danielle stared at something in the distance. I had dozed on the train, and now I felt too awake to sleep, so I examined the books on the shelves. Mostly, they were romance novels with open-shirted guys staring at heaving-breasted women in Victorian dresses. But finally, I found something interesting. A yearbook. It had *The Centurion* emblazoned in gold letters on a black cover. I drew it out and turned to the index, searching for my mother's name, Emily Hill. The first page number led me to the student photos, black-and-white faces, all with the same stick-up bangs that had been in style back then, the same dopey smiles.

Danielle was on the same page, her long, straight hair a darker shade of gray than the others. I wondered what had happened to her. Then, I remembered she was probably dead.

Without thinking, I turned the pages. The book was thinner than my yearbook at home. It looked like there had only been a few hundred students in the whole school. I found another photo of Danielle, a candid shot of her in a winter coat, about to throw a snowball. Danielle hadn't collected friends' signatures in the yearbook. Only one page had an inscription, and that inscription was from my mother, a long block of text about "weird Mr. Oglesby" and "that day in chemistry class." Instead of the usual "Stay sweet" or "Have a good summer" before her signature, Mom had written, "Don't worry. It will be okay."

The date was eighteen years ago. Weird thought that, only a year later, my mother had been pregnant with me. And Danielle, she'd disappeared.

I flipped through the other pages. Finding no more inscriptions, I returned the book to the shelf.

But when I tried to push it in, it wouldn't go. Something behind it blocked its way. With my almost-thawed fingers, I pried the books apart. Suddenly, I wondered if maybe I should put everything back the way it had been. *Exactly* the way it had been. Maybe the old lady was keeping the room as a shrine to Danielle. Maybe I shouldn't even be in here.

But when I reached between the books, I found the obstruction, an old, green notebook with crooked spirals. Was it a diary? No, I had no idea why I'd thought that. It was a notebook for school. Still, I wondered why it was hidden. Probably, Danielle had shoved it on to the shelf when her mother had told her to clean her room. I did that all the time. Probably, the first thing Mom would do now that I was gone was clean out my stuff. But Danielle's mother hadn't cleaned out, and that was understandable. The mess was all she had.

14

The notebook smelled the way old books do, like dust and unrealized potential. I opened it, expecting algebraic formulas or American history notes, and I wasn't disappointed. Or maybe I was. On the first page, neatly copied, was the periodic table of elements.

I was about to close it and move on. I was tired again. A glance at the clock told me it was nearly two, and the cold air didn't help. I wanted to curl under the too-thin blanket on the bed and go to sleep. But then, I noticed the second page.

It was a diary.

The handwriting was feminine but not cutesy like the girls who put hearts over their *i*'s. It began:

It poured all day. Of course, that's nothing unusual. It poured all day yesterday and the day before and the day before that. What does it really matter anyway because, rain or shine, I am stuck in the house with my mother? She's barely let me go anywhere these past few weeks, and since Emily left, I have no friends over either. But I mention the rain so you can understand the <u>utter depths</u> of my misery and also, how unusual it is that I saw a guy (!) outside my bedroom window.

Well, not a guy even, but a MAN. A hot-looking one, from what I could see of him. He was tall (or, at least, his chest came up to the tops of the sunflowers we'd planted) with blond hair and eyes the romance writers would call piercing. I never really knew what that meant before, but now I do. His eyes looked like, if they met yours, they'd go through you like a skewer. And, weird enough, you'd enjoy it.

Even though I didn't know him, I wanted to go down to see him. After all, I hadn't seen anyone except Mom and Old Lady McNeill, who sells milk and eggs out of her backyard, since school ended a month ago.

Now, a NORMAL person could just say, "Hey, Mom, there's some weirdo in the backyard," and then go out and ask him what he was doing there. But I was not a normal person, so I had to sneak.

Mom was sewing or something in her room, so I knew there was half a chance I might make it out if she didn't leave, and if she didn't hear the creaky step when I went downstairs. But the rain would help with that.

Still, Mom has the hearing of a cat, so I crept as slowly and carefully as I could downstairs, stopping every few steps to listen. Nothing. When I got to the kitchen door, I glanced outside and saw him again.

Oh, yes, he was FINE. Jeans ripped in all the right places and a tight, white T-shirt (wet, an added bonus) that made him look like Dylan on Beverly Hills 90210 (because TV is the _only_ thing I am allowed to do). Sure, he was probably a homeless person or a perv. Or a serial killer. But, hey, a girl can't be too picky, especially around here. I had my hand on the doorknob when I heard a voice.

"Where do you think you're going?"

Mom! Instinctively, my hand flew off the doorknob. Wrong thing to do. I took a deep breath and tried to look calm. "Oh, wow, you scared me. I was just going . . . to take a walk." I could feel my heart ramming against my chest, almost like it might burst through.

"In this rain?" Her face was pleasant, but her voice was suspicious.

"I'm bored. It's been raining all week. I haven't gone anyplace all summer."

It was true. Since school had gotten out, Mom had been weirdly overprotective, even for her. She'd always been secretive, strange, which is why I hardly had any friends, but it seemed like, one day, her tiger instincts had gone into overdrive, and now, every little request to go someplace, even the grocery store, was refused.

I don't even know WHY Mom is being so weird. A few years ago, a teenage girl disappeared. Kelly David. Kidnapped, maybe, but they never found any evidence, so maybe she ran away. Everyone was paranoid for a while, keeping their kids inside or only letting them go out in groups, waiting beside them at the bus stop until the bus pulled away. But, gradually, they calmed down. Can't live in fear, right? Mom had calmed down too. But suddenly, she started acting like it just happened. "You know," I said, "lots of people my age have cars and go to Glens Falls or even Albany and don't have crazy mothers hanging over them all the time. Most people are going to college. It's only me who has to be a homebound freak with a freak mother!"

Her hand shot up and struck my face, just like it was nothing. Not even a movie-esque "How dare you!" Just a slap. I stumbled back, and she reached to catch me. But then, she saw something out the window. She pushed past, letting me fall.

"A boy! You were going out to see a BOY?"

"What boy? What possible boy could be out in the boonies on a day like this?"

But, of course, it was true. She'd seen him.

"Why must you do this to me?"

Do this? Me? Me, who'd never had a boyfriend, never been on a date? Not that I hadn't been asked, but I knew better than to try and go out with anyone. I knew she'd flip out like she was flipping out now. My mother is insane. I've *always known that. And I also know that, if I'm going to get away from her and her insanity, I am going to have to sneak away, somehow in the dead of night. It's just . . . I'm scared.*

I looked up from the notebook. Sneak away in the dead of night. That was what she'd done. Would the diary explain why?

She was still yelling, and I was crying and saying, "No, no! What are you talking about?"

And then, her hands were around my arms, icy fingers like handcuffs, and she was pulling me away from the door, up the stairs and to my room. I tried to fight her, but she's surprisingly strong. Finally, she shoved me through the door, slammed it, and I heard her key in the lock.

And here I am now.

I put down the notebook. Her mother had locked her in her bedroom? What kind of crazy person was I living with? But maybe, I thought, her mother had known of some danger, had wanted to protect her. I wanted to read more of the notebook, to find out. It ran on for pages and pages, but suddenly, I felt tired, so tired I couldn't read or think or do anything else but stumble to the bed to sleep. I hid the notebook under my pillow for later reading.

The pillow was old, soft, and the sheets smelled like dust. I wondered if they'd been changed since Danielle had left.

Then, sleep drowned out all thought or reason or anything but darkness.

I woke some time later to the howling of winds and the driving sound of rain or maybe snow. Through it all, there was a tree branch, tapping, scraping on my window, persistent and annoying as my mother's cat. I tried to pull the pillow over my head but ended up with a pin-feather against my cheek. The scraping grew louder. Then, there was a voice. A voice? Impossible. It was just the wind, howling. But it sounded like a voice, a shrieking banshee voice, and it screamed, "Let me in!" The scraping got louder. I remembered the closed, shuttered windows, but now, it sounded like the shutters were open, banging against the house.

Finally, I had to get up to stop it. I'd open the window, break the branch off, and get back to sleep. That was all. I willed myself to stand despite my weariness.

But when I went to the window, it was already open. Open or maybe broken. Yes, broken. A rush of freezing air assaulted my face, and as I stepped closer, intent on finding the branch, a hand grabbed my wrist.

It was an icy hand, too cold, almost, to be real, and I shivered at the touch of it. I tried to pull my own hand away, but her fingers held like a claw machine, and a sad voice said, "Let me in! Please let me in!"

"Who are you?" I said, though even as I did, I knew. My eyes found the window, and I knew.

"Dani," she said.

Dani! Danielle! I stared at her. The face was something like the girl in the yearbook photo, if she'd been dug up from a grave. Her cheeks were white and ghostlike, with mottled blue patches. Her dark hair flew behind her. I gasped and, again, pulled my arm back. But this time, I took her arm with me, scraping it against the broken window, causing blood to run down and onto my own hand. Still, she held tight.

"Let me in!" she begged. "I have been wandering in the woods all these years! Let me in!"

The window was too small to let her in, even if I wanted to, which I didn't, and it was on the second story besides. I couldn't even see how she was standing there. Maybe she was floating, flying like a ghost.

Or a hallucination. Of course! I was dreaming! I was still asleep. Yet her hand on my wrist, the blood dripping down mine, it all felt so real, and her voice was so pathetic.

"Let me in! Please!"

I tried to reason with her. "I can't let you in a closed window, and I can't open it with you holding my arm." Why was I talking to a hallucination?

Her eyes bugged out, huge and horrible, but she must have seen the logic in what I said. She let my arm go. I snatched it back and began grabbing things, books, anything I could find to cover the hole in the window. Once I'd done that, maybe I could sleep.

"Let me in!" Her voice was softer, blending with the wind and snow.

"I can't! You're dead!" Suddenly, I knew she was, knew she was like all the other dead things that haunted me. I had to close the window, let it go. I heaped more objects on, but I saw the pile moving, swaying. "Go away!"

I heard footsteps in the hall. Then, my door opened. "What's this?" a voice demanded. "Why are you in here?"

She stepped forward and I saw her. Fully dressed in a blue dress, a scarf on her head, Mrs. Greenwood wasn't as old as I'd envisioned. Josh had said a hundred or so, but clearly, he'd exaggerated. She couldn't have been more than sixty or so if she'd had a daughter my mother's age, though it was clear that she'd had a hard life, with her daughter disappearing and all. She was tall, with gray hair piled in a bun and eyes that pierced my soul. "Why are you in this room? And why are you screaming?"

"I'm . . . Wyatt. Emily's son. Josh gave me the key. This was the only room open."

"No one comes in this room. No one!"

"I'm sorry. But I . . . I saw her." I glanced at the window. The precarious pile of books had collapsed, but the window was still intact. No broken glass. No blood. No Danielle. "Oh, it was a dream, just a dream, but I could have sworn someone was trying to come in."

"Come in? Who?"

"Dani. She said her name was Dani." Realizing how freaky this would be to the mother of a missing girl, I backtracked. "I mean, I dreamed she said that. I was looking at . . . the photo of her with my mother." Better not to mention the diary. It might upset her to read it. "Then, I had a nightmare she'd come back. Just a nightmare."

"A nightmare? In my daughter's room? My long-lost daughter?"

Long-lost. It was such an old-fashioned way of saying something, and she looked so sad. I knew that she really had loved Danielle. Despite the diary, I knew she hadn't locked her in to control her, hurt her. She'd done it to protect her. And it hadn't worked. Sometimes, things don't.

"I'm sorry. I didn't know." I looked at the window. Nothing out there but snow. "I'll find another room. Which one?" I realized I wasn't getting off on the right foot with her.

"Any room, boy, any room but this one! Now, get out!"

"I will. Of course." With one final glance at the empty, unbroken window, I backed away, grabbing my duffel bag as I did.

"Go!" she yelled. "I'll check in a minute to make sure you've found the right one this time, fool!"

"That's okay." I walked out.

As soon as I reached the hallway, I realized my mistake. My most recent mistake. I'd left the diary on the bed, under the disturbed pillow, where anyone could guess I'd been reading it. Mrs. Greenwood didn't seem like the type to take kindly to snoopers. I had to go back in. It was just an ordinary notebook. She wouldn't know it was

Danielle's. I'd tell her it was mine, my schoolwork.

I tiptoed back into the room to get it. I didn't have to worry about her seeing me, though. She was distracted.

She was at the window, the books and other objects scattered on the ground around her and the glass wide open. She knelt on the sill, looking so far out I worried she'd fall. The room was freezing, and snow swirled through the air. Against it all, I heard her voice, screaming, "Come in! Come in! Oh, Dani, do come! Come back, my darling!" She was sobbing. "Dani, please!"

I grabbed the notebook and ran from the room before she could see me. I chose the emptier of the two spare rooms, hoping I was right this time. I squirreled the notebook away in my duffel bag and hoped that sleep would overtake me before the old woman could think to come check on me.

Wyatt

I fell asleep, eventually, but it was far from peaceful. For hours, I tossed around, alternately freezing and looking for the cool side of the pillow. Danielle didn't return. Of course she didn't. Either she'd been a figment of my weary imagination or she'd disappeared—again—when she heard her mother's voice. No, there was no *either*. She was a figment of my imagination. Period. But still, the wind howled like the opera singers my grandfather worshiped on PBS, and each time I started to descend into sleep, I heard a voice that seemed to say, "Find me!" But there was nothing there. The last time I saw on the digital clock was 5:00 a.m.

The next time was 10:00. Sun streamed through the trees and dotted the walls. I blinked my eyes. The snow and wind had stopped, and there was a silence like I'd never heard.

I wished I could stay in this room forever, alone, unseen by anyone. That was the deal, get away from everything, the people who wanted to talk to me and the people who didn't. Sure, I would have only my own thoughts to deal with, but those would haunt me wherever I went, no matter what. At least, here I wouldn't have to share them.

I hadn't thought about the old lady or, if I had, I hadn't thought much. An old lady had seemed harmless. Mom had kept in touch with her over the years, Christmas cards and things, and when we'd visited the area once, Mom had met her for coffee while I went fishing with my grandfather. So Mom had asked her to let me stay here, to finish out my senior year in exchange for money and chores like mowing the lawn.

I went to the window and looked down. The lawn in question was at least three feet deep in snow. Did that mean I had to shovel the path?

Or, more important, what if the old lady was crazy?

It was a fair question. Danielle's diary made it sound that way. Also, why would she even let me stay? Obviously, she'd been doing okay until now. What if she was a whack job who would murder me in my sleep? What if she'd murdered Danielle?

I fumbled for my cell and, absent anyone else who cared, tried to text my mother.

No bars. Still.

I tried again.

Nothing. Maybe I could go to town or somewhere today, to try and see if it worked. Doubtful. Besides, who did I want to speak to? This place was like one of those novels we read in English class, where people were out on the moors with no one around anywhere and nothing to do but read. You know, like two hundred years ago.

Speaking of which . . . I took out the novel I was supposed to be reading for my online school class, *Wuthering Heights*. I'd tried several times to start it on the train, but it was just too boring, so boring I kept falling asleep. I started again. The chapters where Lockwood arrives at the house he's renting but first stops to meet his landlord were still the same, still boring. No surprises until I came to a part that made me sit upright.

> My fingers closed on the fingers of a little, ice-cold hand!
>   The intense horror of nightmare came over me; I tried to draw back my arm, but the hand clung to it, and a most melancholy voice sobbed,
>   "Let me in—let me in!"

Impossible. It was what had happened last night, exactly what had happened. Now, I dimly recalled that Lockwood in the story had done as I had, gone into a bedroom and found an old diary. But I hadn't read this part. I was sure.

Or had I?

No time to think! My thoughts were interrupted by a knocking on my door, not a desperate knocking like last night, but a calm, businesslike knocking and a chipper voice.

"Wake up, sleepyhead! Everyone must wake sometime!"

It was Mrs. Greenwood. I looked down, found myself still in jeans and a T-shirt from last night. Would she think I was lazy, lock me in a room?

"Are you dressed? I made biscuits!"

I shrugged. No need to prolong the inevitable. "Sure." I opened the door.

The old lady standing there looked nothing like the one I'd met last night. This one could have been in a commercial for Hallmark cards or stuffing or something, a sweet, blue-eyed old lady in a red dress and white apron. She held a tray with what looked like a Denny's Grand Slam on it: eggs, bacon, and biscuits. She smiled. She had dimples and all her teeth.

"I let you sleep in. You must have been tired from your journey." She placed the tray on a small table with a ruffled cloth. "Oh, it's so nice to have someone to cook for. It's been years."

She gave no sign of having met me the night before, much less having yelled at me. In fact, she said, "I see you found your room all right then?"

"Of course. This looks great." So weird.

"Well, don't expect room service every day. This is a special occasion. You can't stay in bed all the time, or soon, you'll find you can't get up. I know."

She must mean when her daughter disappeared, that she'd been depressed.

"Dig in." She spied the book on the bed. "*Wuthering Heights!* Do you like gothic novels?"

Being male, no. "I just started it. It's for school." This was sooo weird. Had last night been all a dream? But then, how had I gotten in this room, in this bed? Had I been here all the time? Was something wrong with me, even more than I'd imagined?

"When you've read a bit more, we can have a nice, long talk about it. And if you enjoy it, I have *Jane Eyre* and *The Woman in White*."

"That's great." I'd given up on thinking about this.

"Oh, forgive my babbling. It's just so nice to have someone to talk to. I'll let you eat and then, perhaps later, you can help me shovel the walk."

This was part of the deal, I knew. My mother had said I'd help around the house. I didn't mind that, but I was weirded out. Mrs. Greenwood gestured toward the tray, urging me to eat more, then left.

As soon as she was gone, I dove for the book. I kept reading. It was long-lost Cathy at the window, and then, as with last night (Had it been a dream?), Lockwood's cries woke his host, Heathcliff. Heathcliff ran into the room, scolded Lockwood, and then, after Lockwood left, Heathcliff rushed to the window, screaming, "Come in! Come in! Cathy, do come. Oh, do—*once* more!"

Just as Mrs. Greenwood had.

Clearly, it had all been a dream, a dream born from reading *Wuthering Heights* while half asleep. The only thing was, I didn't remember reading it.

Whatever.

I realized I was hungry, really hungry. I hadn't eaten anything on the train, and I couldn't remember what I'd eaten before that either. In fact, the past few weeks were sort of a blur. So I wolfed down the breakfast, hoping that food would replace doubt as central in my mind. It almost did. Almost.

In fact, the food was delicious. It had been a long time since I'd really enjoyed food or anything else, but Mrs. Greenwood's biscuits might have broken the barrier. Maybe coming here hadn't been a bad idea. At least, I was inclined to give her the benefit of the doubt that she wasn't crazy, hadn't killed her daughter, and hadn't creeped me out last night. I mean, did crazy people make biscuits like this?

After I finished breakfast, I walked to the window and opened it to see if the cell phone service was any better (or existed) there. It wasn't, but the view was pretty. The snow had finally finished falling, and the sky was bright, reflecting blue on the white. I stared at the vast, snowy lawn.

Maybe my mother had been right. For once. It was a new start, a new place, decent food, a friendly old lady who knew nothing about me. I could be anything, anyone I wanted. I could be better.

Then, I noticed something weird. On the lawn, below the room next to mine, were footprints. Footprints barely hidden in the snow. Even though it had been snowing all night, I could make them out as if they'd been made only hours, not days, earlier.

I opened the window to see something else, the walkway leading to the door where I'd come in. I'd agreed to shovel the walk, and even from a distance, I could tell it was completely blank, white. I'd come in after midnight. That meant the footprints under the window had been made even later.

Through the trees, I heard a sound. At first, I thought it was birds, or the tinkling of a wind chime. It was so blank and white and empty here, I bet you could hear noises from miles away. But, as I listened, the sound put itself together in my mind, and I recognized it.

A human voice.

Singing.

Then, the wind shifted, and the voice was gone.

Wyatt

After it became obvious I wasn't going to find service no matter how many times I raised the phone in the air, I decided to get dressed and go downstairs. I took my plate with me and hunted for the kitchen.

Mrs. Greenwood was there. "Did you enjoy your breakfast?" She was cleaning up after what looked like a baking project. At least, there was a big bowl and flour scattered on the counter and a delicious cinnamony smell coming from the oven. "Wyatt?"

"What? Oh, breakfast was great." Normally, I resented this type of meaningless, extraneous question when it came from my mother. She didn't actually want to know how my breakfast was, after all, just wanted to force me to talk. But Mrs. Greenwood hadn't cooked for anyone in years, and really did want my opinion about the biscuits. And, more to the point, I wanted to interrogate her about 1) cell phone service; 2) internet; and 3) the possibility of going to town and seeing some people, even if those people would probably be backwoods hicks. So I said, "Best biscuits I ever had."

She beamed, so I laid it on thicker. I'd actually been good at that. "Is that pie I smell? Apple?"

"Actually, it's *apfelkuchen*. Apple cake. My mother's recipe. It's so nice to have someone to cook and bake for. There's been no one since . . ."

She broke off, but I filled in. "Since Danielle."

"I am sorry." She picked up the mixing bowl and began to fill it with water. The faucet was old, and it stuck a little. "You came here to get away from your problems, but instead, you're stuck with an old lady and her long-dead ghosts." She began to scrub the bowl a bit too hard with a brush.

So she assumed Danielle was dead too, then. I surprised myself by saying, "No, it's okay. I know how hard it is. See, my best friend died last month."

It was the first time I'd said the words. Back home, everyone knew Tyler was dead. I didn't have to tell anyone, even if they didn't say anything.

She started to reach for my hand, to say she was sorry. I decided that was enough reality TV stuff for one day, so I said, "You need me to shovel the walk?"

"Has it finished snowing? No use starting if it hasn't."

I glanced out at the lawn, at the white walkway. "I think it's done for now, at least."

She wiped out the clean bowl. "The shovel is in the garage. I'll show you." She gestured for me to follow her.

I said, "Um, so does anyone live around here?"

She turned back, surprised. "Oh, there's a farmhouse about half a mile away. Josh, the boy who picked you up. Nice family. They own the hardware store in town."

"Nothing closer?"

"Oh, no. The McNeills were on the other side, but they left years ago."

"I thought I heard . . ." I stopped. Obviously, I was wrong.

"What is it, dear?"

"Oh, nothing. I was just wondering if I'd be able to use my cell phone. And internet."

"Oh, yes, your mother hired a man to hook up the . . . um . . ."

"Wi-Fi?"

"Yes. So you can take your classes on the computer. But I'm afraid you'll need to go to town to use your telephone. Of course, I have that phone." She pointed to a yellow phone with one of those old dials. "We're quite isolated here in the mountains, so I have it, for emergencies."

"Quite isolated here" sounded like something a man in a horror movie would say—right before he started swinging the machete. But Mrs. Greenwood was opening the oven. The room filled with heat and even more cinnamon. She removed a straw from a little broom to test her cake for doneness.

"Some people like it, though," she continued. "They think they're getting away from it all."

Or it just gives them more time to think about their problems.

"In any case, you can take my car to town sometimes, to do the shopping."

I let out a breath and realized I'd been holding it. I'd been worrying that she didn't even have a car or that the crazy lady who'd locked Danielle in the house wouldn't let me out either, and it would be like this movie I saw on TV once, *Misery*, where a woman holds a guy hostage in her house all winter long, and hobbles his feet so he can't walk, and no one even knows he's missing.

But, then again, maybe the diary didn't exist either. I hadn't looked at it today, after all. If everything else last night was a dream, maybe that was too.

But when I finished the walk and went up to my room, I found it right where I'd dreamed I'd hidden it.

The first pages said just what I remembered too. Since I had nothing else to do and was more than a little curious, I turned to the next entry.

Danielle's Diary

Today, I talked Mom into letting me walk to Old Lady McNeill's house a mile down the road for milk and eggs. Mom was baking a cake and she ran out. Big fun. But you'll see what happened . . .

This is the first sunny day in a week, and I feel like a flower that has been kept in a closet, starving for light. I promised I wouldn't be gone long, and I took Ginger our lab, who can't walk far because she's old and puffy. Still, as we started down the hill, I broke into a run. Free of Mom!! I was free of Mom!

And then, I tripped over a root and fell to the ground, scraping my hands and knees. I lay there, struggling, in pain, smelling the wet dirt around me and thinking how stupid

I was. I've lived here my whole life, know every rock and root, including the one I'd tripped on. How could I fall?

Thinking back, I wonder if it was MEANT to happen.

When I tried to pull myself up on the trunk of that same malevolent old tree, I found that not only had I scraped my leg—I'd also twisted it somehow. In my paranoid mind, it felt broken. I couldn't walk at all. I contemplated my situation—could I send Ginger back to tell Mom somehow? Considering she wasn't actually like dogs in movies who did that, probably not. As I thought about this, Ginger began to bark. I looked up to see what she was barking at.

It was a man. Or, really, a guy around my own age, the very same guy I'd seen outside our house a week ago. The one Mom had seen fit to imprison me for looking at. He was about ten feet away, but he walked closer.

I tried to push myself up. Competing instincts warred with each other. A stranger on a deserted road could be a rapist or a serial killer or both. Yet, I knew I couldn't run and, what's more, I wasn't sure I wanted to. Not only has it been weeks since I've seen anyone but my mother—it may have been YEARS since I've seen anyone new. No one new comes to Slakkill. Why would they? Everyone has been here forever. And don't they say you're most likely to get murdered by someone you know?

Of course, it didn't hurt that this guy was gorgeous. As he came closer, I could see that he was tall with white-blond hair that glowed in the morning light. His walk, too, was different than anything I'd ever seen. People in Slakkill walked quickly and with hunched shoulders, as if they were cringing from the constant cold or just weighed down by their pointless lives. The only exceptions were the jocks, who walked with a swagger that revealed they didn't realize they were someday going to end up as beer-bellied car salesmen, like their dads. This guy had neither. He looked open. And, did I mention cute?

Even Ginger must have noticed because she stopped barking as he approached. In fact, she trotted up to him and licked his hand like she knew him.

"Hey, girl." He petted her head.

"That dog would kill you soon as look at you," I joked.

"I can see she's very protective." He laughed. His eyes were the brightest blue I'd ever seen, the color of the ice-blue mint cough drops Mom used to give me when I had a cold. He held his hand out. "Can I help you?"

I started to take it then hesitated. I knew nothing about this guy. Yet, what choice did I have? I was injured, stranded someplace where a car passed maybe every few hours. Mom was inside, probably watching General Hospital. Did I refuse his offer and try to crawl to safety? Even Ginger, my supposed line of defense, was now happily sniffing the guy's very cute butt.

"I'm not going to abduct you, if that's what you're worried about."

But wouldn't he say that even if he was?

"You just looked like you could use some help. I could go away and call the volunteer fire fighters, and they'd be here in an hour or so. It's just, the situation has sort of a romantic quality, like the novels girls like—a fair young maiden takes a tumble and a handsome young man comes to her rescue."

I said, "You consider yourself handsome, do you?"

"Is there any question." He grinned. "Can I help you up?"

I tried one last time to push myself up, then winced. I decided to take a chance. "Yes, please."

I grasped his hand. It felt hard, calloused, a man's hand. But when I tried to stand, I yelped in pain.

"You probably shouldn't put weight on it," he said, and then, before I could protest (even if I would have), he scooped me up in his arms and started to carry me away.

"Wait. Where are you taking me?"

"Just my car."

"Your car?" I saw an old blue Pinto parked by the roadside. Visions of abduction once again began dancing in my head.

He laughed. "Nothing like that. I have some crutches in the back from when I sprained my ankle last month. Should be able to adjust them to fit, and then, I can take you wherever you want to go. Do you live there?"

He pointed to our house, which looked suddenly really old and dirty. Obviously, I should have let him drive me up the driveway, but I knew Mom would freak if I came home in a strange car with a strange guy. The way she'd been acting lately, she'd probably lock me in my room forever. Also, I didn't want the day to be over so quickly.

"Um, yes, but I'm supposed to go buy eggs from our neighbor, Mrs. McNeill. That's where I was going. My mother called and told her to expect me. She's probably waiting outside."

That wasn't true. Mom wasn't friendly with Mrs. McNeill. They'd fought when the McNeill goats had gotten out and terrorized my mother's precious garden, and now, she only let me buy eggs when she didn't feel like going to town. But

I figured it wouldn't hurt to have him think someone was expecting me.

"Okay, Mrs. McNeill it is." He managed to open the car's passenger door and lowered me to the seat. "Just a sec."

He walked around to the trunk and took out not only the crutches but an ace bandage. "Look what I found. Can I put it on you?"

"Um, shouldn't I know your name first?"

"Oh, sorry. It's Zach. You can put it on yourself, if you want. I just thought—"

"No, it's okay. The name was all I wanted. I'm Danielle, by the way. But everyone calls me Dani."

"Nice to meet you, Danielle." He knelt beside me and drew my foot up to his bended knee. He pushed my pant leg up, and when he touched my skin, a cold spark ran through me. I shivered.

"You okay?" he asked.

I nodded. "Just static electricity, I guess." It wasn't, but I didn't know what else to say.

He began to massage my ankle and, with each touch, I felt the same electric thrill.

"You're not from around here," I said.

He smiled. "How do you know that?"

"It's a small town. Everyone knows everyone else."

"Oh, I thought maybe it was because I was so special you'd have noticed me if you'd seen me before."

I rolled my eyes, even though it was true.

"I'd have noticed you," he said. "Pretty girl like you. I bet you're the prettiest girl around here."

"Hardly." I laughed. I certainly wasn't. Emily had been,

but I wasn't even a close second. I'd never even had a boy-friend. Of course, that was partly because everyone was scared of my mother.

He finished rubbing my ankle and began to wrap it with the ace bandage. His hands were firm, strong. "I find that hard to believe. Is this a town with inordinately beautiful girls?"

"I don't know. I've never been out of it. Well, except sometimes to go to the mall down in Glens Falls for school clothes, but that's not a big city either."

"You've never been away from here? And you're how old?"

"Seventeen, almost eighteen. And a lot of people have lived here their whole lives. I'm not some stupid hick, you know."

Although saying it made it sound like I was. And, really, how did I know I wasn't?

But he said, "I didn't say you were. You might be the most brilliant person in the world, but how would you know if you never see anyone else?"

It was like what I'd been thinking, only sort of the oppo-site, sort of turned on its ear.

Of course, I'm probably not brilliant. At least, I'd always been a C student in school. I was always bored in my classes. Besides, what's the point of killing yourself in school when you know you aren't going to college, aren't going really anywhere? Still, I secretly have always thought, hoped I was smart. I also hoped maybe there was something I was good at, best at. And, more than anything else, I hope that some-day, something will HAPPEN.

But, so far, in nearly eighteen years, nothing has.

He finished wrapping the bandage and looked up at me

to see what I thought. I nodded. Actually, it didn't hurt at all.

"You could be really good at something and not even realize it," he said. "I think about that kind of thing sometimes, like what if the world's greatest baseball player lived in a place where they didn't have the game? Maybe he'd never know how great he was. He'd become a goat herder or something and never realize his potential."

I laughed, but I liked the idea of it, that I might still be special somehow and just not realize it, that the best part of my life wasn't already over.

"How about you?" I said. "Where are you from?"

"Me, I'm from nowhere. Or everywhere. My family moved around a lot. I'm twenty, and I've lived in at least twenty towns, almost as many states."

"And now?"

"I've been living in New York City for a while, trying to make it playing guitar and singing, but it's hard. I wait tables, street perform for tips, but there are about a million other guys doing that there. I heard they were looking for an act at the Red Fox Inn in Gatskill, so I tried for it."

Gatskill is the next town over. My friends sometimes go to the Red Fox Inn for dinner, but I never have. "So you work there? You're a professional singer?"

He grinned. "I guess you could say that."

I noticed a guitar case in his backseat. "Will you play for me?"

"Next time, I will. Right now, I think I need to take you to Mrs. McNeill's before I turn into a pumpkin. I double as a waiter at the Red Fox, and they open at five."

I glanced at my watch. It was three thirty. He'd said next time.

"You want to see me again?" I asked.

"Danielle, I want to see you as much as possible."

I smiled inside at the thought of it even as I shuddered to imagine Mom's reaction. He stood and walked to the other side of the car. He took me to Mrs. McNeill's. When the old lady looked through her cataracty eyes and asked who my young man was, he didn't correct her, didn't say he wasn't mine. Even though my ankle had stopped hurting, I held on to him anyway. I liked how it felt to be beside someone.

When he drove me home, I told him to stop at the bottom of the driveway.

"You'll be okay?" he asked. When I nodded, he said, "When can I see you again?"

"I'll walk my dog this way again day after tomorrow, same time. Or I'll try to."

"I'll be here."

And then, he took my hand and pulled me toward him. He kissed me. I knew he was going to do it only a second before his lips touched mine, and when they did, I felt the same electrical impulses, like a wire leading from my stomach to my mouth had become electrified, and I was exploding.

I told Mom I'd fallen near the McNeills' and Mrs. McNeill had given me the crutches and driven me home. She didn't question me, so I mentioned how much Ginger had enjoyed the walk, how I thought she was getting fat and needed to exercise, so I planned to do it every day.

I do. For once, something is happening to me.

7

Wyatt

Mrs. Greenwood was knocking at the door. "Wyatt, the man is here to install the computer thing."

"Okay." Quickly, I stuffed the notebook into its prior spot and opened the door.

It was weird, reading a missing girl's diary. Danielle had been hanging with a guitar player named Zach before she disappeared. Did Mrs. Greenwood know? Did anyone? Probably not, since Danielle had been so secretive. Maybe the guitar player was the reason behind her disappearance. Maybe she'd run away to the city with him. Or maybe he'd murdered her.

Should I ask Mrs. Greenwood if she knew? I, more than anyone, knew the importance of not keeping secrets. Some people were big on them, but I knew that secrets could kill like handguns and knives.

Still, this secret was almost twenty years old. Mrs. Greenwood probably didn't need to be reminded of painful memories that were best left dead.

I thought back to Danielle's diary. What could I ask that would bring it up, yet not bring it up.

"You know what this place could really use?" I said. "A dog."

I knew she'd had a dog when Danielle was alive. Thinking about a dog wouldn't be as painful as thinking about her probably dead daughter.

Which is why I was plenty surprised when she immediately burst into tears.

I mean, really burst into tears. Even the Wi-Fi guy looked up from his work to give me a dirty look for making the sweet old lady cry. I shrugged. I didn't know it would cause that reaction.

"Oh, God, Mrs. G, I'm sorry. I didn't know it would upset you so much. I was just talking. I don't need a dog. I'm so stupid." The Wi-Fi guy nodded. I said to him, "Don't you have work to do? Come on, Mrs. Greenwood. I'll get you some water. Or tea, maybe. Do you like tea?" I took her arm. I had it in my head that old ladies liked tea.

Finally, she started walking with me.

She had calmed down by the time we reached the kitchen. I sat her down and started hunting for a kettle. I thought I knew how to make tea. You just poured the hot water over the tea bag.

"I'm being silly," she said. "We used to have a dog, a yellow Labrador, back when Danielle . . . she was the sweetest thing, and one day . . ." She brushed a tear from her cheek.

I knew what was coming.

"I found her out in the road, dead. She'd gotten out somehow and ran into the street. Cars go so fast here. She didn't stand a chance. I blamed myself for not protecting her well enough, for not taking good enough care . . ."

She sniffed, and I wondered if she really meant the dog, or if she meant Danielle. It must be hard for a mom as overprotective as she obviously was to have a child disappear. And Danielle was her only child too.

"It's not your fault," I said. "Dogs get out sometimes. It happens. You can't protect them all the time."

"I didn't do enough. I used to complain about her. She probably never knew how much I loved her."

I found the kettle and hunted in the cabinet for tea bags. Clearly, if she'd gotten that upset when I asked her about the dog, I couldn't ask her about Danielle. But what if the guitar player had killed Danielle? Maybe he was some kind of serial killer who'd killed lots of other girls too? Maybe he was still out there.

Or maybe Danielle was alive.

But I couldn't ask Mrs. Greenwood. Besides, she'd probably never known about Zach. Obviously, Danielle was big on secrets.

"You never got another dog?"

"Oh, I didn't think I could take care of it. A dog needs walking, and I was getting old."

"This would be a good place for a dog. Lots of wide-open space."

Lots of space to bury a dead body.

But I was thinking it must be so lonely for her. She'd been a widow for as long as my mother had known her, and then, to have her daughter disappear and the dog die, all in one year. It must have been unbearable. I knew something about loneliness, knew what it was to sit in my room, checking my phone for texts that never came, logging on to Facebook to see other people's statuses, happy statuses indicating their lives had gone on while mine hadn't.

Okay, this was depressing.

I found the tea bags and closed the cabinet. It didn't shut completely, overlapping slightly with the one beside it. I tried to lift it a bit, to see if that would help, then opened the other cabinet and closed them in the opposite order. That didn't work either.

"Oh, that's been broken for years," Mrs. Greenwood said.

"I could fix it. I could get a new hinge. Do you have screwdrivers and things?"

I wasn't usually this helpful, but I remembered Mrs. Greenwood saying that Josh's family owned the hardware store. And going there was an excuse to leave the house. I could ask Josh if he knew anything about the Red Fox Inn. Or Zach.

"I don't want you going to all that trouble," she said. "You should do your schoolwork now that you have the internet."

"Hey, hey, hey, it's Saturday. And school doesn't even start again until the sixth. I can take today off and look around town. It's pretty here. Hey, I can run errands for you. Do you have a grocery list?" I added this to prevent her offering to go with me. That would defeat the whole purpose.

"I suppose you're right. It would be nice to get some things fixed around here. Why don't you wait until the cable man leaves, and then, you could follow him into town. You can borrow my Chevy."

Yes! Access to the car. Without even begging. The kettle shrieked to signal the water was boiling, and I was making tea like a pro.

I poured the water, and as I hunted for the sugar, she said, "It's so good to have you here, Wyatt. I've been so lonely since . . . since . . ." She wiped a tear from her eye.

"It's okay. We don't have to talk about the dog."

She shook her head. "Not the dog. No, not that. Since . . . Danielle."

Now, I knew what people meant when they talked about the elephant in the room. It had been standing there the whole time, but we hadn't said a word about it. "Oh, you don't have to talk about her if you don't want."

"I know. But I feel I should explain. When I yelled at you last night. Of course you didn't know anything about it, which room was hers. I should have thought. It's just . . . I haven't been in that room in almost ten years. At first, I sat there all the time. It made me feel closer to her, seeing all her photographs, her stuffed bears and such. The police thought she would never come home, but I was certain she would, unless . . ."

Unless someone had killed her. But I didn't say it, didn't prod her to go on. I just said, "I understand."

"When I saw the light on last night, heard someone in there, I thought for a moment she might be back. Sleep does funny things to the mind, doesn't it?"

"Yeah. I know what it's like to want someone back. Believe me."

She patted my hand. "It's probably a blessing that you're here."

I nodded, but I really did wonder what had happened to Danielle. And if Zach had anything to do with it.

Wyatt

Mrs. Greenwood's Chevy was one of those old wood-covered station wagons from the 1980s. I tried three times before it turned over. "Maybe another day, I can take it for a tune-up. It's not safe for you to drive it like this."

I was setting the stage for another trip to town.

The Wi-Fi guy pointed me in the right direction, but he was going in the other. "Can't miss it. There's nothing and nothing and nothing. Then, there's Hemingway's Hardware and Sporting Goods."

He hadn't exaggerated about the nothing. I pulled onto Route 9, the supposed main road, heading south. About a mile away was a sign, advertising eggs for sale, and I wondered if it was the same Mrs. McNeill Danielle had visited years earlier. Eggs were on my shopping list from Mrs. Greenwood, and I thought maybe I'd buy them there. But when I got closer, I saw that the house was abandoned, boarded up. I remembered, then, that Mrs. Greenwood had said no one lived in the McNeill's house, but it was strange that the sign was still up. After that, there was nothing but bare trees, ice-covered roads, snow, and more snow. The tires on the old car had looked close to bald when I left, so I drove slow. It was the kind of place where people just left things by the side of the road, abandoned. I passed a boarded-up bakery with a *Closed* sign and a hotel with a weather-beaten *For Sale* sign. I saw an old doghouse on its side, then an empty stand that had once held firewood for sale. Then, there was nothing but trees again for a long while. I checked my phone. Still no signal. I didn't even want to talk to anyone, but *still*. Everything was white and gray and empty. It looked like the end of the world and the haze of nuclear winter. My soul felt like the landscape here. It was hard to believe that, back home, there were people wearing bright colors and going to the movies, too many people shopping at malls, buying things they didn't even need, returning gifts they'd just gotten to get other stuff. Here, it felt like they didn't even exist anymore. Maybe they didn't. Maybe I belonged here, here with this mournful woman and the ghost of her dead daughter.

Finally, I saw a building, its sign barely visible through the snowy haze. *Hemingway's Hardware and Sporting Goods*, it said with no irony at all.

I pulled into the nearly empty parking lot. I contemplated leaving the car running in case it didn't want to start again after it stopped. Finally, I decided to chance it.

The hardware store wasn't like anything I'd ever seen before either. In front was a bulletin board with items for sale, cats and snowmobiles. In its center was a Missing Person sign with a photo of a guy about my age. I examined it. The date he'd gone missing was a little over a year earlier. I counted him, Danielle, and the girl Danielle had mentioned in her diary, all missing. This place was starting to look like a rerun of *Cold Case*.

The sporting goods section was a wall devoted to fishing lures and guns. Another wall held secondhand items, waffle irons and battered board games, irons and baby dolls, model Hess trucks and vacuum cleaners. A fancy hairbrush that looked like silver lay on a shelf by a monkey made of coconut shells that someone had bought on vacation. Three golden retrievers lounged in various locations, and there were two white pigeons in a cage with a sign that said *Wedding doves for rent. Ask Josh.* The only other customer was a man in his seventies, examining a television set that had an antenna attached to the top.

"Hey, she's got you running errands already." Josh came up behind me.

"Yeah, I might need a jump-start—or a mechanic—if this car of hers doesn't start again."

He looked out the window. "Oh, that car's not that old. People around here believe in keeping things. We don't need any newfangled stuff when our stuff works just fine."

I thought he was joking when he said "newfangled," but I couldn't be sure.

"I mean . . ." He held up the fancy silver hairbrush with engraved flowers all over it. "Why have a plastic brush when you can have this one that weighs ten pounds, and why have one of those big, ugly flat screens when you can have this cute one?"

I nodded toward the old man, who was trying the television's knobs. "Can you even get cable on that thing?"

"If you can, he'll do it. Jerry knows a thing or two about repairs."

"Well, I'm learning. I'm looking for cabinet hinges. And I had a few questions."

"Cabinet hinges. What kind?"

I held out the old one I'd taken off. "Like this."

He gestured me toward another section, sort of hidden, considering this was a hardware store, behind the duck decoys and the tents and looked around. "We don't seem to have those in stock. I could order it, though, and you could pick it up in a few days."

The internet would probably be faster, but I wasn't really in a hurry. My grandfather always said it was important to patronize local businesses. Besides, I wanted info from Josh. So I said, "That would be great. Thanks."

I followed him to the counter, making conversation about another topic. "So, what's with the pigeons?"

"We rent them out for weddings and stuff. They look like doves, but pigeons always come back home. We've got a falcon too, but he can't stay at the shop because he eats road kill."

"Good to know." Trying to sound casual, I said, "Hey, have you ever heard of a place called the Red Fox Inn in Gatskill?"

Josh thought. He even said, "Hmm." Finally, he shook his head. "Doesn't ring a bell. Gatskill's the next town over, and it's pretty small. I'd think I'd have heard of everything in Gatskill."

"It's okay." I tried to hide my disappointment. "My mom and her friends used to go there when they were teenagers. It's probably closed now. She used to date a guy who played guitar there, a guy named Zach."

"He's not your long-lost father, is he?"

"No, nothing like that." Though that would be a good cover story. "She just wanted to find out if anyone had heard from him."

"Zach Gray." The old man with the TV suddenly came up behind us. "That's Rebecca Gray's grandson. He came to town eighteen years ago, then left."

"Eighteen?" It seemed pretty exact.

"Yup. I remember because that was the year of the big snowstorm." And then, he started in on a long, irrelevant story about the storm itself, the height of the snow, the number of days it fell, and how long it took for the flowers to come back afterward. But I was thinking eighteen years was right before Danielle had disappeared. Maybe he'd run away with her. Or maybe he'd killed her and gone on the lam.

The old man finally concluded his story, saying to Josh, "Will you take twenty for this TV?"

I thought he'd be lucky to get five, but Josh said, "I'll have to ask my dad. He only authorized me to sell for thirty. And he's not here today, so if you want it for the bowl games . . ."

"You drive a hard bargain, son." The old man took out a faded wallet and extracted some folded, soft-looking bills.

After he left, Josh said, "I don't know if you have plans for New Year's."

"Oh, yeah." I nodded. "I'm going to Times Square to celebrate with Ryan Seacrest."

"Whatever, man. If you don't have plans, a bunch of us are getting together. My family has a place on Grouse Lake. It's a three-season house, so it's almost inaccessible right now. Good for partying. I could pick you up if you're interested."

I nodded, realizing at that moment how much I really did miss hanging out with people. "That'd be great."

We made plans for the next day at ten, and Josh said he'd call when the hinges came in.

When I got home, Mrs. Greenwood was asleep on the sofa in front of the TV. An old rerun of *Star Trek* was on, the creepy theme song that sounded more like a theremin, this weird instrument, than a human voice. I wondered if that was what I'd heard earlier, the voice I'd heard on the wind. But it seemed unlikely that the old lady was a Trekkie. I figured her experience with science fiction was more along the lines of H. G. Wells. I tried to tiptoe past her, but she woke up.

"Oh, there you are. I can't believe I fell asleep during *Star Trek*." She picked up the remote and started rewinding. At least she had a real television. "I got cable just so I could still see William Shatner. That is one handsome man."

I grinned. "He's about your age now too."

"Well, I know. He was my age back then. Are you a Trekkie?"

"I can't tell a Vulcan from a Romulan."

"I could teach you."

I smiled. "Maybe later. I want to check out the connection."

Of course, I didn't do virtual school. The week between Christmas and New Year's was sacred, even for the virtually bored. Instead, I went on Facebook. They'd made Tyler's page into a memorial one with hundreds of messages, all talking about how they'd loved him, from people who wouldn't have loaned him a pencil when he was alive. I checked my own. No one was posting on it, only a few invitations to play CastleVille and Texas HoldEm, from people I didn't really know. Bored, I looked through my duffel bag and found the notebook from last night.

9

Danielle's Diary

I saw him again today! It has been three days since I first saw him. I haven't been able to get out, but today I was, and I went, pretending to walk Ginger, limping to the road. And by some miracle, he was there! He smiled. I noticed his eyes again, a shade of blue I'd never seen before.

"I couldn't come before. I'm sorry."

"I know. I came anyway, in case you made it today."

He walked around to open the car door. So polite, so different from the rude boys at school, who joked about how their "women" had better be ready at the door when they honked. I almost wished I could tell Mom about him. She was old-fashioned and liked stuff like that.

"I brought a picnic," he said.

"Every day?"

"So I've eaten a few picnic lunches. It was worth it. I thought we could go to the lake."

That was old-fashioned too, charming like the picnic basket—not a cooler—he'd brought, with its red-checkered lining. He held out his hand to help me into the car. Again, that shock. I shivered.

"Are you okay? Need a sweater?"

I shook my head. "It's a nice day."

It was a lovely day, and as we drove to the lake, a drive I'd made a hundred times before, I began to notice things I never had, the beauty of the black-eyed Susans, how the brown inside was like a dog's nose, and each petal formed a ruffle around. How it and the Queen Anne's lace grew against the craggy, gray rocks, sometimes clinging, sometimes avoiding, like a flirtatious girl. Even the rocks themselves glowed and sparkled. I mentioned that to Zach.

"Do you know why?" he asked.

"Of course. Everyone knows. There are bits of garnets in there, just little flecks It's my birthstone."

He nodded. "A red stone, fiery like you. There's a garnet mine about an hour from here. But they don't use the garnets for rings and necklaces. They make scouring pads out of them, or use them for stone washing jeans."

"That's not very romantic," I said.

"You're right." He touched my arm, maybe unintentionally. "In the right light, they glow just like diamonds. Just like you."

We went silent again after that. I realized I should speak. He wouldn't like me if I didn't talk. He'd think I was a weirdo.

But he spoke first. "I wasn't telling the whole truth the other day."

My heart clenched, wondering what he was going to tell me—that he'd been in jail or was thirty years old? But he said, "I have lived a lot of places, but I've been here before. My grandmother lived here, and my uncles still do. I used to visit them when I was younger, and now, I live with them. Actually, they own the bar where I perform."

I stared at him, mesmerized by his eyes.

"I thought you'd think it was geeky, living with my uncles, or that I was a loser. You were so beautiful, I wanted to impress you."

"I'm impressed," I said.

"It's kind of loserish. I left home, thinking I'd make it as a big rock star in New York, only to come back here with my tail between my legs."

"Are you still going to try to be a rock star?"

"Absolutely. I just ran out of money, so I'm working here for a while. They let me live for free. As soon as I've saved enough, I'm going back."

"That sounds like a good plan." He was so hot I thought he could make it even if he couldn't sing. "It was brave to leave home in the first place. I complain about my mother, but going to the big city all by myself sounds kind of daunting."

He pulled off the road then to a beautiful spot by the river. We waded in the water for a while. He took out the sandwiches. Over lunch, he asked me about my life.

"It's boring. I'd rather hear about you."

"It's not boring. You're not boring."

"There were only thirty kids in my graduating class, and I've known all of them since kindergarten. They'll all stay here and marry each other and have kids who'll stay here and marry each other and have kids who'll stay here and marry each other. A hundred years from now, the people in this town will look exactly the same."

"But that's great. That's what's cool about this place. It's like everything here, the rocks and the trees and the people too. They never change. That's what I loved about visiting here when I was a kid. We had all these traditions—like we'd always eat ice cream at the same places every year, the one near the waterfall and the old-fashioned one on Main Street. And we'd always go to the drive-in movie theater. Do you know how few towns have a drive-in movie anymore, but they do here because it always has to be the same."

"But I've never eaten a snail before."

"A snail?"

"On TV, you hear about people going to fancy restaurants and eating things like caviar or snails. But we don't have any restaurants like that here, and if we did, people would think it was gross anyway. Here, people just eat things like pot roast. Pot roast!"

He smiled. "That, I can help you with."

From the picnic basket, he removed a small container of what looked like salad. I'd noticed it before, but I hadn't gotten too excited about it. Salad wasn't my thing. "Try this?"

"Lettuce? Not very exciting." He didn't even have any dressing from what I could see.

But he opened the container and reached inside to take out one single leaf. He held it between two long, slender fingers. Beyond it, I could see his strange blue eyes, and then, the green itself seemed to glow almost blue too. It was shaped like a heart with little tendrils of smaller *hearts hanging from the stem. I opened my mouth.*

The second the leaf touched my tongue, I was over-whelmed with a feeling of incredible peace. As I chewed, the world grew sharper, brighter. I could pick out the songs of individual birds and smell the pine trees and each flower. In fact, I could even see the flowers bloom-ing.

Zach leaned toward me. His eyes were psychedelic blue. "You know what else is exciting?" he said. "You."

And he kissed me. I kissed him back, and I don't know what was real after that and what was a dream. I could see the reflections of trees on the lake, and I felt like I could jump in and climb them, entering another world, a tree world. Then, Zach was carrying me across a field of flowers toward a ruined tower I'd never seen before. All I knew for sure was that I was in love, so in love, and from this day forward, everything in time will be divided between the days before I met Zach and the days after.

I'm in love.

As I finished the page, Mrs. Greenwood called me, for dinner. Then, we watched *Star Trek*, which apparently is on all the time somewhere, if you have five thousand cable channels. It wasn't as dumb as I thought it was.

I told Mrs. Greenwood that.

She nodded. "Gene Roddenberry, the creator, wanted to show what mankind might develop into, if only they learned from their mistakes."

"Fascinating," I said, imitating Mr. Spock.

"He wanted to end violence. For example, the Vulcans had a very violent past but learned to control it by controlling their emotions."

"Should people control their emotions?" I asked.

"Sometimes, you have to, I suppose. You have to avoid thinking of what upsets you. If not, it will take over your life. I know. . . ."

She meant Danielle, her thinking about Danielle. I wanted to find out more about what had happened to her. Had Zach drugged her? Why? But by the time I went upstairs, I was tired, so tired. I thought it was the altitude, 'cause I just fell into bed and slept with no trouble, the first time since Tyler died.

But a few hours later, I woke once again to an eerie voice, singing on the wind.

It wasn't the *Star Trek* theme. It came from outside my window.

I bolted up and walked across the room, thinking maybe it was Danielle. But there was no one there, only the voice.

Rachel

Sometimes, I like to crouch on the floor and look upward, out the window. Then, I can tell if it's a blue sky, which I know from books means a clear day, the kind of day on which Elizabeth Bennet and her sisters might walk into town in *Pride and Prejudice,* or a gray sky, which might mean a stormy day, the sort of day on which Jo March in *Little Women* might huddle under an umbrella with Professor Bhaer.

Not that it matters, for I never go out. But still, I like to know. It makes me feel like a part of the world.

Even though I'm not.

I'll leave soon, though. I know I will.

I worry that I won't be ready, that I won't know the things I need to know and that people (people!) will think me stupid. I've been doing exercises, trying to remember what I knew of the outside world. If I read a book, I try to picture the objects mentioned. Some things are easy to envision for they are things I own. Chair. Hairbrush. Picture. Others, I cannot visualize at all. Like, in *Emma*, when Mr. Knightley sent his carriage to pick up Harriet, I thought and thought of what a carriage might look like, but I completely failed to envision it. I am certain I have never seen one.

And then, there are items in the middle, items I might remember if I only try hard enough. Dog. When Mr. Rochester meets Jane Eyre for the first time, he has a dog with him, Pilot. At first, I could not think what a dog might be, though I assumed it was some sort of animal, a furry one like the animals I see from my window, which Mama tells me are called squirrels (the small ones) or deer (the larger ones). But, gradually, if I closed my eyes, if I reached back into the far recesses of my memory, I thought I could remember a creature, larger than I had been at the time. I could feel its rough fur between my fingers, and its tongue on my face. It made me happy to think about the dog, so happy I wished for a moment that I could have a dog myself.

But, of course, that wouldn't do. A dog can't live in a tower. Dogs, I now remembered, were vigorous creatures. They needed to run, to play.

But didn't I? I had never tried to escape, had always just listened to Mama. What would happen if I had?

Yesterday, I had quite a shock. I was rereading *Wuthering Heights*, which is my favorite book. I especially like the part where Catherine, who never seems to leave the house either, sneaks out with Heathcliff to spy on the Linton children. Their dog (dog, again), Skulker, bites Catherine on the leg, and she must stay with the Lintons until she recovers.

I liked that part because Catherine is like I am, sheltered from the world. But as soon as she meets the Lintons, they like her. They take her in, and she ends up marrying the charming and wealthy Edgar.

But what upset me was, when I turned to the end of the book, for the first time I noticed there was a page about the author, Emily Brontë.

And it said she was dead!

Long dead from the look of it. It said she had died in 1848.

Which motivated me to look through my other books to learn about *their* authors. The authors, after all, seemed the most like friends of anyone. I learned that Daphne du Maurier was born in 1907, almost sixty years after Emily Brontë had died. And her characters, unlike Brontë's or Austen's, drove around in motorcars!

I could picture a car. Mama had one, and when she took me to this tower on a rainy, gloomy day, it was a car that brought me here. Or, at least, most of the way. The last part, we walked.

I remember the feeling of being in the car. Mama made me put my head down so I couldn't look out, but I felt the motion of the road beneath me, and when we arrived, I felt the grass and rocks beneath my feet. It was the last I'd felt them.

When Mama arrived to see me, I had some questions for her.

"Mama, what year is it?"

She stepped back a bit at the question. "Please, Rachel, you must allow me to catch my breath before you bombard me with questions."

"I'm not bombarding," I said, thinking I probably didn't question enough. But then, I apologized. My tower, I knew, was over fifty feet high, and Mama reached it by walking up steps from the bottom and crawling through a trap door. When she came, she was out of breath and needed to rest. She hadn't always been so out of breath but, she explained, she was getting older.

Sometimes, I wondered what would happen if Mama died. Did anyone else know I was here? Would I die too?

But I didn't ask that question. I would leave before that happened.

When she caught her breath, she reached for a book to read to me. She always read before we ate. She said it was therapeutic. But before she started reading, I said, "Mama, you forgot to answer my question."

"What question is that?"

"What year is it?"

She fidgeted through the pages of the book. "Why do you care so much?"

"Why would I not care?" And yet, it was difficult to put my reasons into words. "Because it is . . . strange not to know such a thing. I understand that you are trying to protect me from . . ." *What? Life? The world?* ". . . those who would do me ill." Mama had told me that the man who had killed my mother had also tried to have me killed, but she had saved me. "Yet, someday, I must go out into the world, and I do not wish to be thought strange. I wish to be ordinary. I'm not mad, after all, like Bertha Rochester, who needed to be locked in an attic."

I wasn't mad, was I? What if I was and I only didn't know it because of the level of my dementia? Did madwomen know they were mad? Or did they think they were sane, and it was the world that was off-kilter? What if everything, my tower, the trees, even the squirrels were all figments of my mad imaginings?

But if these were my imaginings, why would I not imagine something else, something better?

"Am I mad? Is that why you keep me here?" I twisted my neck to see her, for she had moved behind me.

"Of course not, darling Rachel." She reached to stroke my cheek and, simultaneously, to move my face so that I was not looking at her. Yet I detected a strange expression on her face, an expression like panic. "It is not you who are mad but the world, Rachel." She reached for my hairbrush. Even though she no longer had my special brush, she sometimes brushed my hair when she came, for old time's sake. But this time, the brush caught on a knot. I clutched my head.

"Ouch! You're hurting me!"

"I'm sorry, my dear Rachel, so sorry. I do not wish to harm you. I only . . . you must stay here a bit longer. Perhaps you do not trust me."

"Oh, no, Mama. I do trust you." Up until this minute, I had. But why was she becoming so agitated when all I wanted was a few answers to my questions. If she intended to release me, I would need to know.

"I only want what is best for you. I only . . ." She broke down, crying. "I can't lose you, Rachel! I can't. I have already lost so much."

Her face looked so old and sad that I began to weep too. I wept so easily lately, wept reading books, even books I knew very well.

"I'm sorry, Mama. I don't want to leave. I am happy here with my books and with . . . you. I just wondered . . ."

"What, Rachel?" Her face was stormy. "What is it you wonder?"

"It's only that the books I have, I have read so many times. Not that Mr. Dickens and the Brontë sisters do not seem like old friends, but I thought, perhaps, there might be different books, newer books."

It is not what I wanted. I wanted what I had said I wanted, to know what year it was. To know who I was. To know where I was and when I would be released. In many ways, I could see I was becoming a young lady, old enough to marry and have children perhaps. In other ways, though, I was a child, a child who knew nothing and everything kept from me, and I was sick of it. But I was also trapped, trapped and at her mercy. I couldn't have what I wanted, so I would have to settle for newer books until I found a way.

She paused in her brushing, and I heard her take a deep breath in, then out. "Oh, is that all? I can get you new books, all you want.

How thoughtless of me not to realize that an intelligent young lady must have some occupation for her mind. What sort of books do you want?"

I shrugged. I didn't know what kind there were. "I want books . . . that show what it is like to be human," I said, "because I am not sure I know. And if the author is alive, I would very much appreciate it."

"Very well," Mama said. "Should we have dinner now?"

I nodded. Our days were a routine pattern. She came to visit me in darkness. She brushed my hair. We ate dinner, played chess or cards. I sang to her and played the harp. I had taught myself to do both, and I practiced day and night, even if it was only to please her. She said my voice was beautiful. That used to be enough.

But then, I stopped singing, stopped playing the harp when Mama wasn't around to hear. What was the point, I reasoned, of singing when no one was there to hear? Who knew if my singing was even real and not a figment of my imagination? Who knew that *I*, my entire existence, was not a figment of my imagination?

Then, she left, leaving my breakfast for the next day and taking with her my chamber pot, which I was old enough to be embarrassed by. That was all.

Wasn't there more to my life than that?

"I brought ham, your favorite." She smiled and nodded, inviting me to do the same. "I want you to be happy."

I smiled back at her. "Thank you, Mama. I am."

When she left, I began to sing again, and to play my harp. Even though no one was there.

Strangely, I felt that someone could hear me.

And, last night, when I was singing, I thought I heard a voice in my head.

11

Wyatt

New Year's Eve, the night was clear with so many stars it looked like the sky in the movie *Titanic*, when the ship had gone down, and they were waiting in the dark water to die. It was just as cold too. The idea of spending the two-degree night in what Josh called a three-season house (the three seasons being spring, summer, and fall) seemed a little crazy, but the idea of spending it alone, watching Times Square on TV, seemed worse.

Last year, we'd gone into the city. This wasn't a typical thing Long Island kids did, but Tyler had suggested it. One day, during winter break when we were bored, he'd said, "Hey, let's go to Times Square tomorrow."

"I never want to do that, man," I said. "I hear it's suffocating there."

"Never's a long time, *MAN*," he said. "You want to be one of those people who live in New York your whole life and never see the Statue of Liberty or the Macy's parade or New Year's in Times Square?"

"Well, I've seen the Statue of Liberty," I said, "on any one of five field trips with five different teachers who thought I needed to learn—yet again—about how they dewormed the immigrants at Ellis Island. As far as Times Square, if it means getting felt up by street people in twenty-degree weather, I'd seriously rather eat glass."

"Not me," Tyler said. "It's on my bucket list."

I shrugged. "You've got time."

But he just kept pushing, pushing, pushing, and finally, when he said his sister, Nikki, would go with us, I gave in.

In fact, it hadn't been cold. Far from it. Millions of pressing bodies had taken care of that. But everything else had pretty much come true. We were shoulder to shoulder with sweaty strangers, no bathrooms, no food. People who got there after us tried to shove in front.

"Really," a nasal-voiced woman said, "we're meeting friends."

"Yeah?" Tyler said. "Call them on your cell phone and have them raise their hands."

The woman called Tyler a word I don't even say.

"Happy New Year," I told her.

Tyler and I were tall, so at least we could see and stuff, but his sister, Nikki, was smaller. "I can't even breathe," she said.

"Like that's important." Tyler rolled his eyes.

But I said, "Are you okay? You want me to put you on my shoulders?"

"I can't ask you to do that. There's still an hour until midnight." Around us, people were gyrating to music we couldn't hear over the talking. Someone jostled me, separating me from Nikki.

"Wyatt!" Her voice sounded panicked, yelling for me, not her brother. I reached through the crowd. I'd taken off my gloves because of the heat, and I felt for her nubby wool coat. My hand brushed another hand. "Is that you?"

I felt her fingers grip around mine. She squeezed hard.

I couldn't see Tyler. There was someone separating us. I moved closer to Nikki. Finally, I shoved past and found her. "You want to leave?" I asked.

"How can we? Besides, Tyler really wants to stay, but all these people are making me dizzy. Can you just . . . hold my hand? It makes it easier to breathe."

"Maybe if you closed your eyes," I said, "or looked up? Maybe if you didn't see everyone."

"I'll try that." She tilted her head back and looked straight up. I did too, so I could see what she saw. The sky was clear but starless. The buildings cast too much light. She squeezed my hand harder, then looked me in the eyes. "That's way better. Thanks."

I squeezed her hand back, and in that moment, I knew something had changed. She wasn't the girl I'd grown up with. She was someone else.

But the next day, when I'd asked her out, she'd said no.

"I don't want to complicate things. I like what we have. I don't want to ruin it."

It made sense, of course. I was friends with Tyler, and Nikki was his sister. Awkward didn't begin to describe it. Still, it felt like a rejection.

Not that it mattered now.

Josh was picking me up, good since no way could Mrs. G's car navigate the hills in the dark and snow. Still, I figured I should clear it with her. I mean, maybe she'd wanted to watch *New Year's Rocking Eve* together.

But when I asked her, she said, "Oh, no. You get to a point, at my age, where one year seems pretty much like any other. I'll probably just go to bed early."

For some reason, rather than making me feel better about ditching her, I felt worse, like I should be the thing that made this year different. She'd been alone so long. Of course, I wasn't her kid anyway. I said, "You know, I was thinking, if you wanted to get a dog, I could walk it or something."

"Oh, you'll only be here a bit longer."

"I guess. I don't know. I sort of like it. Maybe I'd go to college up here." It was the first time I'd thought about it. A lot of my friends would go to the same college, room together, make college more like thirteenth grade. I wasn't sure I'd want that.

The old woman smiled. "You must miss your mother, or maybe your friends." She stopped. She knew about Tyler.

I shook my head no. The only friend I missed was Tyler, and he wasn't on Long Island. I wondered if she felt that way about Danielle. "Sometimes, it's good to make a fresh start."

Josh picked me up around ten. I was the eighth person in a car that would have been crowded with seven. "I don't see how we're going to get up the hill with all these people," one of his friends, a guy named Brendan, griped.

"Some of us will have to get out and walk," Josh said. "Or you could walk now. It's my car."

That shut him up. I squeezed in, trying not to sit on anyone's lap.

"Everyone, this is Wyatt," Josh said. "He's from Long Island."

"You're staying with Old Lady Greenwood?" said a girl I could barely see under her scarf and hat. "Creepy."

"What's creepy about her?"

"Oh, I don't know. That old house. We used to dare each other to ring her doorbell on Halloween night, then run away."

That was sweet of you. But I said, "She's okay."

"So you've actually been inside the house?" Brendan said. "Are there any secret passages? Jars marked *Eye of Newt*, stuff like that?"

"Well, I did find this one closet she wouldn't let me into. I think it's where she stores the skin of her victims before she uses it." I noticed the car had gone sort of silent. "Hey, she made me an apple cake."

"You shouldn't eat it," the girl said. "Haven't you seen Snow White?"

"I heard she killed her daughter," Brendan said.

"That's not true." I remembered how she'd screamed into the night for Danielle. "And I was kidding about the closet," I added, in case they were too stupid to get that.

"I knew that," the girl said. But then, she turned away, talking to the girl beside her—at least, I think it was a girl. Hard to tell with all the coats. Everyone else went back to what they were doing and saying, and I was left wondering about people back home, if they'd noticed I was gone. We were driving through town now, and by instinct, I checked my phone for texts even though it meant jostling three people. One bar. No messages.

We drove in silence, finally making a sharp turn off the main road onto a side road. Then, there was a dirt path that disappeared down a hill. I wouldn't even have noticed the path if we hadn't been on it. I wondered if it was safe. I decided I didn't care. The trees on both sides of the car came up like cave walls, and ahead, there was nothing, nothing I could see anyway. Finally, the car would go no farther. Josh said, "We'll have to walk from here."

I was glad too. It was hot, and a car feels even more crowded when it's full of people you don't know. Their voices drummed in my ears. I pushed the door open and, feeling the rush of cold air, realized I'd been holding my breath. Everyone else clambered out behind me, and we began the work of trudging through the snow toward a house

I still couldn't see. I noticed some people had six-packs or bags of chips. "Was I supposed to bring something?" I asked Josh.

"Nah, I knew you wouldn't get out much, with Old Lady Greenwood. I brought some chips on your behalf."

One of the guys had a glass bottle of something. "I don't really drink," I said. "I mean, I'm not a jerk about it, but I don't really drink."

"It's okay. You can be the designated driver."

"You better designate someone else to pull this car onto the main road too."

"Don't have that on Long Island, huh?" The guy laughed.

"Nope."

We all stopped talking then, concentrating on walking. A lot of the snow had melted, but it was still hard going, and I realized Josh was right. This wasn't what I was used to. I was a city kid, meant for paved streets and shoveled sidewalks, and the hick kids with their stronger muscles were leaving me in the dust.

I was at least ten feet behind the last of them, even the girls, when I heard a sound too human to be wind.

Singing.

There was no TV showing *Star Trek* here, and I could almost make out words. I wanted to tell everyone to stop, stop stepping, stop crunching snow, so I could hear. But that would look crazy, so I said, "What's that?"

"What?" the girl in front of me said, and they all stopped walking so, for a moment, it was silent, and I could have heard it. But, of course, like all weird sounds, it ceased to exist when pointed out to someone else.

"It stopped," I said. "But it sounded like someone singing. I've heard it at the house too, but this seemed closer."

"Probably a loon," the girl said.

"Are there loons in the middle of winter?" Everyone started walking again, driven on by the cold as much as their boredom with the conversation. At least I hoped so. "I mean, don't they fly south? Besides, this sounded human."

"So do loons."

I knew what I had heard, but I didn't pursue it. It wasn't worth it. Obviously, there was no legendary local ghost everyone had heard of. Maybe it was my imagination. Maybe I was crazy. We kept walking, and a minute later, I heard another sound, an actual bird or animal. Maybe it was a real loon.

The girl turned back to me. "Was that it?"

"Probably," I said, even though it wasn't.

"I'm Astrid, by the way."

"Wyatt."

"I know. You must be pretty bored at Old Lady Greenwood's. Because, if you are, you should get a lift ticket for Gore Mountain. It's not too far. We go all season."

"I ski a little, but probably not as well as you. I'd drag you down."

"Doesn't matter. You could take lessons. My older sister goes to UAlbany, and she's a ski instructor. We've got extra skis. How tall are you?"

"About six feet."

And then, I heard it again, not the bird or the wolf or the loon or whatever, the other thing, off in the distance.

"There! Did you hear that?"

She shook her head. Maybe I was going nuts. Thankfully, we had reached the house. It wasn't a whole lot warmer than outside, but there was wood by the fireplace. "Know how to make a fire, City Boy?" Josh asked.

I nodded. I'd been in Boy Scouts. This, too, reminded me of Tyler. He wanted to get his Eagle Scout and had pressured me to stick with it, to do it together. "Got a lighter? Or do I need to rub two sticks together?"

Josh handed me a long, blue lighter, and I busied myself, breaking off smaller splinters to use as kindling and arranging the logs just right while, around me, people I didn't know talked about other people I didn't know. But I kept listening for the sound from before, which had sounded closer, so much closer, than at Mrs. Greenwood's house, but now, all I heard was the chattering of strangers and the howling of the wind.

But it was a voice. A girl's voice. And somehow, I knew that whoever she was, she was beautiful and also lonely, like I was. I told myself I didn't want to be around anyone, but that wasn't true. I only didn't want to be around people who knew me.

"Need any help?" Astrid asked. She'd taken off her hood, and I could see she was pretty, auburn hair and cheeks flushed pink from the cold.

I didn't really need help, but it was probably better not to be a recluse. Someone had turned on music, loud stuff like Nikki used to like, gothic metal, and someone else was complaining about the music choice, trying to push their own stuff. So I couldn't have heard an outside noise, even if it did exist.

Which it probably didn't.

But Astrid was hot, so I handed her Josh's lighter. "Can you hold this, maybe? And could you see if there are newspapers or anything."

"You mean like these?" She pointed to a pile underneath all the logs.

"Oh, exactly like that. Sorry."

She reached for the papers. "Any particular section you like? Local? Sports? Looks like the Adirondack Phantoms were having a good season in 2011. Sorry, they're a little old."

"That's okay." I took the paper and started rolling it up.

"What I said before, I'd be perfectly happy to ski with you even if you completely suck at it."

"I wouldn't say suck."

"In fact, if I can be totally honest here, there are, like, seventy-five people in my class at school, and we've all been together since kindergarten. It's nice to have a new face in town. We get so few."

"I'll bet."

"So, basically." She put her hand on her hip. "Any guy shows up with all his limbs or maybe even missing one or two, and he doesn't actually pick his nose in public, he's going to get a lot of attention."

"That's flattering." I laughed and stuffed the rolled-up newspaper between the logs. "How do you know I don't pick my nose in public?" I held out my hand for the lighter.

"Do you?" She shrugged. "You haven't so far."

Instead of handing me the lighter, she leaned down across me and lit the paper herself. Her hair, brushing against my nose, smelled familiar, and I remembered last year at midnight. Even though I hadn't told anyone, Nikki and I had kissed at midnight. Would I be kissing this girl tonight? Would something bad happen to her?

Stupid thought. She was hot. She was coming on to me, and I was choosing to be in bed every night, reading a dead girl's diary all alone.

The paper caught, and the flames warmed my face, and she was still there, standing there beside me, warming the other side. "Um, can you hand me the poker?"

When she did, our hands brushed for an instant. I didn't feel the spark I wanted. She was pretty and she was nice, but she wasn't Nikki. I didn't even know what I wanted, maybe Nikki, maybe no one. But I didn't want to live with my ghosts forever.

"Hey, City Boy." Josh threw a corn chip at me. "I don't know how you make a fire on Lawn Guyland where you're from, but here in the freezing north, we do it a little faster."

"Yes, sir." I seized the poker and began moving the logs around until something caught and suddenly there was a good blaze going.

Now, people were splitting off into couples. Astrid and I moved to a chair by the window, far from the fire and everyone, where she said we could talk. But in ten minutes, we were making out, and I had my tongue in her mouth, my hand up her shirt, and she was pressing against me in a way that could have felt really good if there weren't all these people here. And if I didn't feel so dead inside.

I kissed her again. Around me, everyone else was making out too, like it was required. I kissed her, long and hard to get all the voices in my head to stop. I fumbled with her clothes and tried to just go with it. Be normal. Maybe if you acted normal, if you pretended everything was normal, it would be again.

Soon, Josh announced that it was almost midnight. We stood to do the countdown, and I kissed Astrid's bruised lips even though at that point, it was a little redundant. Then, a little while later, someone said we should get going.

I agreed and put on my coat, then helped Astrid with hers.

Then, as the door opened, I heard it again. The voice. A girl's voice. I didn't say anything, though. I knew not to, in case I was crazy. But I glanced in the direction it had come from, and I saw something high among the trees. A light.

Probably just the moon. Or a planet.

I knew it wasn't a planet, though. It was bigger than a planet, and lower. But, obviously, I was hallucinating.

Astrid took my hand and pulled me down the path, but I knew I had to come back. Tomorrow. I had to find out what it was.

When we got to the car, Astrid tried to get me to sit in the back, with her on my lap, but I offered to drive. "I think we're the only ones that aren't wasted, right?" I said to Josh.

Astrid pouted, but Josh handed me his keys.

"Are you sure?" she said, taking the seat behind me.

"Lot of crazy people out on New Year's. Kids get killed all the time." I also wanted to make sure I knew the way back here. "Besides, I'd rather be alone with you, not in a car full of people."

"I understand." But then, she leaned forward and kissed my ear.

"I have to turn this thing around. It's hard with the trees."

I somehow managed to do a three-point turn in the middle of a forest, and drove a long way toward the road. When I finally reached the main route, I looked at the name of the street I'd turned off of. Dickinson. I wondered who Dickinson was, some founding father of this crap town, or was it someone loftier, like the poet? Josh said to turn right, which was south, so I knew the cabin was even farther north. Then, I saw a sign that said Grouse Lake, and I remembered that was what Josh had said the name of the lake was.

Astrid lived closest to town, so I dropped her off last, except for Josh. She made me get out of the car. "So, are we going skiing tomorrow?" She giggled. "I mean, today?"

I thought fast. "I might be a little, um, tired."

"But we're going, right?" Her voice had an edge like an ice-skate blade.

"Oh, absolutely. Just, maybe, tomorrow."

"You'll call me? Or I could call you?"

"My cell doesn't work up here. Let me get your number. I'll call you from Mrs. G's landline."

We exchanged numbers, and Astrid went inside. I dropped Josh off next, promising to bring the car back the next day. "Hey, your hinges are in too," he said.

When I got to the house, the path was covered with a fresh dusting of snow. I'd have to shovel it again. I fumbled for the key, and as I did, I heard a sound in the distant north. Singing. But that was impossible.

Maybe I was crazy.

But if I was, I might as well find out.

Even though it was after two in the morning, I couldn't sleep. I lay in bed, listening to the wind outside. It howled like a lost soul. I wished I'd brought my television from home. Sometimes, when I couldn't sleep, I turned it on and it lulled me into a coma. I could go downstairs and watch. Maybe Mrs. Greenwood was even up, watching *Star Trek*. Instead, I watched the digital clock turn from 2:21 to 2:22. Tyler and Nikki had had a superstition about praying at 11:11 at night. I didn't know about 2:22.

2:23.

2:24.

I heard something downstairs, a key in the lock. I swam through the swampy waters of what had almost been sleep. Who was here? What was that sound? But it couldn't be a key in the lock. There was no one here but me and the old lady, and she'd probably been asleep for hours. I glanced at the clock. 2:49. I'd been asleep, likely dreaming.

Now that I had slept, I couldn't go back. It was like I'd slept a full night.

I felt something hard under my head. The diary. It had been days since I'd read it. I was lucky Mrs. Greenwood hadn't noticed it. Though I'd told her I would do my own laundry, she insisted she'd do it and informed me that the beds were changed Monday.

It was Monday today.

I didn't know why I didn't want Mrs. Greenwood to know about Danielle's diary. Originally, it was because of the way she'd scared me that first night. Now, it was because I didn't want to remind her, as if she needed reminding. Or, maybe, I didn't want to give her hope when there was none. Still, I wanted to finish the diary. In these early lonely days, Danielle had become something like a friend.

Too bad she was probably a dead one.

I didn't hear any footsteps in the hallway, nothing but the wind. The door had been my imagination. Of course it had. My imagination trying to persuade me I wasn't all alone, when I was. Giving up on sleep, I turned on the light and, once again, opened the diary.

12

Danielle's Diary

He's gone! I'm sure of it! He's gone, and the world has ended. Ended!

Every day for a week, he came to me, and it was wonderful. We made love among the trees by the lake, and I saw visions I had never seen before. I used to think this place was ugly, gray, dead. With Zach, it was beautiful.

But now, he is gone. I have walked Ginger out to the road every day this week, and I've returned, having gained nothing but exercise. Has he left town? Or worse, has he died? Been hit by a car? Gotten sick?

Or has he merely decided he doesn't like me anymore?

At night, I have been plagued by the strangest dreams,

dreams in which colors have sounds and something chases me across the sky with spidery, flaming legs. I ran away from it, but also, toward something. Was it Zach? Before I could reach the end, I would wake, sweating, unable to scream.

I began to make plans to sneak away, to concoct a ruse to go to the Red Fox Inn.

And then, yesterday, I did.

Mom has been sick for several days. It's only a cough, but from the way she acts, you'd think she was near death. We are running low on groceries. Earlier in the week, I offered to go shop, but she said it was unnecessary. She'd be better soon. But now, it's been several days. We're out of milk and almost out of bread. I told Mom this.

"We can get milk from Mrs. McNeill," she said, "and I can make bread." And then, a cough racked her body, doubling her up and making her hack grotesquely for over a minute.

When she finished, I said, "I wouldn't eat any bread you made. I could get the plague. Besides, you should rest."

"I've been in bed these three days, and it hasn't helped. I can't sleep for all this coughing."

"Some medicine, maybe. Maybe Dr. Fine . . ." I stopped. I didn't want her to go to the doctor because, then, she'd come to town with me. "I could call Dr. Fine and describe your symptoms. Then, he could phone something in."

"He wouldn't. Dr. Fine isn't helpful unless there's a check involved. He'll want me to go there, and I'm too sick to go out."

Could she be any more difficult?

"Oh!" I remembered the nighttime cold medicine I had in my bottom dresser drawer. Some kids at school said they took it to get high, but when I did, it only made me want to sleep forever and ever. Nothing like whatever I took with Zach. But if Mom took the cold meds, I could go out or do anything I wanted. "I just remembered I have this really good cough medicine. I'll get it for you."

"Nothing will help."

"Try this."

I measured the green fluid into the plastic dose cup, filling it a bit higher than necessary, but only a bit. I didn't want to kill her, only to assure she slept a good four or five hours. I brought it to her, walking carefully so as not to spill it.

"Disgusting color," she said, appraising it. "It must be effective."

"Let's hope so. But it tastes really bad." I wanted to warn her. It would suck if she did a spit take and didn't ingest it. "Maybe hold your nose."

"It's okay. I have no sense of taste today." She raised the cup and drank it all the way down. Yes! "It burns a bit."

"Why don't you go lie down, and I'll make you a cup of tea?"

Amazingly, she agreed to that. I took my time, making the tea, and when I went upstairs, she was already asleep, snoring, the phlegm rattling as it gushed in and out of her nose. Gross.

"Here's your tea, Mom." I said it soft, so as not to wake her. Nothing. Her purse was on the dresser. I reached inside, quiet as I could, keeping an eye on her the whole time my hands searched for her car keys. She had a keychain with an old photo of me in a Lucite frame. One side was cracked, and I felt the scratchy, thick edge. I pulled up on it.

A slight tinkling noise. In her bed, Mom stirred, but she didn't sit upright and accuse me of stealing from her. That was good. I was just being paranoid. I left the tea on her nightstand.

The car didn't want to start at first, but finally, it turned over. I had at least three hours, maybe more. I decided to go to the store first so I wouldn't forget and also, because Zach might not be at work early.

There was a grocery store in Gatskill. No one knew me there. Slakkill is so small that, one summer, when Emily and I got jobs bagging groceries, Mr. Gates, the manager, told us to follow anyone who wasn't from around here. We knew who bought cigarettes without permission, and we knew who bought condoms. Soon, everyone else knew too.

So I went to the grocery store and bought milk and bread and something else.

Then, I went to the Red Fox Inn.

It was a seedy-looking place with dirty windows and a parking lot that was either dirt with patches of grass or grass with patches of dirt. Even though it was only four, there were already cars outside, and I guessed they'd probably been there a while. The rusty doorknob stuck when I tugged it, but finally, it gave way. I was in a dark room that smelled of old beer. My shoes stuck to the floor. I made my way to the bar.

"Hey, girlie." The bartender smiled, showing an incomplete set of teeth. "Aren't you a little young to be in here?"

"I'm seventeen."

"Drinking age is twenty-one. But I'll play along. What can I get you?"

"Nothing." My eyes were barely adjusted to the darkness, and I squinted at him. "I'm looking for Zach. A guy named Zach who works here?" As I said it, I felt a sudden uncertainty. What if he didn't work here after all?

But he said, "I know who Zach is. You and me both are looking for him."

"What do you mean?" But I knew. He was gone.

"He's gone," the guy echoed. "Disappeared. One day, he said he'd done what he came here to do. The next night, he didn't show up at work. I wouldn't have minded so much, but he was bringing the ladies in. Girls like you, they came to stare at him, and the men came to stare at them."

I barely heard this because my blood was pounding, pulsing in my ears like the feedback of an electric guitar. Once, when I was little, my mother took me to the beach, Fire Island, way far away from here. I remember being surprised at how the ocean attacked me, so unlike the peaceful lakes I knew. I just stood there, and it took me down to the sandy floor, so rough against my cheek. That was how I felt, and through it, I could hear the bartender's words: "He said he'd done what he came here to do."

What he came here to do.

What did that mean?

"So what's your name, little girl?" the old man said.

"Me, um, Danielle. If Zach comes back, can you tell him to call me? Or find me? It's really important."

The old man didn't answer for a moment. I looked up at him and saw that his eyes had taken on a sort of fixed look, a little scary. Then, they latched onto me. "Danielle? Wouldn't be Danielle Greenwood, would it?" He reached out his hand toward me. It was old and gnarled.

I backed away. "I have to go." How did he know my name? Maybe from Zach?

He took a step closer, his hand brushing my wrist, almost grasping it. "Wait! I may see him. I'll give him a message."

I pulled my hand away. "No! That's okay!"

And I ran.

I am still trying to understand as I sit here, writing in my journal, waiting. But I don't need to wait. I know what I'll find out.

And I know he is gone.

Rachel

Is it a dream if you're not even sure you're asleep?

Lately, I've been having these dreams, strange dreams. Or maybe, they're fantasies. In my dreams, there is a man. He comes to my window because the door is locked, and he says, "I'm going to steal you away."

But even in my dreams, I know I cannot go with him. At first, I thought it was because of Mama, because she would be alone and miss me. But one day, I realized that wasn't the reason at all. In fact, I am meant to leave Mama. But first, there was something else I had to do, something so important that only I could do it.

I liked that thought. There is nothing like sitting alone in a tower all day to make a person feel worthless, depressed. Often, I've thought that nothing in the world would change if I did not get up in the morning, if I didn't get dressed.

I told Mama this and, not surprisingly, she disagreed. I was important to her, she said. She loved me and would miss me if I was gone.

But how much did that matter, really?

Perhaps the dreams were something I made up myself, to make me feel better. But I didn't think so.

I did not waste time, wondering what it was I must do. I knew that, eventually, I would find the answer. Just like I found the answer to the other question that had been troubling my mind—the question of how my rescuer would be able to reach my window, so high in the air.

In my vision, at first I only saw his face. It was a handsome one, dark hair and eyes the color of the evergreen trees outside my window.

But something lurked in those eyes too, something troubling, as if some tragedy had befallen him, a sorrow he could never quite forget.

Like what happened to my mother.

At first, I merely saw his face, his hands on the window ledge. Then, his whole body as he swung himself through the window. Only I could not see what he swung on.

Until, one day, I told my dream self to look down. I approached the window, looking not just at the man, who had, up until then, fascinated me, but at the mechanics of his being there.

And it was then that I saw how he had come to my window. He had not flown, but almost. Almost. He had climbed on a rope. I knew without asking that the rope had been one of my own tying.

I knew for two reasons.

First, the rope was tied to an iron bench by my window, an object firmly in my control.

Second, the rope was woven from silken strands of yellow. It was woven from my hair.

This may seem insane. How can hair be woven into rope, a rope long enough to cascade to the ground from such a height, a rope long as the trunks of ancient trees?

My hair has always grown quickly, so quickly that it must be cut once a week, just to stay at a length where it doesn't trip me. But, lately, it has been growing even more quickly.

Mama usually cuts my hair on Sunday. She allows it to grow to my waist, no farther.

But, this past Sunday, when I went to bed at night, I felt a tugging. I was sleeping on top of my hair. It had already grown far past my waist, and it had been mere hours since it had been cut.

Thinking this strange, I braided it up and threw the braids over my shoulder, so they just touched the floor.

When I woke, the braids were on the floor, all the way on the floor. But I couldn't see them because coiled over them was more hair, so much more golden hair than I had braided. It grew so fast that I could see it move if I watched it. When I stood, it reached the floor, and if I folded it over, it would reach my head again.

For some reason, I knew not to tell Mama. Rather, I brushed and braided it, a task of hours, and then, I hid it under my covers. I even tucked part of it under the mattress.

When Mama came, I dimmed the lights. "I feel sick today. Please don't turn on the lights. It hurts my eyes." I often got headaches, so this was believable, though I never caught cold. Girls in books got sick from the cold or going out in the rain or being exposed to others who were ill. I did none of those things.

But Mama said, "Oh, my poor dear," and pressed her wrinkled hand to my forehead.

"No fever, at least. Had I but known, I would have brought you a nice chicken soup."

But, of course, there was no way for her to know because she was not there. But I did not say it. I would argue sometime when I was not hiding twenty feet of hair beneath my covers. Today was a day to be sweet, not cross. "Can you bring it tomorrow? Or come back later?"

She never came twice in one day, but I thought perhaps this one time, she might.

"I get so lonely here, especially when I am sick."

She smiled, so I added, "And can you bring me some items as well?"

"What is it you want, my dear?"

I had thought a great deal about this, about a list of items, a long list, to mask my real request.

"My art supplies are dwindling. I need some paper and paints, watercolors and acrylics." She had replaced my paints quite recently, but I hoped she would not notice their nearly full condition in the dark. "Oh, and scissors."

"Scissors?"

I breathed in. "The snowflakes. I have been watching them from my window. They are so pretty, and when they sometimes land so I can see them on the glass, they have shapes, all sorts of shapes like faceted stars. I thought, perhaps, I could cut shapes like snowflakes and hang them from the ceiling, to bring the outside in."

"You wouldn't . . . hurt yourself, would you?"

"Of course not. I just want to create something beautiful. Please."

"Very well. I will bring them."

"Oh, and I'd need some string to hang them."

"Very well. I'll go now to get them. Do you want me to brush your hair before I leave?"

"It will hurt my head. I braided it anyway." I gestured toward my hair, which had already grown another foot since I'd last braided it. "I don't feel well enough to sit up."

"I will bring some tea as well."

By the time she returned, my hair had grown my body length yet again, and I had braided it twice more. She brought the chicken soup, and I allowed her to spoon it between my lips even though I was dying for her to leave. She loved to pretend I was an infant.

After she left, I did not cut my hair. I knew she would not be back until at least the next morning, maybe later. So I waited, braiding and rebraiding my hair, watching it inch away from my scalp. By morning, it stretched across the room and back. I braided it and waited, cutting snowflake shapes too, dozens of them, to make true my lie about why I needed the scissors.

When the sun was high in the sky, my braid reached the ground when dangled out the window. It was sufficient. I tied my hair on both sides with the string Mama had brought, then cut it carefully, the scissors nearly scratching my scalp. Then, I coiled up the braid and stuffed it under my bed.

Oddly, once I cut it, it did not grow so backbreakingly fast again. When Mama arrived, it reached my chest, no more. A little shorter than normal. I hoped she would not notice. I also hoped she would not look under my bed, for if she did, she would see the rope I had begun to make. There was only one purpose for a rope, and she would know it.

I began to cut more snowflakes. I was getting quite good at it, folding the paper over and over into a thick square, then cutting borders and boxes and diamonds to make it resemble the snowflakes on the windowsill. But this time, my hand slipped and the scissors' sharp blade sliced into my fingertip. I gave a cry and felt tears spring to my eyes. A drop of red blood stained the white snowflake. I wiped a tear.

And then, the strangest thing happened. When I examined my finger again, it wasn't bleeding at all.

It wasn't that the blood had been staunched. Rather, it was as if it had never bled. But when I looked at the snowflake, it was still stained red.

Obviously, it hadn't been a bad cut. I was just being a baby.

But when I put my finger into my mouth, the metallic taste of blood that wasn't there still lingered.

Wyatt

I fell asleep with the diary in my hand. When I woke in the morning, the clouds were white and so thick they looked like drifted snow. That was how my head felt too, and I wondered if I was drunk. Had I imagined the singing in the night? The light?

I started to pick up the diary again, to see what had happened. But then, I heard Mrs. Greenwood in the hall outside and stowed the notebook under my mattress.

"I thought maybe we could go to a movie tonight," she said when I opened the door.

"There's a movie theater around here?" It didn't seem like there was much of anything here.

But she nodded. "In Chestertown. It's a bit south of here. They have movies every Friday and on holidays."

Now, I remembered my mother mentioning it. She said she'd grown up in a town so small the closest movie theater was thirty miles away and only showed movies on weekends and holidays.

"I understand if you don't want to go," she said.

"Of course I want to." I didn't.

"It's just such a long drive for me to make by myself. I haven't been since Danielle . . ."

"Of course I'll go." I was a jerk to even think of not going.

"I checked the paper. It begins at eight. It sounds like some sort of space thing."

"And you really like that?" I remembered her watching *Star Trek*.

She clapped her hands. "I love it. After I introduced Danielle to *Star Trek* and *The Next Generation*, she told me about the *Terminator* films."

My eyes widened. "You liked all those machine guns and cursing and stuff?" My own grandfather got mad when I watched a movie with the word *freaking* in it.

"I liked Ahnold—before he became a politician or whatever he's doing now." She laughed. "Does that surprise you?"

"No. I used to know a girl who loved all those movies."

"Your girlfriend?"

"Not really. I mean, I'd have liked her to be, but it was complicated."

"Everything with your generation is complicated. When I was young, you just fell in love and got married."

"We were old friends. If we'd started dating and it hadn't worked out, it would have been awkward."

She nodded. "What did you finally do?"

I looked away. "There was an . . . accident. She died." I knew Mrs. Greenwood knew what had really happened. I just couldn't say it.

"Oh, yes, your mother told me about your friends. I'm so sorry." She looked like she wanted to put her arms around me or something, but she was waiting for permission.

I didn't give it to her. "Yeah, me too." Change the subject. I needed to change the subject. "Hey, I was going to go to the hardware store today, pick up the hinges for your cabinets. Then, I could work on them tomorrow, or later if there's time before the movie."

"I don't think the hardware store will be open. It's New Year's."

Of course, she was right. I should have accepted Astrid's invitation to go skiing. Yet I realized I didn't want to, didn't want to be around happy, bright people, people who didn't know all the bad things that happened, that could happen if you weren't careful, and sometimes, even if you were.

I could probably tell her I was going skiing or make some other excuse to leave, but when I looked at my watch, it was after noon, and it seemed easier to wait until tomorrow. It had probably just been the wind anyway. At least, no one else seemed to hear it. Which was the story of my life lately.

"Is there anything else I can fix for you? I did everything around our house. I'm actually pretty good with electrical."

"What a good boy you are. I can probably find you something to do, but let's have breakfast first."

I reddened a bit at being called a good boy. I didn't feel like one lately, especially since I'd been planning to sneak around on her. "Let me just put on some jeans first. It's cold."

"You're a good boy, Wyatt," she repeated before she left.

I wondered why she had repeated it, but I shrugged it off. Just something old ladies said, I guessed. If you weren't actually committing a carjacking that they knew about, they thought you were a great kid. I put on jeans and a sweater.

Before I went downstairs, I pulled the diary out from where I'd hidden it. I had left it open to the last page I'd read. I meant just to hide it better, but first, I flipped it over. I had to see what happened next.

But the next page was blank. All the remaining pages were.

I knew they would be, but I hoped they wouldn't. Just like part of me hoped Danielle was still alive and writing her diary someplace else.

Wyatt

The movie we saw ended up being one of those dystopian things where it's a futuristic society, and everyone's a drone except the hero, who has to whip everyone else into shape. Oh, and there were robots. Evil robots, which Mrs. Greenwood seemed to enjoy thoroughly, at least, she moved forward in her seat and clasped her hands together every time they showed up onscreen.

Afterward, we got pizza, and Mrs. Greenwood said, "Do you ever think how you'd deal with a situation like that?"

"Like what? Like in the movie?" We'd gotten pepperoni, and it was actually pretty good, even though it was upstate New York pizza instead of real New York pizza.

"Yes. If the world was gone wrong, would you be one of the people fighting against the problem or one of the people ignoring it?"

I thought about it. "I don't know. I mean, everyone thinks they'd be one of the fighters, the Guy Montag or Katniss Everdeen. But in movies like that, there's always one person raging against the machine. And then, there's a million people *being* the machine, just going along, unquestioning. They do what they're told because they don't want to end up in jail or have people think they're crazy."

"Maybe they don't even realize there's a problem."

"Don't realize? Or ignore it because it's too scary to do anything else." The waitress, a girl with dyed black hair, seemed to be listening to our conversation. But maybe, it was just because of what Astrid said last night, because I wasn't from around here.

Mrs. Greenwood looked her up and down, then turned back to me. "Sometimes, I think you can tell yourself there isn't a problem because you don't want there to be. Or because you don't think you're strong enough to deal with it if there is one."

Exactly. "If you're not a hero, does that make you a villain?"

Mrs. Greenwood pursed her lips, and I knew she was thinking about Danielle like I was thinking about Tyler. Probably, she thought about Danielle every day. Any mother would. "I don't think so. That would make just about everyone a villain then. The real villains are the ones who are actually commanding the evil robots to destroy the hero."

The waitress had walked away. "I think I'd like to be the hero. I mean, it's not my nature to be the hero, to be the person who recognizes the problem and takes charge, but I think if you know that about yourself, you can change it too."

She didn't answer, and I wondered if I'd hurt her feelings because she hadn't done that with Danielle. I thought about how it was probably different with parents and kids. Probably parents just had a blind spot where their kids were concerned, preferring to see them as the perfect little babies they were before they got messed up. Or maybe you could just get so close to someone you stopped looking.

"Mrs. Greenwood, I didn't mean . . ."

She shook her head. "I never got to have any grandchildren. I always thought about that with Danielle."

"Well, I've learned a lot from you so far. I never knew my own grandmother."

"I know. That Lina Hill was a stubborn woman."

Lina was my grandmother. I didn't know her. She and my mom hadn't gotten along. She'd never forgiven my mother for getting pregnant with me, I guessed. After my grandmother died, my grandfather contacted my mother. He moved in with us, helped us out, and was the closest thing to a father I ever had.

I wondered if Danielle had been pregnant, if that was why she'd run away from home. Maybe she was still out there. But of course, Mrs. G. wouldn't know about that, and I for sure wasn't going to tell her.

Her hand was on the table, and I gave it a little pat, which was awkward, but it seemed right.

When I got home, I realized I'd forgotten to check my texts when I had service. I had two, though, both from Astrid (who lived in town and apparently had service), one reiterating the skiing invitation, one saying what a nice time she'd had New Year's Eve. I couldn't answer them, but I decided I'd call her tomorrow. When I went out. It probably wasn't good to be alone all the time.

I smiled and listened to the wind howl as I drifted to sleep.

In the middle of it, like a harmony, I heard that same voice, singing.

I would check it out tomorrow.

16

Wyatt

The next morning, I woke from a dream of being chased by evil robots. I felt surprisingly refreshed. I looked down at the snow, which was patchy, indicating a warmer day. I decided to go to Josh's and try to retrace my steps from New Year's Eve, solve the mystery of the bizarre singing once and for all, even if it was just a dream.

I told Mrs. Greenwood, "I'm going to town to get those hinges and also, um, to return some calls I got."

She raised an eyebrow. "Is there a girl involved?"

I shrugged. "Maybe." I wasn't sure if Astrid was someone I was really interested in. But maybe there was another girl. Maybe.

"It's complicated?"

"Not that. Just, I'm not sure yet, you know."

"The course of true love never did run smooth." I thought that was Shakespeare. Maybe.

I laughed. "Okay, yeah. I met this girl, Astrid. She's a friend of Josh's. I thought I'd call and see if we could hang out sometime."

"Hang out? Do you know when I was a girl, people didn't hang out. People actually courted. They went out on dates."

"We do that now too. We just call it hanging out." To her, going on a date probably implied showing up at the door in a suit and carrying a bouquet of daisies. No one I knew did that. But I could let the old lady have her fantasy. "I'm just going to call her today, though."

I thought I'd go to Josh's store for the hinges first. When I saw him, he was putting some kind of weird birdhouse on a high shelf. "Astrid couldn't stop talking about you yesterday. It was pretty boring."

"I'll bet." I examined the shelves of old yearbooks, wondering why anyone would buy someone else's yearbook. "I'm here for those hinges. "

"Sure." Josh motioned for me to follow him toward the stockroom. "But you had an okay time New Year's?"

"I had an awesome time." I overstated it because, really, it was nice of him to invite me, and it wasn't his fault I was kind of congenitally unhappy.

"That's cool. Astrid wants you to come skiing with us. Maybe tomorrow."

"Maybe. Listen." I started to follow him to the register. I noticed the same old man who'd been there the day I ordered the hardware. This time, he was looking at an old school desk. "When I was at the place, I heard this sort of weird sound in the woods. It sounded like someone singing."

"A loon. Must have been a loon."

"Astrid said that. But this was in the middle of the night."

"An owl then."

"It didn't sound like a bird at all. It sounded human."

"It was," the old man said. "People say there's a ghost, a young girl who was murdered by her faithless lover in those very woods. Not everyone can hear it, though."

I turned to him, interested. He had on a fishing hat with flies stuck in it, even though it was the dead of winter. "How can you tell who can hear it?"

Josh nudged me. "Don't mess with him, Wyatt."

"I'm not messing with him. I really want to know." To the old man, I said, "How can you tell?"

"They say it's people who've experienced heartbreak, heartbreak so terrible they'll never forget." He raised his eyes to mine. I expected them to be gray and watery, the eyes of a used-up old man. Instead, they were dark and surprisingly steady. "Have you experienced heartbreak?"

I stared back at him a moment before answering. Finally, I said, "Yes. Yes, I have. Have you?"

Behind me, Josh took a breath. The old man nodded.

"I've heard it too," he said. "Deep in the woods, by the lake. It comes from the ruined tower."

"Tower?"

"There's no tower in those woods," Josh said. "There's nothing but a lake and trees."

"There's a tower," the old man insisted. "I've seen it. And a young girl, singing for her murdered lover."

"Okay, fine. There's a tower." Josh gestured toward some people who'd just come in, a man and a little girl who were petting the dogs. "Look, I need to help the other customers, or my dad gets mad. So can I ring that up for you?"

I didn't know why he was being so impatient. As far as I could tell, his dad wasn't even in the store. But he seemed in a big hurry, so I followed him to the register. "What was that about?"

Josh glanced at the old man again. I did too. He was back to browsing, looking at an old baby stroller, the kind that was like a bassinet on wheels. "That's Jerry. Long ago, the year I was born, actually, his daughter disappeared."

"Murdered?" I whispered. That made four missing kids—that I knew about. This place was so creepy.

Josh shook his head. "She probably ran away or OD'd on something. But it sent Jerry sort of over the edge. He was the town veterinarian, very respected. But after that, he got screwy. He had all sorts of crazy stories about a drug ring in Slakkill. Of course, there was no evidence of any ring, just his druggie daughter, but he didn't want to believe that."

"No evidence." I remembered what I'd thought last night, about parents wanting to think the best of their kids. But what about that salad Danielle had eaten. Was it some kind of drug? Was there a drug ring in Slakkill?

"A lot of people disappear around here." I gestured toward the Missing Person sign on the bulletin board.

Josh did too. "Bryce Rosen—druggie. Every town has them, I guess. And a few other kids have disappeared over the years."

"A few? How few?"

"Runaways. I told you that. But he had this big conspiracy theory. Said it was a ring, that they'd gotten her addicted, that they'd killed her sure as if they'd pulled the trigger. He was in a mental hospital for a while, and sometimes, he relapses and starts babbling about how we need to find the people who did it . . . or stuff about ruined towers. So we try not to remind him about the woods."

I shook my head. I didn't know anyone in my old town who'd disappeared, and until Tyler, no one who'd died young. There was all sorts of weird stuff around this town, the abandoned buildings and the creepy antiques. I said, "How about Danielle. Was she a druggie?"

Josh frowned. "My dad said no. They didn't know what happened to her, though people had theories."

"Like what?"

Josh put his finger to his lips and nodded toward the old man. I looked over at him again. He was holding a doll now, one with curly, yellow hair, and he was sort of crying. I nodded. Josh handed me the bag with the hinges and a receipt, saying he'd put them on Mrs. Greenwood's account.

"So it was a loon, okay?" he said.

I nodded again, but I knew I was going to the woods to look for myself.

I drove Mrs. G's car down the same threadlike, bumpy road as before. It was no less scary in daylight. Maybe it was scarier because, now, I could actually see how narrow it was with the trees attacking both sides of the car. And, anyway, it was almost as dark as night. Still, I was going forward. Going back seemed scarier.

Finally, I reached the point where we'd gotten out of the car and started to walk. I opened the door, scraping a branch and almost slipping on a patch of leftover ice. Luckily, a lot of it had melted. I closed the door, making sure not to slam it. I trudged forward.

The day was warmer than before, but still cold. The freezing wind howled across the trees, and it did sound like a woman crying, but it wasn't the same sound I'd heard before.

When I almost reached Josh's cabin, I heard a noise like something breaking. I stopped, looked behind me. Nothing there. I took another step forward. Another crack. Was something following me? I stopped. No. Probably just a squirrel or even a fox. They had animals like that here. Still, I stood a moment. And then, I heard it, a voice singing. I ran toward it, unconcerned about noises or foxes or anything but finding out what it was.

17

Rachel

Today, I woke knowing something would happen. Something would be different. It is winter. I have learned to tell winter by the cold outside my window and the snow. And, also, the lights from the distance, lights from a town I've never seen. People put them up in winter, and though they're far away, I see them. I watch them twinkle and dream of the day when I will see them close up.

Once, when I was younger, I asked Mama what they were. She said, "People put them up in December to celebrate the season."

"I wish I could go there. They must be so happy." Celebrating sounded like an incredible thing. I had never celebrated anything, other than my birthday and Mama's, and even those were dull. It wasn't that my life was awful, merely that it was the same, day after day, year after year.

Mama didn't let me go, of course. It was too dangerous. But the next time she came, she brought me a package, all wrapped in red-and-green paper with pictures of bells on it. I was so excited. I loved presents. I ripped the paper, carefully, because I wanted to save it in the box under my bed where I kept all my special possessions.

Inside was a box with a green plastic string covered with multi-colored objects, each pointed like an icicle.

"They're lights. You can plug them in the wall and look at them all you like." Mama started to remove them from the packaging. "They even twinkle."

"Oh. They're lovely." I plugged them in the wall. They glowed red and green, blue and yellow, and when Mama changed one of the bulbs, they blinked on and off.

Mama helped me hang them on the wall. I noticed she put them far from the window so that no one would see them, and every night for weeks after, I plugged them in and watched them blink, on and off, off and on. It made me happy to watch them, and peaceful, like I was part of the wide world.

But, one day, I realized that Mama had brought me the lights because she was never going to take me out to see the real ones.

That night, I took them down and hid them away, in the same box where I had stored my paper. When Mama came and asked where they'd gone, I said they were broken.

"I'll bring you a new string," she said.

"It's okay," I told her. "I've looked at them enough."

But that was how I knew it was winter, even before the snow began piling on my windowsill. And, when the snow melts, it is spring and the flowers bloom below.

But now, it had only been winter a short time, and the snow was melting. I opened my window. It was a long way down, too long to see much other than the activities of birds and the occasional deer.

Still, I wanted to leave the window open, to smell the world outside. I would play my harp and sing my songs, and the animals, at least, would hear me.

I began to do this. I sang the saddest song I knew, about a girl in love with a poor boy but unable to marry him. Mama taught it to me. She said it was from Scotland, and I loved it because it was from so far away.

I know where I'm going;
And I know who's going with me.
I know who I love;
But the dear knows who I'll marry.

As I sang, I had once again that strange feeling, the feeling of being listened to, not by birds or squirrels or even deer, but by some sentient, thinking being. I rushed to the window to look.

I saw something, or someone, moving in the distance. Probably, it was just a bear or a mountain lion. Though they were rare, I had seen all sorts of animals in the wood.

I went back to singing. It was silly to hope for what could not happen.

I have stockings of silk;
And shoes of fine green leather;
Combs to buckle my hair;
And a ring for every finger.

Just then, I remembered that Mama had given me these special glasses, which enabled me to see birds and other creatures, very far away. I grabbed them from my table. It was probably merely an animal. A bear. Or a mountain lion. Nothing to get excited about.

Except it wasn't. It wasn't a bear. Bears wear coats of brown or black. This creature wore one of blue. It was clearly a human being. Still, I could see nothing more, not even if it was a man or a woman. It could just be Mama.

But it was not Mama. Mama's coat was gray, and she never walked in the woods. No, this was someone else, someone I had never seen before. It was walking closer to me, struggling where there was no path, holding on to trees to keep its balance, but still coming closer. I could not see the face. Perhaps it was the man I had dreamed of.

Mama would say otherwise. She would say he was coming to murder me, or to steal me away. And suddenly, I was very afraid. What if Mama was right, and it was someone who wished me harm? What if the whole world wished me harm and only this tower could protect me, this tower which seemed suddenly vulnerable? After all, Mama had kept me here all these years. If there was nothing to fear, it would mean she was quite mad.

And yet, I had dreamed of this day, of someone other than Mama coming here, to find me, perhaps to rescue me.

I looked, again, through the glasses. The person was still far away, at the edge of the frozen lake. I could see nothing but the coat. I could not see that it was a man, much less the man of my dreams.

I shut the window and went back to my harp.

Featherbeds are soft;
And painted rooms are bonny;
But I would leave them all;
To go with my love, Johnny.

As I played, I closed my eyes and tried to picture his face. It was silly, of course, for it was merely a dream, a figment of my imagination. My imagination had made him perfect, gifting him with every wonderful attribute of the men in my books, the darkest hair, the greenest eyes, the strongest chin, the broadest shoulders, until he was Arthur and Lancelot, Robin Hood and Perseus all rolled into one, then gifted with the intellect of Rochester and the wealth of Darcy. No man could match up, surely not an ordinary youth with ordinary blemishes.

And yet, I ran to the window to look again, to see if he did. I could not tell yet. But now, at least, I was certain it was a man. The shoulders were too broad, the walk too bold to be a woman. That it was a man was wonderful, yet scary, for I am sure it was a man who killed my mother.

But I was up, and he was down. My tower would protect me . . . if I wished it to.

I was not sure what I wished.

He walked closer. In truth, *walk* was not the proper word for what he was doing. Rather, he struggled over the snow and the trees. Slogged, perhaps, or lumbered. I wondered, for the first time, what he was doing here, and why he continued when it was obviously so difficult. It was not merely uncommon, but unheard of, for anyone to come this close, particularly in winter. In summer, there were children who played and went boating on the lake. The part of the lake that I could see was covered in branches, likely hiding my tower from others' sight. Sometimes, the children came closer, but never close enough to see me. It was almost as if he knew I was here, as if he were looking for me.

To kidnap me?

I stopped singing entirely. I crouched down on the floor, resting my glasses on the windowsill. I peered through them. Now, he was close enough that I could see his face but for his hat and scarf. He could see mine if he possessed glasses. And if he looked up, rather than examining every root or rock that might trip him. He paused in his trudging as if trying to decide where to go next, looking at the stand of trees to his left, the frozen lake to his right. As he did, I saw a bit of hair, peeking out from underneath his hat.

It was brown, dark brown, much like the hair of my imagined lover. Yet, from my reading, I knew that many men had dark hair.

He made his decision and stepped onto the lake. I sucked in my breath. In years past, the lake had frozen solid. I knew for I had seen deer walking upon it. But this year, the weather had been warmer than usual, and though the ice was covered with snow, the animals had avoided it. I wondered if he might fall through, like Amy did in *Little Women*. If he did, with no one to fish him out, he would surely die.

He took another tentative step. Then, another. Then, a third. It was all right. He believed so too, for his steps became faster, more confident. In fact, he nearly skipped, so relieved (I imagine) was he to escape the tangle of trees, dead and living.

And then, he disappeared from sight.

18

Wyatt

I didn't know whose stupid idea this was. Or rather, I did. But was I so starved for adventure, for closure . . . for redemption, maybe, that I'd go out in the cold and snow to look for a ruined tower when no one but a crazy old guy who apparently lived in Josh's hardware store even knew it existed? When the voice I heard was probably a loon?

Yes. The sad thing was, yes. *I* was the loon.

I'd passed Josh's family's cabin half an hour earlier. Since then, I'd been slogging through the woods where there was no path, where the roots of trees seemed to come alive beneath my feet, and the branches reached down to grab me with their stabbing, scratching fingers. Yes, some of the snow had melted, but that made it no less icy, no less slippery. I slid on a patch of ice and grabbed at a tree branch. It grabbed back, scratching my face. I touched my glove to my cheek and saw a wet spot on the black background. Blood.

Ahead, I saw nothing but trees and more trees. Where was the tower? Did it even exist? If it did, I couldn't see it. It must be so far from the cabin, too far for me to have heard singing inside. And yet, when a hawk cried overhead, it seemed so deafeningly loud that I could have heard it ten miles away.

No singing today. I stopped to listen. Nothing but the chill wind, invading my bones. I should go back. But when I looked behind me, I could see neither Josh's cabin nor the car. I might as well go forward.

No, that wasn't true. If I couldn't see the car, that was a reason to go *back*. Go back as fast as I could before the day became darker, colder.

I realized, I had nothing to go back to.

The old lady would be sad if I disappeared, I guessed. But she'd get over it. She'd dealt with bigger things.

I had no friends, and even my mother didn't seem desperately upset to be rid of me. At least, she'd let me go. She was a young woman. She could meet someone, have another child, a better one.

I remembered the old man, his daughter murdered, or maybe dead from an overdose. Did it really matter? He never got over it.

No, I had to stick this out, to solve this mystery once and for all. Also, I felt something pulling at me, as if it meant me to come here, to find out what was out there even if it was nothing. Which it probably was.

Then suddenly, I heard a voice, singing. Still, far away, it sang an old song I'd heard before but couldn't place. I shoved past a few more trees and saw a clearing. No trees at all. But that was impossible.

I realized it was the lake. The lake came up farther here. Did I dare step on it? It would be much easier to walk on the smooth lake than to fight through the trees. But parts of it, I knew, weren't frozen. Near the center was dark, almost black water, reflecting the clouds above. But here, near the shore, it was serene, white, covered in several inches of snow without even a footprint on its surface. It must be safe.

I took one tentative step, feeling it. Solid. I took another. Then, another. This was easy. I took a few more.

Then, I heard a thunderclap, and all at once, I was falling down, down into the freezing water.

19

Rachel

He fell through the ice! I did not know if this was the boy I dreamed of. What I did know was that, whoever he was, he would die out there in the freezing lake and not be discovered until spring, if at all.

And I would have witnessed it. Witnessed it and done nothing.

Something, some unearthly force propelled me forward, told me what I must do. I ran to the bed and seized the rope, my rope of hair, then twined it around one of the pillars in my tower. I knotted it, a good, firm knot such as I had read about in books, a knot that looked like a double number eight. I barely thought, barely breathed as I was doing this. I glanced outside. Was he still out there, floundering in the water? He was. But if I did not move quickly, he would not be. I seized my metal bedstead and dragged it over to the window, I knew not how. I placed one of the legs upon the rope, in case my knot was not true enough. Then, I hung the remaining length of rope out the window. As before, it reached the ground, and then some. Was I insane? I could not slide down a rope! I wove it for *him* to come up. Yet he could not do so if he was trapped under ice. No time for hesitation. I grabbed the quilt and blanket from my bed, threw them out the window to break my fall (and, perhaps, to warm him when I pulled him out). Then, I grabbed the rope, passed it over my shoulder and under my leg in hopes of slowing my descent a bit, and slid down it to the bottom. It all occurred so quickly I remembered nothing except the feeling of my own hair, sliding through my fingers.

I was out of the tower, out for the first time in years.

It happened I did not die. I also did not know how I was going to get back up.

The boy thrashed still. I saw that he had gotten hold of something, a root, and was attempting to pull himself out. Yet, he was unable. I had to save him. I, or he would freeze to death. I grabbed a branch, then ran to the lake and thrust it toward him.

"Here. Take this."

Shock showed on his white face. "Can you pull me out?" He clung to the root, unwilling to let it go.

"I do not know. I have to try. If you hold the root, you will not drown, but you may freeze to death."

"Get over here." He pointed to a spot farther away but still close enough for the branch to reach. "Hold that tree."

I thought him a bit bossy for a drowning man, but I obeyed, gripping the tree with one hand, the branch with the other. I felt it dip with his weight as he grabbed it. I hoped I had chosen well. If it broke, he would surely . . . I could not think about it.

"Pull!" he yelled.

I pulled with all my might, until my fingers ached and felt as if they might break like icicles. He did not budge. Nothing moved. Yet, still, I held the branch while on the other end, I felt him struggle.

"Pull harder!" he yelled. "Please."

I couldn't. I couldn't, and yet, I did, with a strength I never knew I possessed, a strength I didn't possess, a strength nearly mythological. I pulled and jerked until my whole body ached, and yet, it must have been the work of a moment, and then, he was clambering out of the water and onto the shore, shivering and running toward me. I ran away, for the blankets. The blankets to give him.

I threw him both the blanket and the quilt even though, now that my exertion was over, I realized that I too was freezing.

I was cold! I was cold because I was out in the world, out for the first time in so many years. I felt the wind on my face, the snow beneath my feet. I smelled evergreen and fresh air. I was outside! I loved it.

I looked over him. He shivered, still, but I could see his face. His jaw was firm. His hair was dark brown, nearly black, and when he looked up at me, his eyes were green as the trees.

It was him.

I knew it.

"Wh-wha-wh-wh-who are y-you." His teeth chattered.

"I am Rachel."

"W-where d-d-did you c-c-come from?"

I gestured toward my tower, seeing it, from the front, perhaps for the first time ever. It was old and shabby, almost invisible among the gray clouds, with nubby shingles studding its sides, except where they had fallen off. "There."

Wyatt

"There." The girl was stunning. There was no other word. With long, blond hair and skin that seemed almost translucent, she looked like an angel. She gestured to her left, and when I was able to stop shivering and staring at her, I looked too. At first, I thought she was joking, for all I saw was a clump of trees. Was she some unearthly creature, like a sprite or a fairy, who lived among the leaves? But then, I saw it, hidden among them.

A ruined tower.

It was made of wood, shingled most of the way up, and appeared to be very old, too old for someone so beautiful to live in. It rose high among the trees with only one window at the very top. From that window hung a golden rope that reached all the way to the ground.

"Are you a ghost?" I asked. She wore a gown of white, ghostly, as if from another era.

But she shook her head. "I do not think so. At least, I do not recall dying." She reached forward and touched her hand to my cheek. "Do I feel like a ghost?"

Suddenly, the sun came out and shone upon her golden hair. Her eyes were bright blue.

Her hand, though cold, still warmed my own cold face like fire. She was the one who'd been singing. I heard her from so far away. This was why I had come here. I reached up and touched her cheek with my own hand. "No. But I don't understand. How are you here?"

"I knew you would come, that something would happen, that there was a reason. Destiny, or what have you. Every day, I waited, and every night, I dreamed."

"Of someone coming to rescue you?"

She raised an eyebrow. "It was I who rescued you. And now, I do not know how I will get back to my tower."

"You want to go back?"

"It is where I live. Where else would I go? Besides, Mama will worry if she finds me missing."

I gaped at her. When you rescue a girl from a tower—even if she rescues you—you're supposed to take her with you. Though, come to think of it, I didn't know where we would go. I couldn't exactly take her to Mrs. Greenwood's.

Still, I tried again. "But you can't go back. I want to talk to you, to know you. And what about *my* destiny?"

She looked uncertain, and as she did, she shivered. "I'm not sure. Maybe it was only my destiny to save you."

"Do you want one of the blankets?" It would be hard to give it up, considering it was freezing out, and I had just been dunked in water, but it seemed like I should offer.

She shook her head. "I should go back. But I don't know how to get up there. It was so much easier to come down. Can you help me?" She gestured to the sad tower.

"The thing is," I said, "I came here for a reason too. I didn't know what it was, but ever since I came here, I've heard something, something beckoning to me. That's why I came. So I couldn't just be here to fall through the ice so *you* could rescue me. There must be something else."

Man, she was beautiful.

She looked up at me, then down, as if she didn't want me to see her looking. "Maybe. But I do not think I'm supposed to leave. Not yet, anyway. Maybe someday." She glanced up again, out of the tops of her eyes. "But if Mama finds me like this, my rope hanging, she will know I tried to escape. And then, she will make it so I can never come down again. Can you help me back to my tower? Please?"

Her voice became higher at the end, not hysterical but worried. I said, "Isn't there a door?"

She brightened a bit. "There must be. Mama comes through a door to get inside. But she always locks it. I can hear her keys, and the turning of the mechanism each time she comes."

"Maybe we can jimmy it." I'd never jimmied anything in my life, but the tower looked old, so maybe the lock was too.

She took off, walking around the side of the tower. I could tell she was cold by how fast she walked, and how stiffly. I followed her. When we reached the door, it had not one, not two, but three locks on it, and they looked pretty solid. Still, she pulled at the handle. I did too. But without tools, there was no way to open it, and I had no tools.

"Can't you climb back up?" I asked. "You climbed down." I didn't want her to leave, but it was cold, so cold that I worried I might freeze to death if I stayed there much longer.

She shook her head. "I am amazed I came down. You needed to be rescued, so I did. Suddenly, I felt a rush of strength, as if I had drunk a magic potion."

"Adrenaline. I read about that. Like, once, I read about this woman who lifted a car off her father, when he was being crushed." It was weird. She was such a delicate flower, yet strong enough to slide down a rope and rescue me. It was sort of hot, both that she'd saved me and, also, that she needed my help. I could use someone needing me right now.

"I just knew I had to do it."

I thought about climbing ropes in gym class. Or about a hundred rock-climbing birthday parties. This wasn't much higher, if at all. I had no doubt that I could do it myself, but could I lift her? Maybe if I simply bouldered up, I could use the rope to help her, sort of a hip belay? Not that we had any equipment. But if you didn't fall, you didn't need a harness, right?

If I brought her up, could I come see her again?

"I just need more time. More time to understand what it is I'm meant to do." Her yellow hair fluttered around her face.

I decided. "I can pull you up. Is the rope strong?"

"I think so." Her face seemed calmer now. At least, she smiled. "And there is a fire in the fireplace. You could get warm and allow your clothes to dry."

"If I help you, can I come back to see you again?" One of the trees by the tower, its branches weighed down with snow, was shaped like a dragon, its green head crooked toward me, staring. A dragon to be slain.

"I would count on it," she said. "But you have not told me your name."

"Wyatt."

She gazed at me. The sun was fully out now, and her eyes were the color of the sky. "Prince Wyatt," she said.

21

Rachel

Wyatt first attempted to show me how to climb up. He told me that everyone learned to climb a rope in something called gym class at school. I knew about school because of schools in books—*David Copperfield*, *Jane Eyre*, *Little Women* . . . even Ebenezer Scrooge went away to school. Yet, none of the books I read made the slightest mention of rope climbing as a skill learned there. Clearly, this was another instance, one of many, in which my education had been deficient.

After several failed attempts, I said, "Wyatt, I wish, more than you can imagine, that I had gone to your school and learned how to climb a rope. However, it seems that this is not the skill of a day, particularly a frigidly cold day such as this one. Is there perhaps another way you could get me up there?" I was growing worried, not to mention cold. I needed to be in my tower, after all, to keep me free from the dangers of the world. I had managed to persuade myself that Wyatt was safe. After all, he probably hadn't even been alive when my mother was murdered. And he had kind eyes. But what if someone else came? What if someone had followed him? What if Mama came earlier than usual and saw me on the ground?

"Yeah, I was thinking it wasn't going to work," he admitted. "You're not really dressed for it."

I smiled at his attempt to make me feel better. "Yes, I am certain it is merely my apparel that is preventing me from scaling the height!"

"Well, that could be part of it. Anyway, girls as pretty as you don't usually have massive biceps, and I'd like to get to that fire." He shivered.

I smiled a bit more at his comment on my beauty, for it was similar to my thoughts about his. But when he mentioned the cold, I realized he was right. He was wet and cold, and it certainly wouldn't do for him to freeze to death, right when I had just rescued him. Rescuing him was the first definitive thing I had done in years.

Besides, I liked him.

"Perhaps you could climb the tower yourself, then hoist me up?"

"Do you think you could hang on that long?"

I nodded. I felt a bit inadequate about not being able to climb, but just holding on seemed safer. "I hope so."

"I mean, you wouldn't have to hang. There are a lot of footholds on the way up, those shingles. Watch me as I go up. Plus, I have leather gloves on. I could throw them down when I'm up. They might help you grip." He examined the rope. "What kind of rope is this? It's really static."

"Oh, that." I looked down, not knowing what he meant. "It is hair."

His eyes widened, somewhat comically. "Your hair?"

"Um, yes. I have been here a long time. It grew; I cut it. One makes do with what one has. Do you not think we should try to climb instead of talking? I'm cold." Probably, the less said about my hair, the better. He probably thought I was so strange. I *was* strange. I could not believe I was actually here, talking to someone, a man, anyone other than Mama. I knew I should be afraid of him. Yet, I was certain he would not hurt me, no matter what Mama would think.

"Sure," he said. "It's just . . ."

"What?"

He shook his head. "Nothing. It's just . . . cool. And, man, your hair is . . . something."

"Thank you." I thought that was a compliment.

"And it will hold you?" He stared at it.

"It held me, when I came down."

"Good point. And hey, I've already fallen through the ice today. What else can happen? Here's what we're going to do."

He took the rope, the length that coiled on the ground, and wrapped it firmly around my waist several times. Then he tied it very tightly. He was so close to me and his hands were very strong.

Now, I was tied to the tower. But what was he doing?

"It's a sort of harness. You'll have to hold on too, because it's not very good. I mean, it should really be separate, not the same rope. But it's better than nothing."

"What will you do?"

He looked up the height of the tower. The wind whistled through the trees. "Watch me. Do what I do."

He placed his foot on one of the shingles, testing it. Apparently finding it adequate, he grabbed a higher shingle and pulled himself up, then finding a knot in the wood, on which to put his other foot. He repeated this process, climbing higher. "I'll try to lift you," he

121

said, "but you should try to climb too. You'll be tied to me, so you won't fall."

I nodded, shivering. I was cold too. Yet, despite it, I felt a thrill of excitement, watching him, rather the way I imagined it felt for ladies at court to watch their champions at a jousting match. His wet shirt clung to his muscles, which flexed with each new grip upon the tower. He was so handsome!

Higher and higher he climbed, and when he chanced to look back, I waved and smiled.

Finally, after what seemed an eternity, he reached the window-sill. He threw his leg over, bobbling slightly. I gasped. He caught himself and climbed inside.

"You made it!" I yelled.

He said something I could not make out.

"What?" I yelled.

He stood there, breathing heavily. He must be tired, too tired to lift me up right away. I nodded, to show I understood. He pointed to me, then threw down an object. His glove. Then, the other. I slipped them on to my hands. They were big on me, though they had probably shrunk some from being in the water, and they were cold.

They were his.

I studied the rope around my waist. He yelled something else, but it was lost in the wind.

"What?" I cupped my hand to indicate I couldn't hear.

"Try to climb up yourself. If you fall, the rope will catch you."

"I will try."

Remembering what he had done, I searched for a foothold. I found one and stepped on it. It held me. I pulled myself up with my hands on another shingle. I found another foothold and stepped upon it.

I was doing it.

From above, I felt the rope around my waist go slack. I looked up to see Wyatt holding the rope, making it taut so that, if I fell, I would not fall all the way.

"That's good!" he said. "Look up at me! Don't look down."

Of course, as soon as he said that, I looked down. But the ground was not so far below me, and the snow looked soft.

"Rachel! Up here!"

I looked up, but he was still so far away.

"Come on! You can do it."

My foot began to feel uncomfortable. I searched for another foothold and found one. I pulled myself up, then my other foot. I shivered, fearing I would lose my grip. Yet, the exertion made me feel warmer. I found another foothold and pulled myself up again.

"Good for you! Keep going!"

I was closer. At least, I could hear him better. I was doing this! I was doing it!

The rope was taut above me. I took another step up but lost my grip on the tower. My tower. I clung to it with both arms but felt the rope holding me tight. I was worried I would end up hanging like a spider. But no, my tower was angled.

"Careful!" His voice was closer. "You can do it."

I found a handhold, and then, another foothold. The cold air rushed across my dress. I heard birds. I smelled the snow and almost tasted it. I was cold, yet sweating too. I pulled myself up.

"Do that again! All at once!"

I did. It was getting easier, though I was tired. First one foot, then the other, pulling myself up with my hands. I saw him, reeling in the rope, my hair. I heard his voice. "Come on, Rachel. You're doing great!"

It occurred to me that I *was* doing great. *I* was, for he wasn't lifting me. I was climbing. It was like something from a book, but this time, I was the heroine! Suddenly, I knew what I had to do. I found another foothold, then another, going much faster than before.

Ouch! A rough piece of wood jabbed my arm. I cried out, but my cry disappeared into the woods.

"Almost there!" he said. "Come to me!"

I had to go on. Ignoring the pain in my arm, I took two more steps, pulling myself up. I felt his hand, reaching out for me, but I was afraid to take it. I wanted to climb inside by myself.

I reached for the windowsill, and found one last good foothold, a tiny outcropping. I pulled myself up. I lifted myself inside. My heart felt as if it might burst, but good.

"I made it!"

"You did. You're okay!"

I saw, now, that we were tied together. If I had fallen, would he have tumbled out the window as well?

I was breathing hard, my heart pounding. I threw my arms around Wyatt and felt his heart throbbing beside my own. "You saved my life," I said.

"Did I?" His voice was in my ear. "That's perfect. You saved mine, so I owe you."

We stood there a moment, both panting, both shivering. I knew he was the man I had dreamed about. How could he not be, for he was the only one who had come? But did he know?

Finally, we broke apart. I said, "Perhaps you should warm yourself by the fire. I'll get a blanket. Then, you can tell me what you are doing here."

He walked to the fireplace and sat beside it, then took the poker and used it to rearrange the logs. His shirt was wet and clung to him. I thought, perhaps, I should suggest that he remove it, to hang it by the fire. But would that be too presumptuous? Yes. I noticed him touching it, and I wondered if he was thinking the same thing. Yet, there was nothing I could do, nothing but gaze at him with the fire's light caressing his face, unable to believe he was actually there.

"Will you tell me what you are doing here as well?"

I came out of my trance. "What? Oh, the blanket. I forgot." I rushed to the closet and took down the bright green blanket. I returned and draped it over his shoulders.

"Thank you."

"Perhaps . . ." I stopped.

"What?"

I looked away. "Perhaps now that you have the blanket to cover you, you should . . ." I felt my cheeks grow warm. I spit it out. "Your shirt would dry more quickly if you draped it by the fire."

He didn't respond for a moment. Then, he said, "Oh. Oh, I suppose it would."

"I will not look," I whispered. I crossed the room, back to the window. Outside, the air was cold, so I closed it up, to keep the heat in. Then, I gazed out. The hole in the ice had filled with snow, so it was barely visible.

"Rachel?"

The sound of my name startled me. Yet, I loved it. "Yes?"

"Since you saved my life, and I saved yours, I feel really, like I've known you. Like we're sort of closer than other people who've known each other an hour. Will you tell me how you got here? I've been hearing you, or something. A voice from the woods. I've been hearing it for days. But I don't think anyone else can hear it. I didn't know if you were real."

I turned to face him. He was wrapped in the blanket, his shirt draped on the mantel, warming. He had removed his shoes, but he still had on his pants. The green in the blanket brought out the green in his eyes. I walked closer.

"I think I am real," I said, though I wondered. Could you be real

125

if no one saw you, if no one knew you were there?

He reached out his hand to me. "I think you are too."

And the next thing I knew, I was sitting beside him, and his lips were on mine. Mine were on his, and all the loneliness of my life was over, evaporated, as if it had never been there at all. He tasted like the breeze, the snow, the pine trees, and I worried that I would wake to find that it was all a dream, all a lovely dream. But his hands on my hair, his lips on mine let me know he was real. He was real.

"I'm sorry," he said. "I didn't mean to. It's just . . . I feel like I was meant to come here, to find you."

I kissed him again. "I feel that way too."

22

Wyatt

I had been shivering. Now, I was warm, warm from the fire in the stone fireplace on one side of the room, warm from the girl in my arms. This was it. This was why I was here. To find her, this strange, unearthly, beautiful girl, locked in a tower yet so brave that she slid down a rope and fished me out of the ice. Seeing her, I realized that I was like that too, in my own tower, a tower of the mind, enchanted and unreal. Would I be as brave as her, given the opportunity? Could I save her as she saved me? This girl was different from anyone I'd ever met. She made me feel like a hero.

I glanced around. The room was from another era—wrought-iron bed and a rag rug. The walls were painted bright blue, like the sky. "So, who are you?" I asked.

She looked down. "Well, it's hard to say. I don't really know, except that my name is Rachel. On my last birthday, I was seventeen. I've lived here since I was a child."

Unreal. "And before that?"

"I lived in a house, with Mama."

"Mama." Such an old-fashioned word. I didn't know anyone who called their mother Mama. It was like something they said in books.

"She's not really my mother, though. My mother is dead. She was killed when I was a little baby. I don't remember her at all."

I thought about the old man in the hardware store, the one with the dead daughter. Could she have been Rachel's mother? If so, he didn't know about it.

"Mama brought me here to keep me safe. She said the people who harmed my mother might come after me as well."

It was all kinds of crazy. Yet, everything seemed crazy up here, from Danielle eating her psychedelic salad to Rachel locked in this tower. But maybe the whole world was like that—it was just more noticeable in a small town. I gazed at her, trying not to look like I was. Her skin was so pale, like it had never seen the sun. It was almost translucent, and her hair hung around her shoulders like an angel's wings. She believed what she was saying. That was for sure.

"So why did you come down to save me? Weren't you worried I'd kill you?"

She smiled. "I thought about it. But then, I realized you were too young to have killed my mother. You looked no older than me. And I could not simply watch you die when it was in my power to help. Then, my existence would be worthless indeed. I sometimes wonder if it is anyway. Besides . . ." She broke off, shaking her head as if she had said too much.

"We all wonder about that sometimes," I said.

"Do you? Do other people wonder that? I do not know any other people."

"I think so." There was something intelligent about her face, something older than her years. "What were you going to say?"

"Nothing. I don't want to . . . burden you, tell you too much and get you into a mess."

I looked around. Outside the windows, I could see only the tops of trees. Inside, I could only see her.

"I think I'm in it," I said.

"You don't have to be. You could leave, climb down to the bottom and never see me again."

"No, I couldn't do that. Now, I know you're here. I can't just leave you."

"Why can't you?"

"I don't know." Though I had an idea. It was because of Tyler. I hadn't done enough there. I wasn't going to make that mistake again. "Besides, I feel like I'm supposed to be here, like I found you for a reason. Why else would I hear you when no one else did?"

She sat very still for a moment, her face illuminated by firelight. Her hand was still in mine, and I wanted to kiss her again, but I didn't want to spoil it, so I just sat there. Her fingers were so delicate, interlocking with mine.

Finally, she said, "I have these dreams, strange dreams."

"Dreams?" I thought of Danielle at the window. But maybe that had been real.

"They don't feel like dreams at all. I mean, not like dreams you have when you're asleep and forget an hour later. These dreams feel like prophecies, and when I started having them, things changed."

"What sort of things?"

"Well, for one thing . . ." She gestured toward the rope of hair on the floor. "My hair grew. It grew very fast."

I nodded. "That's weird all right. What else?"

"When I was little, Mama used to brush my hair with a special brush, a silver one with a pattern of exotic flowers, orchids or lilies, I think."

"What?" I had seen the brush, or one like it, somewhere. Where?

"A fancy silver brush. And then, one day, it disappeared, and I came here. But I have been dreaming of that brush, and dreaming of it all the time, as if it is the key to . . . something, to escape. And then, you showed up."

I nodded. "And that's weird?"

"Other than Mama, I haven't seen another human being in years. But more than that . . ."

Again, she stopped speaking and stared at the rope of hair on the ground.

"What?"

"More than that, you were in my dreams too. I don't want to frighten you, but there was a boy, tall and broad shouldered, with dark hair and green eyes. Do many people have green eyes?"

I shook my head. "Some. But most people have brown. Or blue." I looked into hers, which were a bright sapphire color.

"Do many boys look like you?"

"Exactly like me? No. So you're saying I was in your dream?"

She nodded. "I am certain of it. You are meant to be here."

"Then I'm certain too." And I was, in that instant, I was. There had to be a reason I was here, a reason I'd heard a voice beckoning since I'd gotten here, a reason I'd left home, even. "But what was I doing in your dream?"

"That is where it grows dim. There were people, somewhere. They wanted me to help them. They needed me to. It had to be me, only me. But I don't know why or how. I thought perhaps when you came, you would tell me. But you don't know either?"

I shook my head. "Sorry. But maybe we could ask someone." I thought of the old man again. Maybe he would know. Or Mrs.

Greenwood. I wouldn't tell them about Rachel. It would freak them out, and I wouldn't want to get the old man's hopes up if Rachel wasn't his long-lost granddaughter after all. "Would you want me to?"

"I'm not sure. I wouldn't want anyone to know I was here." She glanced out the window. "Oh, my, it is getting dark already. I don't want you to leave, but . . ."

I looked outside. The sun was already low in the sky. I glanced at my watch. It was already past four, and around here, it got dark early in winter. I had to get back to my car, this time without falling through the ice. "I don't want to leave either. But I should."

"Come again tomorrow. Please?"

"If I can. If not, the next day." I stood up.

She put her arms around my neck again. "Please come back. I never knew how lonely I was until you came."

I kissed her. "Me either. Don't worry. I will. I promise."

The trip down the rope should have been easy compared to the trip up, but it wasn't because I didn't want to make it. I didn't want to leave. My hands ached until I felt I might fall, and even though my clothes had mostly dried, I felt bone cold. I finally reached ground and struggled across the trees to the car, then drove to Mrs. Greenwood's house, but I was already plotting how to come back.

I felt the chill of cold in my legs, my arms. Even my hair felt cold. But for the first time since Tyler died, I felt like something made sense.

23

Rachel

I watched Wyatt climb down the rope, his dark hair against the snow-whitened pines. For an instant, I wondered if I should call him back, ask him to take me with him. But I didn't. I couldn't.

Mama would be disappointed, for certain. But part of me said that it would be her own fault, for trapping me here, imprisoning me away from the world. That was what she was doing, wasn't it? I remembered being outside with Wyatt, the sting of the cold air, the feeling of branches scraping against me. Why should this be so unusual?

No. Mama was protecting me. But could she not protect me by bringing me someplace else, someplace where I could at least go outside? I knew from books that there was a wide world out there. I hadn't seen it. If Mary, the heroine in *The Secret Garden*, could travel all the way from India to England to live with her uncle, why could I not travel to hide?

Nonsense. Mama was an old woman. It would be too difficult for her.

But what if the man who had killed my mother was gone? Or even dead? What if all my hiding was for naught?

Oh, this was too much to think about. It had been a day of great excitement, easily the most exciting day of my life. I had rescued someone! I had met a boy, a real boy who liked me, who thought me pretty. I had kissed him. For some girls, this might be the stuff of an ordinary afternoon. For me, it was incredible.

My arm throbbed. I pulled up my sleeve and examined it. I found a scrape, forgotten. I remembered how it had happened, climbing up the tower wall. I touched the scrape with some satisfaction. A cold breeze blew in through the window. Wyatt was out of my sight. I pulled up the rope and coiled it round and round itself until it was small enough to store under my bed.

I yawned. It had been a tiring day, and though I knew that Mama would be here later, I decided to take a nap.

I crawled under the covers, taking my pillow into my arms. It was merely a pillow but I had, many times, imagined it was my true love. Now, he had a name. Wyatt.

Wyatt.

I felt like I could smell him in the air as I drifted off to sleep.

But I did not dream of him as I would have liked. Instead, I dreamed of people, people I had never seen, their faces pleading with me to save them, save them somehow from themselves. But I didn't know how. Sliding down a rope and rescuing someone from the ice seemed like child's play compared to what they wanted from me. In fact, I did not know what they wanted at all. But they seemed to think I did, and they grew closer, their hands reaching toward me, touching me.

I woke, sobbing, to someone shaking me. The room was dark.

"Who's there?" I asked.

A laugh. Then, a gentle voice, soothing. "Who would be there, Kitten? It is only me."

Mama. How many hours had passed since Wyatt had held me, since I'd been that different, not helpless, girl he'd held in his arms.

"Mama, you're here."

"Of course." She stroked my hair. "But why is it dark?"

I wiped my teary eyes with my arm. "I was tired. Maybe still a little touch of fever."

"Oh, I am sorry." She reached for the light switch. "I had hoped you would be better."

The room illuminated, and she looked around. I imagined she could see that everything had changed since she had been there last. Indeed, her eyes showed suspicion. But there was no difference.

My sleeve felt wet where I had been crying. I pushed my sleeve up, then remembered the scrape on my arm. If she saw it, she was sure to ask how I got it. I pulled my sleeve down, the better to cover it. But it did not hurt anymore, and when I looked, it wasn't there. Had it been my imagination?

The eagle eyes traveled the room. "Is everything else . . . all right?"

I nodded. "Only I am lonely. I get so lonely, Mama, all by myself."

24

Wyatt

I was about halfway back to Mrs. Greenwood's house when it hit me. There was a *girl* in a tower out in the middle of nowhere, trapped. No one but me knew she was there. How was I sure she wasn't a figment of my imagination? Maybe it was all a dream, born of my own loneliness, my need to be a hero to make up for everything that had happened. Maybe I'd crashed through the ice and pulled myself out.

Maybe I was lying on the ground, dying of hypothermia, and the girl was merely a vision.

A beautiful vision. I remembered her blond hair, her lacy dress, her skin, a shade of white I had never seen before, almost transparent. Was it because she had never seen sun, or was she an angel?

And how was it, if she was real, she'd been looking out her window at the exact moment I'd fallen through the ice? Was it because

135

she was so lonely she looked out her window all the time, seeing nothing? I knew what it was to be lonely, but she had been alone far longer.

I pulled in to Mrs. Greenwood's driveway, got out of the car, and started toward the house. Then, I remembered the hinges. I decided to tell Mrs. Greenwood I hadn't been able to get them, that I needed to go back tomorrow.

Because, of course, another possibility had occurred to me, that Rachel was Mrs. Greenwood's granddaughter, that somehow, Danielle had had a baby, then disappeared. Maybe she was so scared of her mother she hadn't told her. How cool would it be to reunite them?

I looked for the hinges on the seat, then realized they were in my pocket. When I drew them out, I saw, attached to the bag, a long, golden hair.

She was real.

But I couldn't tell anyone, least of all Mrs. Greenwood, about Rachel, not until I was sure who she was. I needed to find out.

Besides, even though I'd only known her a day, I thought I was falling in love with her.

25

Rachel

In the night, it began to rain. I could count on three fingers the number of times I'd seen rain in January. The rain would make the way here impassable. He could not climb the tower in the wet. I would not see him. Having been alone all these years, I yearned, now, to see him.

What was it Shakespeare said—The course of true love never did run smooth.

I turned on the light and surveyed the room. I noticed the scissors Mama had gotten me, lying on my nightstand. I picked them up and tested the blades. Dull. Still, I could try.

I drew it quickly across my wrist.

A small amount of blood showed, seeping out.

The cut didn't hurt enough to make me cry, but the thought of not seeing Wyatt did. I imagined that it would rain forever, that I would never see him, that I would always be alone.

Soon, a tear leaked from each eye.

I dabbed at them with my forefinger, then dabbed at the wound. It stung from the salt.

Then, it disappeared.

26

Wyatt

I woke to the rain on the roof. Some might call it a patter, but it was more like a deluge. My mother once said that, when it rained up here, you might as well cancel your plans. I knew what she meant, but today, my plans were with Rachel.

I knew I could never climb that tower in the rain.

I decided it might be a good idea to start the online courses I was supposed to be taking. That way, I could skip a day when the sun came out. So, after breakfast (Mrs. G. made waffles, which was the only good thing about the day), I logged on to start virtual economics.

No connection.

After unplugging and replugging the computer and an hour on the phone with the service provider, then another hour talking to someone in another country who clearly knew nothing about how bad it could rain here, I faced the fact that they were going to have to come service it. Tomorrow.

I went downstairs to see if Mrs. G. was watching *Star Trek*. Because this was what my life had come to.

"It's not on now," she said.

"I thought it was always on."

"I wish. Do you want to play Rummikub?"

"What's that?"

She reached down under the end table and pulled out a small leather suitcase. "It's a game, sort of like gin rummy, only with tiles. You have to build groups of three or four of a kind, or straights. Your mother and Danielle used to play all the time. I haven't played since . . ."

I couldn't imagine my mother doing anything so nerdy, but maybe it was just that dull up here. "Okay?"

That was all it took for her to start putting together racks and piling on tiles. The piles were numbered and came in four different colors. She explained that you had to make either a group, meaning several of the same number, or a run, which meant all the tiles were the same color, but consecutive numbers, like 2, 3, 4, and 5. There had to be at least three tiles in each run or group. "But the fun part," she said, "is you can steal from other groups that are already down. For example, if there are three 4s down, and you need one to make a run, you can take it—just not on your opening turn."

I didn't make my opening turn for about fifteen minutes because she said your tiles had to add up to fifty before you could start. Meanwhile, Mrs. Greenwood was building runs and groups, then stealing from them to make more. "It just all comes back to you," she said.

"I wish it would come to me in the first place." But, actually, I was just as glad to have her beating me. She seemed to enjoy it.

Still, she said, "You must have something."

"You're just better at this than I am."

"Nonsense. You're a smart boy. That's what I like about this—it exercises the brain, helps with problem solving."

I thought about the problem of how I was going to see Rachel. What if it rained for a week?

The joker Mrs. Greenwood had just put down laughed at me.

After she'd beaten me for the third time straight (and I suspected she was holding back), I asked her if there was anything else she needed repaired.

Maybe she saw the look of quiet desperation on my face. Or maybe she was just as bored of playing Rummikub as I was. In any case, she said, "You know, I think the library might have that internet service. Is there a way to bring your computer there and work?"

My head shot up quicker than a cartoon character's. "What? Yes. Yes, there is a way. Where's the library?"

"Well . . ." She played with the Rummikub tiles. I dimly remembered that Nikki and her friends used to make necklaces out of them. Nikki . . .

"It's a little far," she said.

What around here wasn't? "That's okay. Where, exactly, is it?"

"You pass the hardware store and get onto the Northway. Then, you get off in Gatskill."

Gatskill? That had been where Zach had worked, at the Red Fox Inn. "About how far away is that?"

"At least half an hour I'd say. And you should drive slowly in this rain." She glanced at her watch, a skinny gold thing I bet she had to wind each morning. "Maybe it's too late to get started. They probably close at five."

It was nearly two now. It probably was too late. But on the other hand, I was sure the bar was just getting started at five.

"No, I'll go. I'd like to get something done today." I started to put away the Rummikub tiles.

"Such diligence." She placed her hand on my wrist, stopping me. "I'll put them away."

"I'll get gas for your car too." It was the least I could do, since I was the only one driving it.

"Sweet boy." She made me a little map, which I took with me. I took my computer too, even though I had no intention of using it. I felt bad lying to her in a way I hadn't felt bad about lying to my own mom. Maybe it was because I was still suffering with what had happened to Tyler or maybe it was because I knew she'd been lied to before, with great consequence. Still, I did lie, I just felt bad about it.

I went to the library first. It was surprisingly packed, by which I mean I saw eight or nine people, and I actually had to wait to talk to the librarian, an old lady who looked like she'd died a few years ago. Maybe everyone's internet was out.

"Red Fox Inn?" she said when I finally asked her. "It used to be on Route Eight, just a ways down from the grocery. I'm not sure it's there anymore, but I don't drink."

"Thank you." I started to turn away.

"Do you want a book while you're here?"

"Um, maybe later. I have to get there first. It's sort of . . . ah, a scavenger hunt."

She sighed.

"Don't forget we close at five."

It had finally stopped raining. In fact, the air was cold. I found Route 8, which I had passed on the way to the library, found the grocery store, and, very eventually, found the Red Fox Inn.

Or what was left of it, which was merely a skeleton of a building, burned out by fire. A sign still remained, its charred letters saying *Red Fox Inn*. I started to drive away, when I saw there was a second building, a little shack or house. It had looked equally abandoned at first, but then, I noticed some movement. When I turned, I saw a grimy window shade drop down. I got out of the car.

Then, I stopped. Was I crazy? I mean, really, was I crazy? I was out here in a rural area, exactly the type of place where people disappeared and were never seen again. Add the abandoned, burned-out building and some kind of squatter living in it. Possibly, it could be some harmless Boo Radley type—or it could be Jason Voorhees from *Friday the 13th* parts one through twenty. In fact, I'd passed a boarded-up summer camp on the way there. Sure, it might just have been closed for the winter, but what if it wasn't?

I got back in the car.

But then, I remembered Rachel, saying she thought there was something she was destined to do, trapped in a tower over her poor, murdered mother. Who had put her there? And why? Would she ever get away? There was something weird going on in this town, and finding the guy who had given Danielle those creepy leaves seemed like the key.

I thought too, of Mrs. Greenwood, all alone. I needed to find out what had happened to Danielle.

Then, someone tapped my window.

I jumped. It was just like *Zombieland*! And me without my shotgun. My feet searched for the gas pedal, not finding it.

"Can I help you, son?"

The face at the window was an old guy, but he in no way looked dead. In fact, he was sort of a harmless old guy, older than anyone I'd ever seen, blue eyes surrounded by a spiderweb of wrinkles, looking out from under a Yankees cap.

Running him over would probably be considered an overreaction. I rolled the window down, which took a minute because Mrs. Greenwood's car had these crazy window cranks you had to turn.

Despite this, the old guy left his hands on the glass the whole time. On the up side, I could see his hands, and he didn't have a knife.

Still, it could be in his pocket. I put my right foot over the gas, just in case. I shivered. The air was cold now.

"Yeah, do you live here?" I asked.

"That, I do. Are you lost? Need directions back to the Northway?"

I relaxed a little more. Zombies didn't usually offer directions back to the Northway. They just ate your brains.

"Um, no. I'm okay. But do you know anything about this place?"

"The Red Fox? Sure, I'm the owner. At least, until it burned to the ground—Poof! One second it was there, the next gone. I didn't have money to fix it up. It was named after me, Henry Fox. I used to have red hair." He flipped up the Yankees cap to show his balding scalp. "Back when I had hair. But you won't find much around here except ashes and memories. There's Mahoney's about a mile down Route Eight if you're looking for someplace to watch the bowl games. In fact, I was headed there myself."

"Oh, thanks. No, I was just wondering. If you're the owner, maybe you know a guy that used to work there. His name was Zach, played in a band there. It would have been about seventeen or eighteen years ago."

The old man looked confused. This wasn't what he'd been expecting. Then, a glimmer of recognition filled his eyes. "I do remember Zach. Nice kid. But that was a long time ago. You couldn't have known him."

"No, I . . . that is, my mother knew him. From school. She's on the reunion committee and trying to find people. Zach hasn't been to the Facebook page." I knew as I said it that the old guy had never heard of Facebook, but that was okay. Harmless babbling was okay. "Do you know any of his relatives? Does he still have family in Gatskill?"

"Who's your mama? I know most people in these parts."

"Emily Hill."

"Emily Hill . . ." He got a strange look on his face, then smiled. "Nope, don't know her."

"It's okay. She hasn't been here in a long time. I'm staying with an old friend of hers, just for the Christmas holiday."

I didn't know what made me lie except, in that second, I realized that not a single car had come down the road in the time we'd been talking. And something about his questions was making me nervous.

He asked another one. "Who you staying with?"

Again, I lied. "Astrid. Astrid Brewer. She's my cousin."

"I thought you said she was a friend."

"Well, she's like a cousin because we're such close friends. I need to get back soon, for dinner. So do you know anything about Zach?"

The old man shook his head. "No, can't say we've kept in touch. But he was friends with my brother, Carl. Maybe he would know something. If you give me a phone number, I could call if he does."

"Great." I was just looking for a way out of there. I found the receipt from the hardware store and wrote down my essentially worthless cell phone number. "Leave a message if I don't answer."

"I'll do that. Hey, I'll be seeing Carl tonight at Mahoney's. Sure you don't want to come?"

Poor old guy. He probably just wanted companionship, and here I was, treating him like an ax murderer. But I shook my head. I was entertaining enough old people already. "Nah, I gotta get back. Thanks, though." I handed him the paper.

He took it. "I'll be sure and ask."

"Yeah, thanks. See you around."

I waited, as politely as possible, for him to back away. Then, without bothering to put the window up, I tore out of there.

I went to the library and spent the next hour on old micro-films of the town's newspaper. There was nothing about Danielle's disappearance, not anywhere. They weren't treating this as a cold case, but as no case at all. The police obviously assumed she'd run away.

I went back home, had dinner, and went to bed. Right before I turned in, I noticed it had begun to snow again.

27

Rachel

He didn't come. I knew the rain would make it too difficult for him. Yet, somehow, I hoped he would come anyway. Now, Mama has left, and today is over. And, with it, any chance of seeing him. Perhaps I imagined him. It would not be impossible.

When I was a little girl, I imagined a playmate for myself, a little girl with red hair and freckles. Her name was Sarah, and she liked all the same things I liked, peanut butter sandwiches and playing with dolls. When we had tea parties, she would always let me have the last cookie. I taught her songs, and we danced and played games. She never neglected me.

What if Wyatt too was imaginary, like Sarah had been? What if I was slowly losing my mind?

No. The thing about Sarah was, she always did what I wanted her to do. Always. And that was because she was me, and I was her. She never disappointed me. She always showed up. Wyatt disappointed me precisely because he was real. He was a real boy who could not climb my tower in the slippery rain.

I walked to the window and opened it. A blast of cold air met my face, but I was still warm from the fire inside. I stared down, remembering yesterday, the feel of my feet on the sodden, snowy ground, the first time I had felt it since I had come here so many years ago. I glanced at my bed. The rope was under there. So strange, to have the means of escape at my disposal yet not go. Was I really not leaving because I wanted to stay? Or was it because I was afraid to leave this, my comfortable cocoon? If Wyatt didn't come back, would I continue as I had been before, all alone, no contact with anyone? Could I be content to stay here alone? Had I ever been?

I gazed into the moonlight and saw that the rain had ended. Indeed, it was snow falling now, giant, lacy flakes that had already begun to whiten the trees.

I glanced at the rope again. Would he come tomorrow? I pulled the rope out from under the bed and tied it using the figure eight knot. Then, I threw it out the window so it dangled and fell all the way to the ground.

I closed the window as best I could and went to bed. In my darkened room, I tried to imagine he was there. After all, I had seen him before, in my dreams. But now that he had been there in the flesh, I could dream him no longer.

That's how I knew he was real.

28

Wyatt

When I woke the next morning, it was still dark. The house was quiet. Still, I opened the window, half expecting to see Danielle again. Nothing there. But by the slim circle of moonlight, I could tell it had snowed all night long, snowed deep enough to obliterate any memory of grass. I stood for a second longer, listening for a voice on the wind. For a second, I thought I heard it. Then, it faded away. I started to put down the window. It was old and hard to pull up on, and as I struggled with it, I felt a chill run through my arms. Then, my entire body. At the same time, I noticed a car pull up in front of the house beside a bank of snowy evergreens. Its lights went out, and it disappeared. This was strange. Few cars passed in the morning. Eighteen wheelers, yes, but few cars, and fewer stopped. Probably, the driver was waiting for someone. Still,

I'd remember to look when I came down.

Now, I dressed quickly in warm clothes, bringing extra jeans and a sweater in case of another mishap. I crept into the hall. Mrs. G. wasn't up. I'd beaten her, for once. What luck. I tiptoed down the dark stairs and left a note telling her I was going skiing with Josh.

At the last minute, I went into the hallway coat closet and found a coat. I was careful to choose one from the back, so Mrs. G. wouldn't notice it missing. I took the car keys and stepped outside.

The car was in the garage, which was an old one without an electric door. But the driveway was completely snowed in. That meant I had to shovel it first. The road was already clear.

As I shoveled, I noticed the car was still there, out on the road, far in front of the house, motor running.

Finally, I put down the garage door and pulled onto the road.

The car followed me.

The road was otherwise deserted. I glanced at the dashboard clock. Six thirty. I decided to change my plans and go to the grocery store the next town over, which was south instead of north. I found a safe place, then pulled off the road without signaling. The car soared past me. It was some kind of sedan, an Accord or Taurus, dark blue or black. I made a U-turn and sped in the opposite direction.

A minute later, I saw the same car, behind me again, its lights blazing in the window.

Finally, I reached the grocery store. Again, I turned off without signaling, without warning. Again, the car soared past me.

I had to wait a few minutes before the store opened at seven, but I could see the employees inside. I knew the guy would be back in a minute. Then, he was. The light was good enough, now, that I could see it was an old, dark blue Taurus. Whoever it was stayed in the car. The store opened its doors, and I walked around, choosing random items, fruit and donuts for breakfast. Why would anyone be following me? Me, who knew nothing, who wasn't even from around here? Could it be because I'd asked about Zach? But no, I hadn't even given my real address. What if it was someone looking for Rachel, someone who'd seen me go to her? But even that seemed insane. No one knew about Rachel. She said she hadn't seen anyone but the woman who took care of her, a woman she called Mama even though she wasn't her mother, in years. Still, I had to lose the guy before I went to her. I approached the register. The car was still out there.

The cashier was a girl about my age. I remembered what Astrid had said, about everyone knowing everyone around here. "I think that blue car's been following me. Any idea who it is?"

She glanced outside, squinted, then shrugged. "Doesn't look familiar. You from around here?"

Considering the circumstances, I said, "I'm from Long Island, staying at the Big Spruce Lodge."

"Shame. We don't get many new people here."

"I'm staying a month. I'll stop by again. You always work mornings?"

"No, during school I work nights."

"Perfect. I'll stop by.

She nodded. "I'll look for you."

She was still watching me as I walked out the door. Which was good because she could be a witness if anything happened later on.

Clutching my groceries in one hand, my keys in the other, I sprinted for the car. It took a minute to open the door since Mrs. Greenwood, of course, didn't have remote door locks. I got in, locked the door, and waved to the check-out girl. I drove to the exit, signaled left, but turned right. The guy still followed me. I accelerated. It was about half a mile to the expressway entrance, and I wanted to be going fast, real fast, when I got there. The guy kept pace with me.

As soon as the expressway signs came into view, I started to signal. The guy signaled too.

I took the ramp and made like I was going for the southbound entrance. The guy followed me. We were going close to eighty. At the last minute, I swerved left, taking the northbound entrance.

The Taurus missed it and soared into the southbound lane. I headed north.

I'd lost him. But it didn't explain why he'd been following me in the first place.

The distance between exits around here might be ten miles or more. I had lost him in a real way. Still, I would keep one eye on the rearview.

To further evade the guy, I got off at a later exit, then drove back. No one was on the road but the snowplows. I followed them until I got to the back road I'd taken to the cabin, then realized it hadn't been cleared. Fortunately, the trees protected it a great deal, so the snow coating was light. Still, I pulled over earlier than before and began to slog through the snow. It was even harder than the first time, but now, I had a goal. Rachel. Beautiful Rachel, Rachel who knew better than me or anyone what it was to be all alone.

My legs ached, and it was hard to lift them in and out of the soft snow. Still, I did. The pain felt good. It made me feel alive and like my life had purpose.

I knew what that purpose was too, to persuade Rachel to come with me, to run away with me. It was the only safe way. I was certain the guy who had followed me was really after her. He knew about her, somehow. She had told me about her mother's killer. He wanted to find her. Maybe I had tipped him off. If she came with me, we could find someone, the police, the FBI. Someone who wasn't me to get to the bottom of this. After all, what reason did she have to stay, other than some woman who was holding her captive?

And suddenly, I heard a voice in the distance, singing something. But it couldn't be. The tower was tall, and surely, the window was closed against the cold and snow. Was I delirious from the frigid weather? Or was some supernatural force calling me toward her?

29

Rachel

He would come today. I was certain of it. I sensed him. And, more than that, I sensed that he was struggling to get to me.

I loved him. Though we had barely met, there was some power greater than me, greater than all, that bound me to him.

I looked out the window, certain I would see him in the distance. Nothing. Yet I knew he was coming.

For every reason and no reason, I began to sing. Even though the tower was high and the weather was windy, I knew he would hear me. I knew it would urge him on toward me.

Wyatt

Finally, I could see the tower in the distance. The voice, Rachel's voice, grew louder in my head, and though my legs were numb with the walking and my body was near freezing, I kept going, pushing through trees and obstacles in my way.

Then, suddenly, I was there before the tower. It looked older than I remembered, maybe because of the freshness of the white snow. It looked so dilapidated I might be able to bring it down with the slightest push and rescue her that way.

No, not that way. I could see the rope, her strange, magical hair, hanging to the ground. Above it, I saw her face. She was waiting for me.

I waved to her.

She waved back.

I looked behind me one last time, to assure myself no one had followed me. Nothing. I waved again and yelled, "Hello!"

The sound carried. She jumped up and down, yelling, "Hello! I'm so glad you're here!"

"It's nice out! Can you come down?"

"You'll help me back up?"

"Yes!" I didn't want to. I wanted her to come with me. But that conversation could wait for later. I wanted her to come down now.

She had gone back inside to get something. She threw it down, and I saw it was a braid, shorter than the one that hung from the tower. I looked up. She was already climbing down.

As she made her way down the rope, I tried to think about how dangerous this was, how crazy, freaky dangerous. I'd done rock climbing at a gym at home, fake rocks, tons of safety equipment. I was good at it, but here—people got killed falling from lesser heights.

And yet, we had done it before. I was willing to risk it to see her.

Finally, she dropped down beside me, and I took her in my arms.

"Missed you," I said. "I couldn't make it in the rain."

"I knew." She shivered. "Cold here."

"I brought you some stuff." I gestured to the coat I'd stolen. "There's a hat and gloves in the pocket. I thought we could play in the snow. Have you ever done that?"

"I think, maybe when I was a little girl. I remember building a snowman with Mama. But then, she got scared and we had to go inside."

"We can build a snowman. Put it on."

I picked up the coat and held it so she could step into it. Then, the hat and gloves. Once dressed, she twirled around, modeling, and I wondered if that was some instinct all girls had, twirling, modeling, even if they'd never seen a television or even met another girl before.

I had a strange sense of *déjà vu*, looking at her, as if I'd seen that

156

girl in that coat before. I shook it off. Of course I hadn't.

"How do I look?" she asked.

"Adorable."

I kissed her. The wind picked up the fresh snow and flung it around us, and I felt like this was the first day I'd ever lived, like Tyler and Nikki and everyone at home didn't exist, and we were the only people in this beauty of a white world. "So what should we do?"

31

Rachel

I stared around at the green and white trees, feeling the ache in my muscles, the cold on my face. The air was silent, waiting.

I looked at Wyatt. "I'd like to make a snow angel."

"A snow angel?"

"Yes. I've read about them in books. You lay on the ground and flap your arms until it looks like wings and a full skirt."

"I know what a snow angel is." Wyatt glanced around. "It just takes a lot of room. We sure can't go on the lake."

"Please. If I made one, I could see it from my tower, even after you leave. There's a clear spot back there, behind those trees. I can see from the window."

I suddenly realized I'd staked it out. I'd been doing it for years, planning my escape, thinking of how it would be when I left. Why had I never tried it before? Was I so afraid of falling, of dying?

I had no life to lose. Until now. I breathed deeply, letting the world into my lungs.

It was as if saving Wyatt from the ice showed me that I could do something, that I wasn't helpless, worthless after all.

I grabbed his arm. "Come this way!" I felt like a different girl.

"You show me then," he said, laughing. "I'll follow you."

"I will!" I knew there was a clear path nearby. I'd been tracing it and retracing it.

"We have to pass that tree." I gestured toward the big one, the one that had always frightened me as a child, its gnarled branches resembling a monster. It almost completely blocked the path.

I reached behind me for Wyatt's hand. He grabbed mine, squeezed it.

After we passed the monster tree, there would be two more. Then, the clearing would become visible. It was so incredible to think I'd be there, in person.

The only thing Wyatt had not brought was warm shoes. But I ignored my frozen feet as I pushed through the snowy tree limbs, then held them for him.

As he clambered through, one branch slipped from my grip. It sprung back, hitting him in the face and sending a pile of snow onto him as well. "Oh, sorry."

"You did that on purpose!" But he was laughing.

"No, I didn't!"

"Okay. Just let me hold the next one for you."

"Not a chance." I ran as fast as I could toward it. Which wasn't very fast because of the snow. I had never walked in anything like it before. At least, that I remembered. The snow was white and sparkly with a hard crust on top. But when you stepped on it, your foot sank down, down, and you had to lift it high to get out. Wyatt was gaining on me.

He grabbed me. "Let me go first, actually. Not very gentlemanly to make you do all the pushing."

"You just want to get back at me." I struggled against him, and then, I reached the tree.

"Maybe," he said.

I pulled up a huge, snow-covered branch, held it back, and then, again, flung it in his face. "Gotcha!"

Even though that time, he must have known it was coming, he didn't duck. He let it hit him full in the face. "You think you're so funny!"

I laughed. "I'm hilarious."

He started to run fast, overtaking me. He reached the last tree. I hung back.

He pulled back the branch. "Come on, Rachel." His voice was low, enticing.

"Sweet Rachel. I'll hold it for you. I won't throw snow in your face. I'm the bigger person."

"I'll bet." He was holding the branch so a huge pile of snow was aimed at me.

"Okay, then. Take your punishment. Admit you lost."

I sighed. "I suppose I have to. You're more powerful than poor little me." In a way, I wanted to feel it, all that snow against my face.

I stepped toward it, closing my eyes. But he didn't release it. He let me in.

We had reached the clearing. The sun had risen, and the snow sparkled with a white glow that had every color of the rainbow. I jumped up and down and into his arms. "We made it! We're here!

Isn't this the perfect place to make an angel?"

"Do you know how to make one?" he asked.

"You'll show me."

He smiled. "The trick is getting up and down without making footprints in the angel. You have to fall back flat. I'll show you." He broke away from me and walked a few steps to a clear area, away from the trees. He stood straight and just fell. Then, he flapped his arms and legs like scissors until an angel appeared.

"Now, help me up," he said.

"How?"

"Careful. Just stay off to the side. Help me balance."

I did what he said, and he was able to rise, only stepping in the tiny spot below the angel's "skirt," where her feet would be. Then, he backed away.

It really did look like a real angel, with full skirt and spreading wings. What a wondrous accomplishment! Suddenly, the cold in my feet, on my face, felt like a gift.

"I want to make one," I said. I ran over to the other side of his, where the snow was white and unspoiled. I stood, smelling the air, the moment, so that I might never forget it, no matter what else happened. I knew that smells brought memories, but I'd had precious little to remember before now. How amazing, when you thought of it, that most of my life had been spent reading, waiting for Mama to come. Only now was I living.

"Go ahead," Wyatt said. "It's soft."

"I know." My voice was a whisper. I held my arms out, wavered, then fell. The snow caught me. I lay there a moment, letting it hug me. Then, I remembered what Wyatt had done and flapped my arms and legs as hard as I could.

"Did I do it right?" I asked.

"Absolutely." He was beside me now, holding out his hand.

I reached up and took it, feeling the connection between us like a shock of electricity. Then, I rose slowly, careful only to step where the angels' shoes would be. I stepped back.

My angel was enchanting, perfect in the morning light. I almost thought she would take flight. I couldn't believe I was here, part of this strange, wonderful world I'd only read about in books. I stared at Wyatt. He was so beautiful.

"Thank you," I said.

"For what?"

"For bringing me here."

He shrugged. "You brought yourself."

I made three more, barely noticing the cold, but finally, Wyatt said, "Let me make another."

I stepped back, so he could do it. But this time, when I went to pull him up, he pulled down on my arm so I tumbled beside him. He took me in his arms, kissing me.

"I've never met a girl like you. You're so brave. And when I see things through your eyes, they're wonderful."

"They are." I kissed him back. I felt a warmth rising from within me. "I feel the same way. I think I've been waiting for you, always."

"Then come with me," he said. "Please. We can find help."

I wanted to. I really wanted to. And yet, I couldn't leave Mama. I imagined her finding me gone. But more than that, I knew there was a reason I had to stay.

"I can't go," I said.

"Because of Mama?"

"Yes, but more than that. Because of who I am. I know there is something I have to do."

"How can you possibly know that?"

I wasn't sure I should tell him. Yet my feet were frozen, his eyes were bright green in the snowy light, and I heard my voice saying, "Come to my tower, and I'll show you."

32

Wyatt

It was easier to reach her tower, having done it once before. We embraced once again when she reached the top, and I was newly amazed that she was real. Real. Not some crazy dream I had in the delirium of the cold. She was real and warm, and for once in my life, I had earned the right to her, earned the right to kiss her.

And that feeling made me brave enough to speak when we finally parted. "Rachel, did you ever think that maybe it is me you are meant for? I was the one who heard you singing. It was impossible. No one else heard it from miles away, but I heard you because I was meant to find you. I was meant to rescue you."

"I know you were meant to find me." She gazed deep into my eyes in that way of hers. "Though, if I recall, it was I who rescued you. But there is something more. Meeting you is merely a piece in the puzzle. I believe I am . . . unusual."

I looked at her. She was so beautiful, unearthly beautiful, beautiful in a way that sort of put her out of my league. And, thinking about it, her singing was pretty incredible too—not to mention making that rope out of her hair. Who did that? I said, "Of course you're unusual."

She shook her head. "Not merely in the ways you are thinking. Let me show you."

Before I could say anything else, she walked to the bed and drew a pair of scissors out from beneath the mattress. She held up one finger, opened a blade, and quickly sliced it, hard, so it started to bleed.

I clutched my own finger. "Man, why'd you do that?" I knew a girl at school who was a cutter. I never understood it until Tyler died. Then, I sort of did, the way sometimes, when you hurt one part of yourself, it relieves another. Still, I'd never tried it.

I stared at Rachel. Her blue eyes filled with tears as she gazed at the drop of blood welling on her fingertip. She held her other hand up, silencing me, telling me to stay away. The tears flowed from her eyes, and I longed to hold her, longed to comfort her. Yet, I also longed to shake her for hurting herself. I didn't want anyone to harm her.

Then, she held her finger to her tearstained cheek. For a second, the blood mixed with the tears. She withdrew her finger and held it toward me.

"Look," she said.

I did, though it pained me. But her finger no longer bled. In fact, I couldn't see a cut, not the slightest scar. It was healed perfectly, as if she had never cut it.

"Can normal people do that?" she asked.

I gaped at her, speechless. Did she mean what I thought she did?

"My tears . . . they heal. Can you do that? Can other people?"

I shook my head.

"I didn't think so. I was uncertain, but in books, people need bandages when they are hurt. I don't."

"Does it only work on yourself?" I asked. "Or can you heal others too?"

"I don't know." The air in the room felt strangely still, as if there wasn't enough of it. "I don't know others, except Mama."

"You know me."

She held up the scissors. "Shall I cut you then? I thought you might scream like a baby when I cut myself just now."

"You don't have to." I held up my hand, rough and scratched from clutching at the branches and ice the other day. On the cheek she hadn't touched, a tear still glistened. "May I?"

She nodded.

I brushed the tear away with my wounded palm. Her face was so soft, so wild and strange. I wanted to kiss her again, but first, I pulled my hand away and looked at it.

It was perfectly healed.

"Wow," I said.

She nodded. "Wow. So you see, I am a special girl. I am waiting to find out why, to find out what it is I must do."

"But what if being up here is preventing you from finding out?"

"It didn't prevent your finding me."

"That's true. But maybe that's why—I'm supposed to take you away." I was talking in circles, and I knew it. I just couldn't believe she was supposed to stay here.

She shook her head, then stared off into the distance. "I don't know." New tears sprung to her eyes. "I wish I understood. Why are you here? What brought you here? Why are you the one who came for me?"

I thought about it, but the only reason I could think of was a bad one: because I *needed* to do something good, to make up for the other things. Was that enough of a reason? Enough for her?

I decided to tell her. I hoped she wouldn't be disgusted by me, but I had to find out.

33

Wyatt

The sun had finally risen high in the sky, stretching its fingers through the many branches and lighting the room. I tried to make myself comfortable, but I couldn't. There would be no comfort for me. Telling this story might help, but probably not. Probably, only doing something would help.

"I used to have this friend named Tyler," I explained. "He lived next door, and he and I were best friends, almost like brothers. You know what I mean?"

Too late, I realized of course she didn't. She'd been locked in a tower her whole life, no friends, nothing. Which was mind-blowing, when you thought about it. Locked in a tower. You could say it a hundred times, and it still seemed like something not real, like something from a book you read a long time ago, before you were old

168

enough to question how crazy it was.

She'd been locked in a tower. Oh, and her tears had healing powers. That too. What else? Maybe, if you dropped her out the window, you'd find out she could fly.

I looked at her. Her skin was the same translucent white as the snow outside, and her eyes saw right through me.

"I'm sorry," I said. "I know you don't really know what I'm talking about."

"Don't be. I've read books. My favorite was called *A Little Princess*. There was a girl named Sara, and she had to stay in an attic, which was like a tower. She thought she would be so lonely, but then, she discovered a little girl named Becky in the next room. They became friends and had so many adventures. I used to long for a friend like that, just on the other side of the wall. In fact, at night, I pretended there was someone there. Was that what it was like?"

"Sort of." I didn't want to say it was nothing like that. Tyler wasn't some theoretical soul mate, some pretend friend like in a book. He was a real person, a person who let you copy his homework if you left yours at home, a person to throw a ball with. When Tyler and I went out for the travel baseball team in seventh grade, he made it and I didn't. So he said he wouldn't do it either because it wouldn't be fun without me, even though he really wanted to do it. That was the kind of friend he was. "Yeah, it was like that. We were best friends. His parents were divorced, and after his mother got remarried, we became even better friends. He was over at my house all the time."

"That's so nice," Rachel said. "I always dreamed of having a friend like that. You must miss him, being away from him."

"I do." I felt a lump forming in my throat, but I swallowed it. "Anyway we always hung out at my house. Tyler said we couldn't go to his anymore because his stepfather worked the night shift. I wished I could go over his house more so I could see his sister, Nikki."

"Nikki?"

"Yeah, Nikki. Nicole. I'd known her since we were little kids too, and I never really thought of her like . . . well, you know. I never thought of her. But last year, I suddenly started noticing that she was, you know, pretty. I'd known her my whole life, and she should have been like a sister, but suddenly, she wasn't."

"I understand. Like Laurie and Jo March."

"Exactly." Even though I had no idea who Joe March was, he sounded familiar. I thought maybe he was from one of those girl books like Nikki had liked. I'd look on Wikipedia when I got back. "Anyway, one day I decided I'd go over there, just to say hi to her. And Tyler too, of course. I wouldn't make any noise or disturb their stepdad. We'd pretty much had the type of friendship where you could just walk over without knocking, so I didn't tell Tyler I was coming.

"But when I got there, Tyler's stepdad was awake anyway. I knew because he was screaming and yelling. I could see them through the little window in the front door. Just barely, but they couldn't see me."

I could still picture the scene, through the thick, mottled glass shaped like a flower. Tyler's stepfather—his name was Rick—was mad about something. Maybe someone had already woken him up. Anyway, his face was practically purple, and I knew I didn't want to knock.

"I started to back away. He was calling Tyler's mom all sorts of names, and then, he hit her. I couldn't believe it. Tyler sort of freaked then, and they got into it, struggling on the floor. I couldn't move. I didn't really know what to do."

"I wouldn't either," Rachel said. "It sounds terrifying."

I remembered it so well. I had stood frozen, both figuratively and literally, in the November cold, while Ty and Rick were hitting each other. Nikki and her mom ran for safety. I was glad at least for that.

Finally, it was like a spell had been broken. I ran home.

"I didn't know what to do," I told Rachel. "If I should call the police or something, but I thought Tyler might call them, and it was over anyway, so I didn't. After a while, I called Ty on his cell phone." I realized she probably didn't know what a cell phone was. "It's a little phone where you can talk to people privately. Like this." I took out my phone and, even though I knew it wouldn't work, I turned it on, so she could see the lights. Weirdly, it had bars. Maybe because I was up so high. Josh had told me his phone worked in the hills. There were three texts too, all from my mother. "I asked him if he wanted to come over, hang out, or go to the mall—that's a place a lot of teenagers go, to buy stuff and hang out. He sounded a little weird, and I knew why. He said he'd see if he could go. A few minutes later, he called me back and asked if Nikki could come over too. Of course I said okay.

"So we went to the mall, and all the way there, Tyler was quiet, and Nikki was sort of crying, and I didn't know what to say, what to do. Part of me felt like I'd seen something I shouldn't have, and if Tyler wanted to talk about it, he would have told me himself. It felt like spying. But another part said that Tyler was my best friend, and he was in trouble. I wanted to know how often this happened, though I sort of knew. That was why I wasn't allowed to go over there. Part of me was angry at him for not telling me. I mean, he was my best friend."

"It was probably hard for him to talk about it," Rachel said. "He was embarrassed. At least, I think he might have been."

"No, you're right," I said. "And, eventually, when I decided to break down and ask him, that's exactly what happened. He got mad at me, for knowing, for spying on him. I said, 'I wasn't spying. I was just coming over your house like a normal person. I can't help what I saw, man. I want to help.' And Nikki took my side. She said she was glad I knew, that it was hard, not having anyone to talk to about it. She said she'd wanted to tell one of the counselors at school but their mom said not to. If they told the counselor, the counselor would have to tell the police or something. Then, they'd come and take them away."

"'Isn't that a good reason to tell someone?' I said, 'So they'd come and get you some help, arrest that bastard?'

"Nikki looked at Tyler, and I could tell they'd had the same conversation before then. Tyler said, 'My mom's worried about us all getting separated, that they'd put me and Nikki in foster care. She says she's going to leave Rick as soon as she can get enough money together to take us to live with my aunt Mel in Florida.'

"'Do you believe her?' I asked. Tyler's mom didn't even work anymore. She used to be a nurse before she'd married Rick, but then, she'd quit.

"'Sure,' Tyler said. 'Why not? In any case, I don't want to get separated from Nikki.'

"I told him they could move in with us, but Tyler shook his head. 'I have to stick around to protect my mom.'"

Rachel was sitting, hands folded in her lap, staring at me, and I knew she understood. I said, "I know now there were things I could have done. If I'd told my mom, maybe she would have given them the money for the ticket to Florida. Or maybe the police would have arrested Rick, and then, it would have been over."

"But you didn't do that?" Rachel said.

Her voice didn't sound judgmental. I shook my head. "I didn't know what to do."

"I wouldn't have either."

"I just figured—I don't know what I figured, that it wasn't my place. I knew Tyler would be mad at me if I told. Now, I realize he was too scared, they all were, too scared of what might happen.

Sometimes, people are more comfortable with sticking with what they know, even if it's bad, instead of taking a chance on something that would probably be better but might be worse."

She nodded. "Like this tower. I've been here for years. Obviously, I could escape. I left when I saw you fall through the ice, when I needed to leave. But I've always thought that maybe, there'd be something really bad out there, or someone, someone who'd hurt me, kill me. Or maybe I'd just starve to death. Here, Mama feeds me every day, like a . . . pet. I have no idea what's out there. So I stay."

She stood then, and paced the room, perturbed. "We all like to think we'd do the right thing, the heroic thing if we had to. But usually, we don't because that's not the comfortable thing. The easy thing is to stay put in your comfortable tower, even if that tower is actually a prison."

"But you saved my life."

"Because I couldn't just watch you die, drown in the icy lake. Sometimes, you have to act. It's a matter of life and death."

I felt my stomach drop. "It was a matter of life and death with Tyler. I just didn't know it. I didn't recognize it."

"What do you mean?"

I shivered, remembering what had happened next.

"A week went by, then two, and nothing changed with Tyler. They didn't move out. Their mom didn't leave their stepdad, and I didn't say anything because I didn't want Tyler to be mad at me or whatever." I shook my head. "Like that would be a big deal."

It was hard to go on. I drew in a deep breath, and even though it was cold in the room, and my feet were wet, my face felt hot.

Rachel touched my hand. "Are you okay?"

I shook my head again. "No. No, I'm not, but I have to tell you anyway."

She took my hand in hers. "Okay."

I breathed in, then out. I could picture the scene, like it was frozen in time, my mom and I at the breakfast table, English muffins and I Can't Believe It's Not Butter. I couldn't see that table without remembering. It was a big part of the reason I'd left.

"We were eating breakfast. It was a Saturday. Tyler and I had played a big game the night before, and my muscles ached. Football. I was going to call him at nine, you know, to rehash it. But suddenly, there was this really loud noise.

"My mother and I looked at each other, and she was, like, 'What was that?' and I said, 'I don't know,' but I did, and suddenly, I was screaming and running to the door, and my mother was pulling me back. She was saying, 'Don't go out there.' She'd call 911—the emergency number. Then, there was another loud noise and a woman screaming. I could tell it was a woman, maybe Nikki or Tyler's mom, and somehow, I knew Tyler was dead. I knew he was dead, and I was crying, screaming, yelling to my mom to call the police, and she did, but it was too late. It was too late. Then, the door to their house opened, and Tyler's mom came running out. She was covered in blood, and I knew it was too late. But my mom was on the phone with the police, and I let Tyler's mother in. I waited a second to see if anyone else was behind them, if Tyler . . . or Nikki . . ."

I stopped, unable to speak anymore. Tears were streaming out of my eyes, down my face and into my mouth. These tears didn't heal anything at all. They were salty, and they hurt. I looked at Rachel, and she was all wavery like one of those weird paintings at MoMA, and I saw that she was crying too. She put her arms around me, her face against mine, her tears, her magical tears, blending with my own, and I didn't know if it was the tears' healing powers or just having her near me, but I felt a little bit better. A little bit.

We stood there a moment, clinging to one another, weeping. Finally, I said, "He killed them. She said she was leaving him, and he killed her kids. He killed Tyler and Nikki, and when the police sirens started coming, there was another shot, and he killed himself. And I knew all about it, but I did nothing."

The room felt so cold, and I started to shiver, shiver uncontrollably, worse than the day I fell in the lake. Rachel held me tight. She said, "It wasn't your fault. You couldn't have known. You couldn't have seen it coming."

"You don't think so?"

"No. I didn't see it coming, even when you told me. To believe that would happen, you would have to be so negative. You would have to think people are evil. You're not like that."

I shook my head. "In the days after that, I felt so many different things, sad, angry, guilty, but mostly just numb, like part of me was dead. But other times, I felt like I could just go over there, just go and change it, see Tyler and tell him to run, tell him to leave. A couple of times, I started out the door before I noticed the police tape, before I remembered the ambulances that had come for their bodies. And on the day of the funeral, I felt like if I just told someone, maybe I could fix it. I knew it wasn't true, that nothing was going to bring Tyler back.

"Still, I felt so guilty. I told a friend, this girl in my class, Megan. I told her how guilty I felt, like I could have prevented it."

"What did she say?" Rachel stroked my back.

"Nothing. She didn't say anything at all." I remembered her stony face, then her back as she turned away. "I'm sure she hated me."

"I bet she didn't," Rachel said. "That would be so unfair. It wasn't your fault."

"Do you really think so?"

"Of course it wasn't. You couldn't have predicted the future. No one else even knows what they would have done. Everyone thinks they'd do the heroic thing, but you never really know." She pulled away from me, angry and fierce. "The person whose fault it was is dead. It wasn't your fault."

"I wish I could be sure."

"You should be sure." She stroked my hair. "You're a hero. You came out here, all this way to find me. Who else would do that?"

"Lots of guys."

"I haven't seen any of them." She walked to the window and opened it. "Helloooooo! Are you out there? Hellooooo?"

I laughed. "They must have fallen in the lake."

"Oh, I see."

"Okay, maybe not that many guys have the same kind of time on their hands as I do." Though, in Slakkill, that probably wasn't true.

"So you just came to rescue me because you had time on your hands?" She glanced out the window again. "Maybe I should look for those guys."

"That didn't come out right."

"Try again, then." She closed the window, looking at me the whole time. Then, she walked toward me and put her arms around me.

"You're so incredible," I said.

She kissed me, my cheeks, my eyes. I kissed her back, stroking her hair, her hair, and for a moment, holding her, I forgot.

She took my hand and led me to a little sofa in the corner, the type of sofa my grandfather would have called a settee. She placed her arms around my neck and pulled me down, down with her until I was on top of her, feeling her beneath me. I felt alive, alive for the first time since Tyler had died, not just pretending like with Astrid, just going through the motions. I felt that finally, there was something worth living for. She pulled me toward her, my mouth on her mouth, and I felt her heartbeat beneath me. I was alive.

"I think . . . I love you, Rachel. I know it's too soon. I've only met you twice. But you saved my life . . . twice." I really felt like she'd saved my life today too, like I'd been dead, but now, I wasn't.

"I know," she said. "I feel the same way. And you will save my life too. You will."

"Let me save it," I told her. "Please come with me."

"Not now." She kissed me again. "But soon. I love you. Soon."

34

Wyatt

I wondered about the car, the one that had followed me—whether it would still be there when I returned to Mrs. Greenwood's house. Probably not. Probably, it hadn't been about Rachel at all. After all, I hadn't told anyone about Rachel. In fact, I hadn't told the guys at the Red Fox I was staying with Mrs. Greenwood. I'd given them Astrid's name.

Astrid. I felt bad about not calling her. We'd only made out New Year's Eve, which was practically required by law anyway. Still, I knew she'd really liked me. Or, at least, liked the fact that I was a guy she hadn't known since kindergarten. I wasn't usually the type of guy who led girls on, then ditched them. Of course, that could be because I'd never had a girlfriend at all before. Still, I should probably call Astrid, let her down easy, not be a jerk.

I was thinking about this as I passed Hemingway's Hardware. I actually reached into my coat pocket for the phone, wondering how far I'd go before I lost reception.

It vibrated.

I fumbled in my pocket for it, my reflexes slowed by the very urgency of it. Finally, I picked it up.

"Were you, like, ever going to call me?"

It was her.

"Hey, I was just thinking of you."

"Right."

"Really. I was going to call you. I had my hand on the phone." I slowed down, so I wouldn't lose her. On one side of the road, up on a hill, was a monument company someone was running out of their home. The business announced itself with a pink, granite tombstone that said *Fiske Cemetery Markers*.

"I'm so sure," she said. "You know, I'm not completely stupid. Or maybe I am because I thought you really liked me. Obviously, you were just using me."

"That's not true. I've just been really, really busy."

"Forget it. Just stop having your creepy friends call my house. I'm not your answering service."

"I wasn't . . ." I was out of town now, and trees and abandoned buildings were the only things visible on either side of my car. "What creepy friends?"

"Don't act like you don't know what I'm talking about."

"I don't know." I sort of did. The guy at the Red Fox. I'd told him I was staying with Astrid's family. Had he looked her up? I remembered her saying everyone knew everyone around here. Had the guy found her, and then, she'd told him I was staying with Mrs. Greenwood?

"I didn't give anyone your number. Did you tell them where to look for me?"

"What? What?" The phone was breaking up. "Barely . . . didn't . . ."

"What did you say?"

The call dropped.

Should I go back to where I had bars? No. She'd just yell at me. Besides, I was suddenly worried about Mrs. Greenwood. Why hadn't I thought about it before? If the creepy guy was stalking me, maybe he'd break into the house, bother her, wait for me. I mean, sure he was an old guy, but she was an old lady. And, since I had taken her car, she couldn't even leave. No, I had to get back to check on her. I knew firsthand the kind of sick shit people could do. I felt bad about Astrid, but she lived in town, with her family and people. Mrs. Greenwood was totally alone. Even her dog was dead.

I drove faster. I'd call Astrid too when I got back. I hadn't wanted to hurt her feelings. I just didn't want to be her boyfriend.

When I reached the house, everything seemed normal. The driveway was cleared, as I had left it, but the front path, which I hadn't shoveled, showed no footprints but mine. Mrs. Greenwood hadn't gone out, and no one else had gone in. She'd obviously spent the day with William Shatner.

I exhaled. I wouldn't have to add endangering a sweet old lady to my list of crimes.

I parked the car and went inside. "Mrs. G?"

Sure enough, I heard the weird singsong of the *Star Trek* theme. I'd been right about Shatner. I went into the living room.

"You know," I said, "some channels show reruns of *Boston Legal*. He's on that too."

"Oh, hello, Wyatt." She turned away from the commercial to look at me. "I like my William better young. How was skiing? You know, Danielle used to frequent a ski store that rented equipment by the month. It's probably a lot cheaper than renting at the slopes."

For a second, I forgot I'd allegedly gone skiing. Reminded, I said, "Yeah, Josh was telling me about that."

I felt guilty about lying to her, especially when she asked, "Did you see anything interesting?" It was almost like she knew.

"Anything interesting? Like what?"

"Oh, I don't know. Birds, animals. You city types seem to find that kind of thing fascinating, no?"

She didn't suspect. She was just making small talk. But maybe I should tell her anyway. She could help Rachel. Rachel could live with us—if I could talk Rachel into it. After all, Mrs. Greenwood had already taken me in.

But something held me back. Rachel had been adamant about not telling anyone.

I said, "Nothing really. Do you want me to get dinner? I make a pretty mean spaghetti with cut-up hot dogs." I'd bought hot dogs on one of my trips into town.

"I have a chicken in the oven. It will be ready soon. Come watch *Star Trek*."

But suddenly, I wanted to be alone for a while. The events of the day had been pretty amazing. Pretty weird. From being chased in the morning to falling in love in the afternoon to confessing everything about Tyler. I felt empty. I glanced at the screen. "I've seen this one. I think I'll go upstairs and change. My socks got wet."

She nodded, not taking her eyes off Captain Kirk. "Okay, about six o'clock, all right?"

I glanced at my watch. The episode would end at six. I nodded, then realized she couldn't see me. "Okay, I'll be back."

I trudged to the stairs and started up. The house was already dark, so I flipped the switch to turn on the stairway light. As I walked up, I noticed the photos, as I had the first day I was there. The woman in the wedding dress, I now knew, was Mrs. Greenwood. Like her daughter, she had been beautiful once. The photos reminded me of something, I wasn't sure what.

Then, I remembered.

I could still hear *Star Trek* in the background. I had close to an hour when she'd be concentrating only on that.

Instead of turning into my own room, I looked behind me. Nothing. I touched the doorknob on my left. No one sprung out at me. With one more glance over my shoulder, one last listen for footsteps, I turned the knob. I stepped inside. I closed Danielle's door behind me.

Danielle's room looked the same as that first night. No broken glass on the floor. I hadn't expected it. The broken window had been a dream, a figment of my imagination.

And yet, I expected the room to look somehow different. I expected it to be different now that I knew Danielle was dead.

After Tyler died, his mother had come to stay with us for a while. When the crime scene people finally cleared out of their house, my mother and I had offered to go over and clean out Tyler and Nikki's rooms. The house was being sold to whoever would buy it. Mom suggested that I, as Tyler's best friend, would know what was most important to save and what he might have wanted given to friends. I didn't know, though. Tyler hadn't thought about what he wanted to leave people. He hadn't planned to die. He wouldn't have. You don't consider your own mortality at sixteen. He wasn't like my grandfather, who had talked about what he'd leave me for years before he had. Death in the elderly seemed inevitable. Death at sixteen is usually sudden and seems escapable, as if you should simply be able to rewind, turn the page back, and get on with the course that had already been charted. I should have told a guidance counselor or someone about Tyler's stepdad. Then, Tyler would have lived, played football, taken the SAT. He'd have gone to prom, then college, done all the things he was supposed to do. Death, in Tyler's case, wasn't an ending. It was like one of those books where they don't tell you what happens to the characters because there's a sequel. Only, in Tyler's case, the sequel had never been written. Instead, I was in Tyler's room, looking at each binder in a backpack he'd never use, thinking I couldn't just throw them away, that he'd need them. Then, realizing he wouldn't. He never would. So I separated out the textbooks to give back to the school (trying not to think of the kid next year being assigned a dead guy's American History text) and stuffed the rest of his backpack into a black forty-gallon trash bag. I did that with every drawer in his desk. Yet, I felt like I was looking for something, a note maybe, a sign, some sort of last words of wisdom for me. Of course, there was nothing.

That was how Danielle's room was too, now that I knew she was dead. It seemed unfinished, its contents pointless, worthless. I looked around for the photo, the one that made me sure she'd never come back.

It had been in the yearbook. The shot had been taken on a winter day. Danielle wore a coat—the same coat, I now realized, I'd taken from the closet to bring to Rachel. She held her arm up, threatening someone, the cameraman, with a snowball. Her hood was up, covering her dark hair, which made it easier to recognize her face.

It was Rachel's face.

Danielle had been Rachel's mother, not the old man's long-lost daughter. I remembered Rachel saying her mother had been killed, and how Josh's friends had joked about Mrs. Greenwood killing Danielle.

Maybe it wasn't a bad joke. Obviously, Danielle had gotten pregnant, had a baby. Maybe Mrs. Greenwood had found out about it, had killed her. Or maybe just sent her away?

Or maybe she really didn't know anything about it.

But who had taken Rachel? Who was protecting her now? Was it Mrs. Greenwood? Or someone else?

Whatever. It was better for now to leave Rachel where she was, far out of the way in a tower in the woods, where no one could find her. No one could hurt her. I had to make sure she didn't leave.

Carefully, carefully, I pulled the page from the yearbook. The paper was thick, sewn in, and it came out with barely a shudder. I folded the paper so the photo wasn't creased and hid it inside my shirt. I walked to the bedroom door, opened it. The hallway was empty. Downstairs, Spock said, "Fascinating." My watch said five thirty. I shut the door, walked to the desk, and opened each drawer, searching for something, some evidence of what happened to her, a note, a clue. As with Tyler, there was nothing.

With one final check of the hall, I shut the door and tiptoed to my own room. I hid the photo in Danielle's diary. That, I stowed in my backpack. I'd bring it to Rachel tomorrow.

I used Mrs. Greenwood's land line to call Astrid.

"Thanks for calling back." Her voice was sarcastic.

"Sorry, sorry. I was in a dead zone."

She muttered something I assumed was unflattering, then said, "So are we ever getting together?"

"Of course." I hated lying. "Look, I'm sorry someone bugged you. Did they leave a number?"

"You think I'm an answering service?"

"No, no. I just wanted to give them this number so they wouldn't bother you again."

"But why did they call me in the first place? Did you give them my number?"

Her voice was shrill. I had to keep mine calm, so Mrs. Greenwood wouldn't hear me. I waited until she was finished.

"I don't know," I whispered. "I must have told someone we were seeing each other, and they looked it up."

"Well we're not seeing each other, are we?"

"No," I admitted. "Look, I'm really sorry. It's just . . . I met someone else."

"You are such a jerk."

The line went dead. Terrific.

I went downstairs to have chicken with Mrs. Greenwood, but my thoughts were about Danielle and Rachel. Mrs. Greenwood said something I didn't hear.

"What?" I asked.

She said, "I remembered the name of that ski place. Beaver Brook Outfitters. We used to buy all Danielle's equipment there, from her first pair of skis when she was a little girl."

"So you skied too? When you were younger?"

"Oh, yes. We loved skiing. And Danielle took to it from the first day of ski school. I used to worry because she was a bit reckless." She laughed. "Well, not a bit. *Quite* reckless. While the other children were carefully snowplowing down the slope, Danielle was flying, flying. I always worried she would crash, that she would leave me."

She got a faraway look on her face.

What had happened to Danielle?

35

Wyatt

I left even earlier the next morning, to avoid being followed. No one there, at least that I saw. Still, I took a winding route, just in case.

When I reached the tower, it was dawn. I could barely make out Rachel's hair, hanging down already. Just seeing it there made me feel sort of giddy. She was waiting for me. I climbed the rope with ease, and when I reached the top, the window was open.

"You're here!" She ran to me. "And early! I'm so glad. You have no idea how it feels, wanting to see you, wanting to say your name, yet having to hide it, having no one to talk to."

I kissed her. "I get it. Once, when I was about twelve, I had a crush on this girl, Caroline, and all I could talk about was Caroline this, Caroline that, and do you remember when Caroline said that, until my friends wanted to kill me."

187

Rachel frowned. "Were you in love with this girl, this Caroline?"

"Of course not." I didn't want to upset her. "It was a crush. Every guy in school had a crush on her." I held her tighter. "The only girl I love is you."

"I'm sorry. I haven't—I've never felt this way about anyone else, never *known* anyone else, except the characters in books I read."

The sun had almost risen. I had a fleeting thought, that maybe she just thought she loved me because she'd never known anyone else, that once she escaped her tower, she'd find someone she liked better.

But, no. She was right. I had found her for a reason. It was meant to be.

"Besides," I said, "I barely remember anything about Caroline, except that she wasn't as beautiful as you."

She led me to her sofa and sat down, then kissed me. "I wasn't worried. You are my destiny. I have seen your face in my dreams."

"I've seen your face before too, but not just in a dream. Let me show you."

I opened my backpack and removed the carefully folded year-book page. "Here. I found this. I think . . . I'm sure this is your mother."

She stared at it, stunned. "It is me . . . just like me." She shook her head, then looked back at the photo. "Who is she? Where did you find it? It is me! But it cannot be me because I have never seen this place." She pointed to the background, the school.

"Her name was Danielle Greenwood. She was the daughter of the woman I'm staying with. They say she disappeared about seven-teen years ago, right around the time you were born."

"That is so sad." She touched the photograph with one finger, reverent as if it was one of the religious icons in the churches I'd visited on vacations. "But to have her picture, like she was a truly real person, a mother who might have given me cookies when I came home from school instead of a pretend character in a book. I can't quite believe it."

"She was real all right. She kept a diary—I brought that too. And I think your mama is right to protect you, to tell you to stay hidden. Okay, the tower's a little weird, but . . ."

She tore her eyes from the photo. "I know, I know. But I wish I could be a normal girl, like everyone else. Go to school. Would your friends like me?"

It was hard to look at her without wanting to touch her, to stroke her hair. But it wasn't like our relationship was only physical. "Of course they'd like you. You're so sweet, and . . ." I stopped, wondering if that was true, if people would see her as I did, or if they'd just think she was odd. Sometimes, people at school wanted everyone to be the same and think the same. But she was so beautiful, and somehow, her very strangeness was what I loved about her, that she made me feel less weird.

I wondered, maybe, if everyone felt weird sometimes, if they just didn't tell anyone.

"And what?" she asked.

"And you'd have me. I think the coolest thing about you is that you didn't go to my school. You're different, unspoiled."

"Of course." She touched my hand. "But tell me about it, your school. The books Mama brings me, they seem very old. I worry that it might not be the same."

I tried to think how to explain school to someone who'd never been. It was strange. I wished we could watch a movie or something. "What do you want to know?"

"Everything. Start with the first thing you do in the morning. Do you walk there?"

Somehow, I knew she was picturing *Little Women* or *Little House on the Prairie*, one of those books girls liked. "No. I live too far. I drive now—I mean, when I went, but when I was younger, I took the bus."

"And a bus is . . . ?"

I laughed. "It's a vehicle. It picks you up near your house. It's big and yellow . . . orange and ugly. A lot of people sit in it, fifty or sixty, two on each seat."

"Sort of like a train?"

"Not as cool as a train."

She got a faraway look in her eyes. "I remember a train once, before Mama brought me here. It was nighttime, and we had a private compartment, away from everyone else. Mama wouldn't let me come out. She was too afraid. I felt sick, and she told me to look out the window, that moving while looking at the other stuff, not moving, was what made me sick. But if I saw movement, I'd feel better. She was right. I stared out, and most of the time, there was nothing outside—just like my window here. But, sometimes, there were towns and houses and stores lining the track. You could tell the name of each town by the signs on the businesses and the post office. Finally, I went to sleep, and when I woke, Mama was carrying me away." She stared off, remembering. Finally, she said, "So you went on the big yellow-orange ugly bus. Were your friends on the bus too?"

"A lot of them." I thought of Tyler and Nikki. We'd waited for the bus together, of course.

"It sounds wonderful."

Sitting there, in the still room, I could almost smell the bus exhaust, hear the farting sound the vehicle made when it stopped, the screaming kids, and the bus driver, shouting at us to be quiet. "It was sort of loud. Every once in a while, the bus driver would flip out at us for being so loud."

"Flip out?"

"It's an expression. Get mad, upset."

She nodded, like she was still picturing someone flipping over. "I don't even know what loud would be like. My world is quiet, so quiet. Sometimes, I sing just to keep myself company."

"I know. I've heard you."

She looked at me, surprised. "You have?"

"When I was at my friend's cabin one night, it was quiet outside. The sound carries here, I guess. I heard you sing. That's how I knew you were here. I'd heard you before, but this was closer. But no one else heard you. They said it must be a bird, a loon. But I knew it wasn't."

"You were meant to hear me, and they were not. I had heard you too, for days before, or rather, sensed you. I knew you were coming."

It was so weird when she said things like that. Yet, I believed her. I reached over and took her hand in mine. It was small, so small, and cold. I squeezed it.

"Tell me more about your school, when you arrive. What does it look like?"

I tried to picture the school, how it would look to someone who had never been there, who'd never been to a school at all. I closed my eyes, remembering me and Tyler walking up to it, any given day.

"The building is brick. The bus parks in the back by the basketball courts." She wouldn't know what that meant. "Basketball is a game we play. There are no trees or anything back there, but there are trees in the front, not as big as these trees. When we get there, there are already lots of people. Everyone finds their friends, their little group. At seven thirty, we go inside."

"And inside?"

"There are hallways, white tile. Well, it used to be white, but now, it's gray from all the people stepping on it for so many years. The walls are white too, but they're covered with posters and signs, so you can't really see the walls."

She leaned forward. "What do the posters and signs say?"

"Um, different things. If there's a student government election—where they choose the people who run things—they put up signs saying things like *Vote for Lisa Amore* or whatever. Or sometimes, they think of slogans. Like, once, this girl named Sara Mitts ran for president. Her signs had a picture of a shoe on them, and they said *If the shoe fits, vote Sara Mitts*. Or, sometimes, there was a pep rally."

"What's that?"

"Um, football, it's a game, a contest. People get pretty excited about it."

"Like the jousting contests in *The Once and Future King*?"

"Sort of like that. People at school sometimes acted like it was like that. Yeah, we'd challenge other schools to see who was the fastest and strongest, so yeah, just like that. Anyway, before the team competed, they'd have a pep rally, to sort of get people excited about it." I pictured the school gym as one of those long jousting arenas like they had in movies, the cheerleaders like ladies of court, waving ribbons instead of pompoms. "The band would be there, playing the school fight song, and people cheer—they scream stuff like, 'Let's go, Spartans!'"

"And you were on the team."

She seemed impressed. I nodded.

"That must have made you feel like a hero."

"It did." It almost was like being a knight, the deafening applause as I ran into the school gym, Tyler behind me. I remembered smiling so much my face hurt. Where had it gone? What had it come to, if you could just be there one day and gone the next. It all seemed like a wasted effort.

I changed the subject. "Sometimes, they have a school play or a dance. They put up posters for those too."

"A dance! At your school? How fun that must be!"

"It wasn't that big a deal. They were mostly . . ." I stopped. I'd been about to say the dances were lame. I'd never gone. I didn't even know anyone who went, except to prom. But I realized that would sound ungrateful to say that to someone like her, like complaining about the food in front of a starving man. "I mean, they were fun. They'd usually have some kind of theme, like . . ." I reached back into my mind, trying to visualize the posters. "Under the Sea, or Western, or Winter Wonderland."

"Winter Wonderland?"

"I think . . ." I pictured the posters. "They decorated everything blue and white, and the girls wore white dresses too."

She gestured to her own dress, which was white and lacy. "Like this one?"

"Exactly. If I'd taken you to that dance, you could have worn that."

In fact, that dance had been last winter, a few weeks after the New Year's Eve when Nikki and I had kissed. I had thought about asking her, even though she'd said no to me before. But I'd chickened out. I couldn't tell if it was better that I hadn't asked her. Would it have changed anything if I had? Would it have been like one of those time-travel movies, where every different decision upset the space-time continuum, changed the future just a little bit? Would Nikki be alive today if I'd gone?

I couldn't think about it. I said, "I'd pick you up at your door, and I'd want to say, 'You look so beautiful,' but I wouldn't say it."

"Why not?"

"I'd be scared silent, in awe of you, that you would even go out with me. It would make me shy."

She nodded. "That answer is acceptable."

"But I'd help you on with your coat. My mom would tell me to. We'd walk out to the car together."

"Would you hold my hand?"

"Of course." I took hers now. "I'd use the ice as an excuse, to keep you from slipping as I walked you to your car."

"You wouldn't need an excuse." She squeezed mine.

"I know." She was so sweet, and I wanted to make her happy. She'd had so little happiness. I realized now that my life—all of it, even the bad things—was a gift. It hadn't been perfect, but it was my life. Mine, and I'd lived it.

Bolder now, I said, "We'd go inside, and everyone would stare at me, at us, wondering how I got you to agree to go with me when you're so beautiful."

She smiled. "How did you?"

"I asked. None of the other guys did. They were intimidated, afraid to. But me, I was just so stupid. I just asked you, and you figured it was better to go with me than to sit home and cry from loneliness."

I gave her a goofy look, and she giggled. "Oh, I am sure I found you attractive—in a funny sort of way."

"So before you could realize your mistake and dance with someone else, I'd lead you onto the dance floor. The band would be playing . . ." I realized I had my phone. I scrolled through the playlists. The first slow one I saw was "I Will Follow You into the Dark," which was a guy saying he'd go with his girlfriend if she died. Morbid, much? I wished I had some classic songs like "Unchained Melody" or "When a Man Loves a Woman," but I didn't have those. I'd never been the kind of guy to download songs girls liked. Finally, I found "The Only Exception" by Paramore. I'd liked them at one point. There was no speaker, of course, so I turned up the sound on my phone as loud as it would go. Rachel was right. It was quiet here, and she could hear it. The voice started coming out of that tiny speaker.

I held it to Rachel's ear. "They'd be playing this, and I'd lead you out onto the floor."

I stood. Rachel did too, and I put one arm around her, swaying to the music. The song was a little depressing too, about someone who didn't believe in love, but I liked the chorus, where it said:

Darling, you are the only exception
You are the only exception.

Because that was how I felt about Rachel, exactly how I felt. The song was about me, keeping my distance, not taking chances with people because I was afraid. But Rachel was different. Rachel was worth the risk, any risk. The only exception.

I tightened my grip on her.

"This is so nice," she said. "I've never danced with anyone before. Would you try to kiss me on the dance floor?"

"I would try. Would you let me?"

She leaned in toward me and whispered, "I might."

You are the only exception.

"I bet I would then," I said.

And then, we were kissing, kissing and holding each other, the music in our ears, as we sank slowly to the stone floor.

36

Rachel

I had expected Wyatt to try, again, to persuade me to go with him. I had thought of nothing else since he left. Perhaps he was right. Perhaps my destiny was not here, in the tower, waiting. Maybe I was meant to go with him. I had decided that, if he asked me again, I would hear him out.

Which was why I was quite surprised when he said, "I think you're right that you should stay here at least a little longer."

I reached to brush a lock of hair from over his eye. "Really? Why? This is quite a reversal from before."

"I know."

"What is the meaning of it?"

He gestured toward the picture he had given me.

"I don't know. Just a feeling. But I have something for you." He reached into his pocket. "Take this."

He handed me an object, the same object he had used for the music. Now, I held it. It was rectangular, smooth and black with bits of color on it.

"What is it?"

"A phone. A telephone. You can use it to talk to other people. I noticed it worked up here, probably because you're so high. It doesn't work in the woods, mostly."

I shook my head. He would think I was stupid. "I don't know how to use it."

"It's easy. Everyone can use a phone. Here, do you have paper?"

I gave him some, and he began writing, first numbers, then a sort of diagram. "This is what you press to call me, and here's the number. Or you can just go to 'Contacts' and look for 'Greenwood.'" He pressed a button that looked like an arrow.

"My goodness! It looks like something from the works of H. G. Wells!"

He laughed. "I don't think you'll be able to time travel with it. But look." He pointed to some numbers. "Here's a clock."

"Oh, I have a clock. I asked Mama for one last year." I didn't want him to think I was some idiot who didn't know what a clock was, for heaven's sake! But my clock was round and had hands. The one on his telephone only had numbers.

"Okay, well, I'll call you at eight. Before I go to bed."

This was unbelievable. "And I will be able to hear your voice, inside of this little thing?"

"Yeah. We can talk all the time."

"I cannot wait. You must leave now, so we can try it."

He laughed. "Okay. Maybe you could read the diary after I leave. It would tell you about your mother."

"My mother." I felt a weird empty sort of feeling in my stomach.

I had just met my mother, and now, she was dead. Still, I knew I would look at the photograph, read the diary, until I saw him again.

"I love you, Rachel," he said.

"I love you too. Now, go. Go, so I can talk to you."

37

Wyatt

I realized there was someone else I should talk to, someone who might know about what happened to Danielle, crazy as it sounded, crazy as *he* sounded.

"I have to go . . . darling." The word sounded crazy old-fashioned, like something romantic guys would say in movies my mom watched late at night when she thought no one heard. Yet, it sounded right when I said it to Rachel. She was like a girl from one of those books they made us read in Language Arts class, like Cathy Earnshaw, only not batshit crazy, or like Daisy Buchanan, only nice. I repeated the word because I liked it so much. "My darling."

She touched my cheek with her soft hand. "My own, Wyatt. Wyatt. I don't want you to go."

"I know. I don't either. But you're safe here, and I need to get some answers. I love you."

"I love you too."

"Remember, this is my number." I pointed to what I'd written. "Don't answer if anyone else calls." I thought of the weird phone calls. If someone was really following me, I sure didn't want him to find Rachel.

"All right. I promise. But call soon."

"What time does Mama come?"

"At night, nine or ten. Call before then."

"I will. I can't wait to hear your voice again."

It should have been easy to reach the ground. I'd done it before, so I was used to the rope. My feet had memorized the tower's shingled surface. Yet, it was hard because I didn't want to go.

But I had to leave. I had to go to Hemingway's, to find the one person besides Mrs. Greenwood who might know something about what happened to Danielle.

The whole way, I tried to think of an appropriate reason, a reasonable explanation why I was there. After all, it was a hardware store, not a grocery store. Maybe there were some people—adults—who would go to one every day, but guys my own age didn't think home repairs were fun. I didn't want Josh to think I was stalking him. Unfortunately, Hemingway's wasn't like Home Depot, so big you could probably keel over in the aisle and go unnoticed. Around here, people wanted to talk to you.

So, when Josh greeted me at the front (crushing any hopes I had that he might not be working that day, it being the last few days of break), I said, "I need a washer. Mrs. G. has a leaky faucet."

"All work and no play . . ." Josh grinned. "What size?"

"Yeah." I tried to laugh. I hadn't anticipated this question. I looked around, trying to see if the old man, Jerry, was there, if I'd made the trip for nothing. "I'm not sure. Mind if I just look around." I didn't see him. I didn't know why I'd been so sure he'd be there.

Josh looked dubious. "Sure. But usually, people bring in the old washer or the faucet or something. It's hard to judge otherwise."

"Is there a standard size?"

"Nothing's standard in Slakkill." He gestured toward the aisle where the washers were. "The houses are old. Most faucets are washerless these days, but don't tell the people who come in here. They want to repair the one they have for the fifteenth time, instead of buying a new one that will last the rest of their lives."

I spotted Jerry. He was, as usual, browsing through the yard sale items. I said to Josh, "Would it be better to buy a new one?"

He shrugged. "If you can talk her into it."

"I can try. Is there some kind of catalog with pictures of the faucets. Maybe she'd like a pretty new one."

"I could give you some websites if she, you know, believes in the internet."

"Paper would probably be better."

"I can print something out. Just give me a minute."

"No problem." I gestured toward where the old man was standing. "Take your time. I'm going to look at your secondhand stuff. I want some board games."

"Board games?"

"The old lady, she's been kicking my butt at something called Rummikub. I thought maybe if I got a different game, the playing field would be more level."

Josh shook his head. "Beating up on the elderly, nice. Oh, I think we've got Battleship."

"Perfect. I'll look for it." There were board games over where the old man was standing. "Take your time. I want to make sure it has all the pieces."

"Good idea." He walked away.

I headed toward Jerry in the opposite direction of Josh. I wanted to see what he was looking at, but on the way, something caught my eye. A hairbrush. The same silver hairbrush I'd seen before. I remembered Rachel telling me her mama used to brush her hair with a fancy hairbrush. I picked it up. The bristles were made of boar's hair, and the back had an intricate design, flowers as Rachel had said, orchids or lilies. It was ten dollars. I decided to buy it for Rachel.

I approached the guy. "Hello?"

Nothing. Maybe he was deaf. I walked closer and raised my voice slightly. "Hello?"

He jumped, then, like he hadn't realized anyone was there. He'd forgotten he was in a public place and was just caught up in his own little world. "Oh, you scared me. Hello."

"I'm Wyatt. Mr. . . ."

"Jerry. Do I know you?"

I held out my hand. "We met the other day. You were in here buying a television set."

"Yessiree, it was a good one too."

"It actually worked?"

"You bet it did. Watched the Sugar Bowl on it."

I fought the urge to ask which teams had played because, if he'd watched it on that TV, maybe his house was some kind of portal to 1985 or something. But I didn't ask. I remembered how it had been with my grandfather, after he'd lost it. He didn't remember things that had happened the day before, but the past, he remembered really well. I wanted to ask Jerry about the past.

I picked up the Battleship game. "I think I'll buy this. I want to play it with my friend, Danielle. Do you know her? Danielle Greenwood?"

He took his hand off the set of hot rollers he'd been contemplating and stared at the ceiling, like he was trying to remember. "Danielle Greenwood . . . I think Suzie has a friend named Danielle."

"Suzie?"

"My daughter, Suzie. She's about your age. Do you know her from school? She's a cheerleader."

I nodded. "I think so. Does she know Danielle?"

"Yes, I've seen her at the house. Pretty girl, long, dark hair, right?"

"Yeah." I wondered what year he was thinking it was, how old Suzie had been when Danielle disappeared.

He shook his head. "I know Danielle. Poor girl."

"Why?" We were getting someplace now.

"I'm sorry to break it to you, boy, but I don't think you'll be able to play Battleship with Danielle Greenwood. She's disappeared."

"Disappeared?" I looked to see if Josh was anywhere around.

"Yes, disappeared. The police think she's just run away, but Suzie said she's dead."

In the empty store, the word *dead* sounded like a door slamming.

"You know about Danielle?" I asked. "You know what happened to her?"

"I don't know, but Suzie does. She said she couldn't tell me, though. If she told anyone, they'd kill her, and they'd probably kill me too."

"Who are they?" The game felt suddenly heavy in my arms. I put it down, the hairbrush on top of it.

"The people with the rhapsody."

"Rhapsody? What's rhapsody?"

"A leaf. A drug, actually. It grows somewhere, maybe deep in the woods, and people will kill for it."

"Is that why they killed Danielle?"

"I told you *Suzie didn't tell me anything*!" He stomped his foot.

"Don't you think I'd remember if she had?"

He was shaking. I placed my hand on his arm, to calm him. It was rigid, but under my touch, he relaxed. "I'm sorry. Of course that's true."

He looked into my eyes, pleading.

"Do you know where Suzie is? Do you?"

"What? No. You said she was missing."

"Missing? Suzie?" His face crumpled, and he began to cry.

"Wait. I could be wrong. If you tell me more about it, I could help you find her, maybe."

"I told you I can't talk to you. Leave me alone!" He was flailing his arms now, beating his fists into me, the shelves, everything, and all the while, sobbing. "I can't tell! I shouldn't have told! Now, Suzie will be lost forever!"

I heard footsteps, Josh's footsteps running toward me. He grabbed the old man. "Jerry. Jerry, it's okay. He won't tell anyone. Look, we got some new stuff in. I saved it behind the counter, old clocks like you like."

"It's no use," the old man was sobbing. "Suzie's gone. He's right. She's dead."

"No, it's okay. We'll find her. There's a box on the counter over there. There are cameras too."

"Cameras? Do they have any pictures in them?"

Josh nodded. "Some might."

Finally, Jerry calmed down enough that Josh could escort him to a new box of old junk. He was still looking at it when I left with the Battleship game, the old hairbrush, and more confusion than I'd felt before.

38

Rachel

For hours after Wyatt left, I could do nothing but stare at the photograph he had shown me and read the diary he had left. My mother's diary. Her photo. Up until today, I had known I'd had a mother, and yet, she had never seemed quite real. Now, I looked at her picture, and I saw a girl like me, but not like me, a girl who had attended school as I hadn't, who'd had a true love, as I had.

What had happened to her?

It was so sad that, though I could see her, we would never touch. I would never hear her voice.

I gazed upon the photo again. That's when I realized she was wearing a coat. But not just any coat—the same coat I'd had on yesterday. I shivered, realizing it. The coat must have been in the closet where Wyatt was staying.

Now, it was here, under my bed!

I checked the clock. It was seven, an hour, still, before I'd planned to speak to Wyatt, longer still before Mama would arrive. I glanced out the window to make sure she was nowhere in sight. No. Nothing but trees. Even Wyatt's footprints had already been covered by a fresh layer of snow, like they had never existed. He might almost have been a product of my desperate imagination.

I looked at the object he had given me, the telephone. No, I could never have imagined that. He was real, and he loved me. He would take me away with him if I only asked.

But, for now, he had given me this token of my mother's existence.

I reached under the bed and drew out the coat. It was the first object I had ever owned that Mama had not given me. That made it the most precious as well, even more so because I knew it belonged to my mother, my real mother.

I lifted it to my face, sniffing it, trying to find a scent, a sign of her. I wondered what she had done when she wore this coat. Who had purchased it for her? What had she been like?

But I smelled nothing but the odor of age. Mama's clothes smelled like this too, as if they were coated with a thin layer of dust.

Perhaps, I detected the slight smell of something else. Cinnamon.

Of course, that might simply be from the house where Wyatt lived, a smell of something baked yesterday, not when my mother was alive. But I preferred to think otherwise, that my mother had smelled of cinnamon, perhaps from a spiced cider she had drunk when wearing this coat, so many years ago.

I shivered at the thought of it, and in that moment, swept the coat around and onto my shoulders.

It fit perfectly. I buttoned it up and tied the belt around my waist. I made my hair into a ponytail and slipped it between the coat and my back, then lifted the hood over my head. I walked to the mirror.

Hair hidden, I looked exactly like the girl in the photograph.

I sort of hugged myself and then slid my hands deep inside my coat pickets, imagining my mother doing the same.

I gasped.

She had certainly done the same thing. I knew that, for when I reached into the pockets, I touched an object.

I drew it out.

It was a letter, a letter addressed to Danielle Greenwood.

The return address said Emily Hill.

Wyatt

Mrs. Greenwood went to bed early that night. She knocked on my door at seven thirty to say goodnight, like she always did. I'd been thinking she missed having someone to say goodnight to. She always watched television in bed, usually late-night shows, but tonight was earlier. I heard a situation comedy with lots of canned laughter.

When I was sure she was snug in her bed, I crept downstairs and picked up the kitchen phone. It was the old kind, the kind my grandfather had had, that attached to the wall. Mrs. Greenwood said she had it because it would work even during an electrical outage. Grandpa had said the same thing, but I didn't believe it. I thought the old people just wanted the old things. Maybe someday, I'd be desperately clinging to my old cell phone or computer, when there was something way cooler.

I checked for the dial tone. I could see the full moon through the sheer kitchen curtains. I imagined Rachel, seeing it too. Could she see it through her tower's one window? I tried to figure out which way she would be facing. Was I facing that way too?

Then, suddenly, I heard a sigh. I jumped, but the sigh was not beside me. Was it her, sighing over the moon?

I began to dial my phone number.

She answered immediately. "Is it you?"

"Yes. Can you see the moon through your window?"

"I can. I hoped we were seeing it together."

"Now, we are."

"Now, we are. But Wyatt?"

"Yes?" I was whispering.

"Something has happened. Two things, actually. I've been waiting for you to call so I could tell you."

"Me too. I mean, I've been waiting to hear your voice." I sounded like a girl, but she had that effect on me.

"I know. I mean, me too, but I have to tell you what happened."

"What happened?" I hadn't really taken her that seriously when she said something had happened. I mean, what can happen when you're stuck in a tower all day? And yet, her voice sounded strident with urgency. "Is it Mama?"

That would be urgent. If something happened to Mama, what would happen to Rachel? She would be all alone in a world she knew nothing about.

No, she would have me.

But she said, "Nothing like that, but right before you called, someone else did."

"Who?" I hadn't thought about it, obviously, in my excitement to talk to her. The phone had barely rung since I'd been here, but that was because of not having service. With service, other people—Mom, people from school, *Astrid*—might call and talk to her. I should have told her not to answer other calls. Wait, I did.

"Oh, Rachel, you shouldn't answer unless it's this number." I hoped it hadn't been Astrid. She would have gotten an earful for sure. "I'm sorry if anyone said anything—"

"Listen! Wyatt, it's important. A man called, and he said he might have information about Zach."

"Zach?" For a moment, I couldn't remember who Zach was.

"About Zach," she insisted. "About my father."

"Rachel, you didn't tell anyone where you were, did you? Or who you are?"

"Of course not! I just said I was your sister. And that's when he said he had news about Zach. Here, wait. I wrote it all down: His name was Carl. You spoke with his brother, Henry. He wanted you to meet him at the Red Fox Inn tomorrow. He left his number." She recited a number which I scrambled to write down. News! This was awesome! If it wasn't creepy.

"But wait, if the guy didn't tell you Zach was your father, how did you know?" I twisted around to make sure Mrs. Greenwood wasn't there. I could still just barely hear the television upstairs.

"That's the other thing that happened—the other amazing thing I had to tell you. I found a letter."

"A letter? Like in the tower? From Mama?"

"No, from a girl. Emily Hill. Do you know her?"

"Um, yeah. Emily Hill is my mother. There was a letter from her?"

She nodded. "It was in the coat, the pocket of the coat you gave me."

"The coat?" Danielle's coat? Was it possible the letter had been waiting there all along? "What did it say?"

"It was from your mother to mine. My mother was pregnant, and your mother was worried about her."

"Why?" In retrospect, it made sense, but I was surprised to hear my mother had been worried all along. Then again, she was probably worried about normal stuff, like whether Danielle's mom would throw her out of the house or if Danielle would go to college.

"She said Danielle was talking crazy, about hallucinogens."

The rhapsody!

"Danielle said it was destiny."

"What was?" Had my mother known about Danielle? About everything before she sent me here? No, it was crazy.

"Emily didn't say. She was trying to get Danielle to calm down, saying it would be okay, but . . ."

She broke off.

"But what?"

"I have to go." Her voice was a whisper.

"What? Wait, Rachel. You have to tell me more."

"It's Mama. She's early."

"Okay. I'll come tomorrow morning, early."

And then, the line went dead.

I stood there, holding the phone, wondering if it had malfunctioned somehow. No, it hadn't. Rachel had hung up on me. Then, I wondered if I should call my own mother, should see what she knew. She definitely knew about the baby. Had she sent me here on purpose to make me part of this?

I dialed her cell phone, but it rang and rang. No surprise. She was probably working late. Without my cell phone, I couldn't text her. I'd call tomorrow.

Instead, I dialed the number Rachel had just given me.

Someone answered immediately.

"Is this Mr. Fox?" I said.

"Not the Mr. Fox you met," a smooth voice said. "This is Carl, his brother. I assume this is Wyatt?"

"Yes." I glanced out the window. It was snowing again. "Did you have something to tell me?" I didn't want to give too much away. This might have been the guy who'd followed me. I wanted to ask him.

But he said, "I talked to your sister before. Henry said you were looking for information on Zach Gray. I have it."

"Great . . . um, what do you have to tell me?"

"I actually can take you to him."

"Your brother said he moved."

"My brother, fact is, he's losing it. He's got total recall for a football game he watched six months ago, and then, he can't remember something that happened yesterday." He laughed. "Zach moved to New York City, wanted to be a rock star. But then, he moved back."

"Oh." That was weird. "Wouldn't people know he was there?"

"He's sort of a recluse, I guess. Doesn't come out much. But I could take you to see him."

Everything in the world told me to say no. No, I couldn't meet him. But, finally, I said, "The supermarket in Gatskill? I could meet you there."

"You're really making this difficult."

"Sorry. Someone followed me yesterday." Probably you. "It was weird."

"Well, it wasn't me. I don't get out much. I've been sick." He coughed, a bad smoker's cough that came up all the way from his chest, and he kept coughing for almost a minute. "Can we just meet outside the Red Fox? Maybe at noon?"

"Can we make it earlier?" I wanted to see Rachel.

"I can make it as early as you want. Eight?"

"Eight's fine. How will I find you?"

"I'll find you." And then, the line went dead.

40

Rachel

I could hear Mama's footsteps on the stair. Usually, she was easy to hear, for her steps were labored, which reminded me that she was old. But, of course, I had never needed an early warning before. There had never been any danger. Now, I fumbled with the strange phone. I thought, at first, to stuff it under the mattress. But, at the last minute, I dropped it into a tall, empty vase in which Mama had placed some fake flowers. She would never look there.

Mama's footsteps grew still closer, then paused. I heard her fumble for her keys. If she would but allow me to open my own door, I could let her in. But no, she did not trust me.

I sighed. I wasn't trustworthy. I had done exactly what she feared—allowed someone inside. She would see it as endangering myself.

But Wyatt was not a danger to me.

I had begun to wonder if there was any danger at all. But, indeed, the letter, and then, the strange phone call had confirmed that there was, that Mama's fears were justified.

But she had no reason to fear Wyatt. But still, I wouldn't tell her about it. She would, as Wyatt had said, flip out.

I heard her key enter the lock. Phone hidden, I sat on my bed to read.

Just as I did, she entered. Her face was lined with urgency.

"I heard voices. Is someone here?"

Calm. Keep calm. "You heard . . . voices?" I knew she had heard only one voice, my voice talking to Wyatt. But I tried to make my face a blank. "How could anyone be here. I am in a tower, at least five stories up and in the middle of a vast forest. I have not seen anyone but you in years."

Her glance darted around the room. "Don't take me for a fool. I know I heard something." She walked to the closet and threw open the door. Nothing, of course. Then, under the bed, the very bed upon which I sat. Fortunately, I had moved the rope, just that day, to the back of one of my bureau drawers, under my clothing. That would have incited justifiable suspicion indeed. But there was nothing.

"Are you finished? Perhaps I have a boy under my pillow." I lifted it up to show I had none. "Or a tiny little man in that vase over there."

She sighed and embraced me. "Oh, darling, I am sorry. I worry about you, and I could have sworn I heard voices. It must have been my ears playing tricks on me."

"Had you allowed me to speak, I would have told you that the voice you heard was mine. I was reading aloud." I tuned to an oft-dog-eared page of *Jane Eyre*, one I might have been able to recite even without looking upon it. I trusted she had not heard my exact words. "'I am not talking to you now through the medium of custom, conventionalities, or even of mortal flesh:—it is my spirit that addresses your spirit; just as if both had passed through the grave, and we stood at God's feet, equal,—as we are!' Is that not so beautiful that you need to read it aloud?"

"Of course it is, my darling." She stroked my hair. "And I should not have doubted you."

"I forgive you, Mama." Though I did not.

"I'm glad." She opened the hamper she had brought with her. "And if you have not, you will when you see what I've brought—your favorite roast chicken!"

This did cheer me somewhat. How sad that, before I met Wyatt, food had been my only pleasure.

"And I thought," she continued, "that, after dinner, we could play a round of Rummikub!"

41

Wyatt

I couldn't call Rachel because, of course, Mama might still be there. The phone was on vibrate, but around here, it was so still, so quiet, that even vibrate was loud. So, instead, I went upstairs. Through Mrs. Greenwood's door, I could hear the TV, still blasting, another sitcom. How could she sleep through that? But maybe her hearing wasn't good. I thought about going in and turning it off, but seeing her in her jammies would be . . . awkward.

I couldn't sleep anyway. What had the letter said? And what would I say to Zach when I met him. "Hey, dude, you know you fathered a child seventeen years ago, and she's, like, locked in a tower?" Maybe he was a total waste case from all the drugs he'd taken.

In the darkness, I swore I could hear Rachel singing. I wondered if she ever heard me.

216

It was weird, when you thought about it, my mother moving to Long Island and getting pregnant at almost exactly the same time her dear friend Danielle. Rachel didn't know her birthday or anything about her parents, but if the dates in Danielle's diary—the date her mother had met Zach and the date he'd left—were true, her birthday was very close to mine.

I thought about that a while, listening to a late-night show with a comedian who must have been hilarious. Then, the audience laughter turned into the drone of an infomercial which, thankfully, I could only hear if I tried. Finally, Mrs. Greenwood must have gotten up and shut off the TV because I couldn't hear anything.

I could not sleep. I fell asleep, then woke an hour later, slept then woke again. Outside my window, the wind howled and rattled the glass. When I finally went into something approaching REM sleep, I was roused from it once again, violently, like my mother shaking me when I was late to school. I heard a tapping noise, like someone banging at the window, and a voice crying. Was it Rachel? No, just the wind. I pulled my pillow over my head, ignoring it.

The voice said, "Let me in!"

Imagination! Way too vivid, for sure. With one hand, I searched the nightstand for my earbuds, to muffle the sound. I couldn't find them. In doing so, I knocked over a glass of water, soaking my bed and probably the earbuds I was looking for. I stood and walked across the room, searching for the light switch for the ceiling lamp.

Across the hall, the banging continued, and the voice. "Let me in!"

I crossed the hallway to Danielle's room. I didn't turn on the lights. I didn't need to. The room was illuminated by a strange bluish-white light. As I entered, I heard glass breaking. I looked to the window.

It was Danielle. She looked just as she had the first night I had arrived. But, this time, she didn't wait for me. Instead, she reached through with one glowing hand, unlatched the window, opened it, and stepped through.

"Whoah!" I said.

She shook her head, then pressed her finger to her lips. She started toward me.

Instinctively, I knew I must step aside, must follow her. Now, I would pursue wherever she went. I felt an icy chill as she passed, but maybe it was just the wind through the broken window.

She went only to my own room. Once there, she surveyed the unkempt bed, the messy desk, the spilled water, until she found what she sought.

Beside my bed was the plain brown bag from Hemingway's. She slid her hand inside it and brought out the hairbrush. She ran her finger across the flower pattern, as if to make certain it was the right brush.

Then, she began to take down her hair. It had been in a ponytail, but once down, it was very long, almost as long as Rachel's hair, but dark instead of blonde.

She brushed her hair. As she did, the hairbrush opened to reveal that it was, in fact, a box. Carefully, she held it up, then turned it over.

Out fell an object. She tried to catch it in her hand, but it tumbled onto the floor.

From her glow, I could see that it was a key.

I leaned to pick it up.

She handed me the hairbrush and motioned that I should replace the key inside it.

I did and closed the box. She watched as I attempted, unsuccessfully, to open it. It wouldn't budge. She took it from my hand, brushed her hair, and repeated the process, then handed it back to me. I closed it and placed it on my nightstand.

She started to walk away.

"Wait!" I said. "What's it for?"

She didn't answer, which was maddening. I knew she could speak. I'd heard her screaming just moments before. But she merely continued to walk away.

"Wait!" I said.

Again, she pressed fingers to lips. "Shh, you'll wake my mother again."

"But . . ."

She shrugged and continued out the door.

Blackness began to swirl around me. I didn't, couldn't pursue her. I was suddenly so tired, more tired than I had ever been before. I fell to the bed and didn't even see her cross the threshold of my room.

In the morning, I woke comfortably tucked into bed. I looked at the nightstand. It was dry, and my earbuds were where they belonged. The hairbrush wasn't there.

I checked the hallway for Mrs. Greenwood. No sign of her.

Slowly, careful not to make a sound, I crossed the hallway to Danielle's room.

Had I expected to see broken glass? A mess where snow had made its way in? I wasn't sure. In any case, I didn't see any of it. I peered out the window.

In the circle of lamplight, I could see that footprints dotted the doorstep. I couldn't tell where they started, but they definitely ended at the door.

Had Danielle returned last night?

Or was it someone else?

Again, checking carefully, I traversed the hall. I spied the Hemingway's bag on the floor. I reached inside.

The brush was there, as it had been last night in my dream . . . vision . . . visitation. I drew it out, as Danielle had then. I tried to open it.

It didn't work.

I drew it through my own hair. Nothing. Still, when I shook the brush, I could hear the key rattling inside.

I gasped.

I understood. I thought. Rachel would be able to open the box by brushing her hair. That's what Danielle had been telling me.

I took the brush with me.

It was cold even inside the house, so I put on a sweater, grabbed my coat and gloves, and went downstairs.

Mrs. Greenwood's car keys weren't where I'd left them. Strange. I finally found them, then left a note for her, saying I'd gone skiing.

I thought about calling Rachel before I left, but it was too early. I'd see her later. And by then, I'd know about Zach, her father.

I got into the car and drove down the still-dark road to the express-way. I drove slow because something about the day was dangerous. I could barely make out the snow-dappled boulders that lined the road. I imagined myself running off it, dashing against those rocks, no one knowing who I was, where I'd come from.

And Rachel would never know what happened to me.

I slowed further and moved to a different lane.

In the first morning light, I thought I heard a voice, Rachel's voice, saying, "Call me." Crazy. But I didn't have my phone anyway, and I'd be there soon. Aloud, I said, "I'll be there soon. An hour, maybe."

Finally, I reached Gatskill. The streets were deserted. I passed the library, then almost missed the Red Fox Inn. As I was about to pass it, I noticed something. A light in a window. Someone was there.

With a deep breath, I pulled into what was left of the parking lot and got out of the car. The wind whipped through the trees, rattling them like dead bones. Its whistle was almost a warning. Almost. I reminded myself that the real danger was in the place I had just left. I trudged toward the door. The snow was high here, as if the wind had collected it. I left footprints where there had been none.

I hesitated. Last chance to leave.

Before I could knock, the door opened.

"Are you Wyatt?"

I stepped back, but I nodded.

The man was just as old as his brother, maybe eighty, maybe more. Like his brother, he had startling bright blue eyes.

"I'm Carl." He held out his hand. "Come in."

"I'd rather not." Even as I said it, the wind kicked up, and a chill ran from the bones in my shoulders down my body to the ground. "I'd rather stay out here."

The man shrugged. "Suit yourself. But it's cold out there, and you said you wanted information on Zach."

"You said you knew where to find him."

"I might. But first, I need to know why you're looking for him."

I looked down. "No reason. I mean, nothing bad."

"Are you sure?" The man's eyes narrowed. "You haven't been completely truthful so far. I mean, you told Henry you were staying with the Brewers, but that's not true, is it?"

I shook my head no.

"Didn't think so. You're really staying with Celeste Greenwood."

It wasn't a question, but I nodded anyway. "But how did you know?"

He laughed. "Little thing called Caller ID."

"Oh. I forgot they had that here. So many other things are a little . . . retro." I could feel the warmth coming from inside. In fact, he had a fire going. Somehow, that made it seem even colder out.

"So why are you looking for Zach?"

"I know someone who wants to see him."

"Who? Old girlfriend? Or creditors?"

"No, nothing like that. No one who wants anything from him, just someone who liked him once, a girl, a friend."

"A girl and a friend, but not a girlfriend?"

I decided to lie. This guy would never know. I could tell the truth when I met the real Zach. "My mother, Emily Hill, she was a friend from school."

The guy opened the door farther, taunting me with the heat. "So you're saying Zach is your father?"

"No, n-nothing like that." I could barely keep my teeth from chattering. "J-just a friend."

"Why don't you come in? If I was wanting to kill you, deserted as it is here, I could have done it by now. Or the cold would do it for me."

I looked inside. The fire was inviting, and there was a dog lying by it, wagging its tail, almost like Josh's hardware store.

I stepped forward.

The door slammed behind me.

From behind a pillar, the guy I'd met on the first day, Henry, stepped forward.

"Okay, Wyatt, why don't you tell me why you're really looking for Zach?"

42

Rachel

After Mama left, I lay in bed, missing Wyatt, but I knew it was too late to call. Wyatt had told me that the phone in his house would ring and wake everyone. That's why I had to wait for him to call me.

I was sorry. For all the disadvantages of my upbringing, the one advantage was that I had never missed anyone. Now, I did.

Since I couldn't call Wyatt, and I couldn't sleep, I did the only thing that interested me.

I took out the letter.

It was surprisingly crisp looking considering the date on it was almost eighteen years ago. It was written on white paper with blue lines and stuffed in an envelope that was the wrong size. The handwriting was pretty, in purple ink.

Dear Danielle:

Are you okay????? I'm worried about you. Your last letter has me so freaked out. You have to know that it sounds a little (please don't take this the wrong way) crazy. Is it pregnancy hormones? Fear of your mother? Those weird hallucinogens you took before you got pregnant? All understandable (especially about your mother—she sounds a lot different than I remember her!). But please hold it together. I wish you could come stay with us until your baby comes. I know it's hard for you. But my parents are just barely managing not to throw me out of the house due to my own, er, delicate condition. I can't spring you on my mom—especially since she (again, no offense) never liked you very much. This would sort of prove her right and <u>I hate to prove her right</u>!!! Is there someplace else you can stay? I read once about a home for unwed mothers. Do they actually have those, do you think? Or is it just something in books? Also, my mom mentioned that sometimes, when people want to adopt a baby, they'll find a pregnant girl and pay all her living expenses until she gives birth. I told Mom I am not doing that, but maybe you would. It would allow you to run away.

I know what you'll say, that someone is after your baby, that that druggie Suzie Mills told you Zach was dead, and that you need to protect your baby because she's some kind of magical creature or whatever. But that's the part that sounded crazy. I know we always wanted to think of ourselves as special, but face it: We're not. We're like maybe a million other girls who met a guy who said he loved us—then found out he didn't. Zach is probably in the city with some other girl.

Honestly, Dani, you need to get out of your fantasy world. The child you're carrying (which you somehow already know is a blond girl) is not the key to thwarting an enchanted drug ring. There is no destiny, no prophecy. She's just a baby!

Please tell me you're getting some help.

I love you but—again—I'm worried.

Emily

After reading the letter four times, I fell asleep.

I woke to the morning's first light, and I said, aloud, "Call me."

It may have been my imagination, but I thought I heard him say, "I'll be there soon. An hour, maybe."

But by eight o'clock, I still hadn't heard from him. Perhaps, I thought, I could simply call and, if the old lady answered, hang up (that's what Wyatt had called it) or say I had made a mistake dialing the number. Did people do that? And then, Wyatt might realize it was me and call. Probably.

I knew! I'd say I was a friend of his, if the woman answered, a friend from town.

I turned on the telephone and touched the square that said, "Phone." A list of names and numbers showed up, Mom, Josh, Astrid. Who was Astrid? Celeste Greenwood. I touched that number. The phone began to make a noise, more like rattling than ringing. It did it twice, then someone said, "Hello." I drew in my breath.

It was not Wyatt.

I had meant, if someone who was not Wyatt answered, to remain calm, to simply say, "Hello?" and ask to speak to him. That would, I suspected, be a perfectly normal thing to do.

Instead, I sat, mouth slightly open, listening to the voice on the other side of the phone, saying, "Hello? Hello? Who is this?"

The thing is, I knew that voice. It was too familiar not to recognize. And I knew if I recognized her voice, she would also recognize mine.

I touched the part of the screen that said, "End call."

43

Wyatt

"I told you why." I try to act like everything is normal, like it's not creepy at all. "He was a friend of my mom's. She said to look him up. No big deal. If you don't know anything about him, I'll go." I made like I was going to walk out.

I saw a flash of silver, a knife. Then, it was against my neck.

"Stop right there," Carl's voice said.

I did what I was told. I stopped. He signaled me to sit down on a dirty sofa. I sat.

"Now, listen you little punk." Even in the dim light, I could see spit flying out his lips as he spoke. "We know you're lying. Not just suspect. Know."

"You couldn't because there's nothing—"

"Zach never went to school with your mother or anyone else

around here. He came into town for a month or two. He did two things while he was here. One was work at the bar, and I think you know what the other thing was."

Involuntarily, I nodded. He'd gotten Danielle pregnant. But why? Why would he come to town, specifically to meet one girl? Or maybe he left when he found out about her being pregnant. Except, judging from her diary, she'd never told him.

Carl nodded. "So you do know about Danielle."

"Danielle's dead. That's all I know. I'm staying with a woman, her mother. You know that, of course."

I was trying to play dumb, real dumb, but also, nice. Specifically, I was trying to be a kid you wouldn't want to stab.

"She talks about Danielle all the time, so I got curious. That's all."

"That's not all," Henry said behind me. "The old lady, she wouldn't have known about Zach unless Danielle told her. And Danielle wouldn't have told her."

Did these guys know Danielle? It sounded like it. "Okay, I found her diary. She talked about Zach. But the diary ended after she found out he skipped town."

Now, I wondered, *had* he skipped town? Or had someone killed him? Had these guys killed him?

"I don't know what happened to Danielle any more than you do. Any more than anyone does. Her poor mother . . ." I realized Mrs. Greenwood definitely hadn't had anything to do with Danielle's disappearance. "Her mother's always crying about her, and I found the diary, so I thought this Zach guy might know something. That's all. Obviously, if he's d—gone, he doesn't know."

"We don't care about Zach," Carl said. "We want the daughter."

"Daughter?" I tried to look confused.

"The daughter. The one you've been visiting. She's hidden

somewhere, and you know where she is." Henry was there again, with his knife. They wanted Rachel. Would they really kill me to get to her?

I wasn't telling them. I didn't know what they wanted with Rachel, but I knew it wasn't good. If they were looking for her because one of them was her long-lost grandpa, they wouldn't have lured me here, and they wouldn't be threatening murder.

I made my choice. I would do what I hadn't done with Tyler and Nikki. I would be brave. They wanted Rachel for some bad reason, and I wasn't going to let them have her.

I looked at Carl, felt the knife digging into my neck, and said, "I don't know what you're talking about. I go out to ski with a girl named Astrid. That's all."

And then, I closed my eyes and waited.

But instead of the sound of a cut to the jugular, I felt a rough hand on my arm. Carl's voice said, "Well, let's see if you remember after a few hours downstairs."

He grabbed me, opened a door I'd thought was a closet. Instead, there were stairs, leading to gray darkness. Henry took my other arm, and they frog-marched me down.

44

Rachel

Mama was the lady Wyatt had been living with, the lady Wyatt called Mrs. Greenwood. And, since Mama was Danielle's mother, that made her my own grandmother, my real, true grandmother. My face was warm, yet I was shivering. I drew my mother's coat out from its hiding place and wrapped it once more around me. I inhaled deeply, the scent of my mother's house, my grandmother's. How I longed to go there. I felt, finally, that I had a history. If only I could see them.

But Mama would be angry if she knew. She did not want me to see, to talk to anyone. A boy climbing through my window would still be strictly forbidden. But perhaps, the fact that Mama knew him, knew that he was kind and good, would make up for the fact that he had entered my bedroom.

Probably not.

And that he kissed me.

Definitely not.

And yet, I wanted desperately to talk to her, to someone. Even more than I usually wanted to talk to someone.

Where was Wyatt?

It was very early, still. I knew I was being unreasonable. But those who are not trapped in towers could not possibly understand the special concern of those of us who are. We get lonely.

Still, I walked over to my window, opened it, and leaned out.

The cold air on my face made me feel alive. Below, the coat warmed me. I scanned the snowy ground below to see if he was coming. No one there except a bird, perhaps a hawk, circling overhead, looking for its morning meal. I wondered if hawks ever got lonely. They did not flock together, as other types of birds did, crows or blue jays. No, a hawk's life was a solitary life. Like mine.

I threw my head back and yelled his name: "Wyatt!"

The sound was swallowed by the morning. No one heard, not even the hawk.

Still, I stood, staring, watching the still, silent, painted world until I started to shiver and had to close the window.

Now, the clock said ten. He had said he would come early. Where was he?

Wyatt

I struggled against them, but they were strong, freakishly strong for such old guys. Did they have some kind of magical strength? I couldn't resist them. I had expected the stairs to lead to a cellar, or even something smaller, a hole in the ground, or an abandoned well like the one the killer in *The Silence of the Lambs* used to imprison his victims, small and dark.

The landing of the stairs was dark, but Carl immediately turned me and led me to a door, which opened on to another stair.

"Where are you taking me?"

For all the world, it looked like hell. When the door opened, a dull, red light pervaded the room, and it was warm, warmer than I'd been in weeks. The door slammed behind me, and I continued down the dark, creaky stairs. I struggled, but struggle was no good. It only made me more afraid of falling. Henry had a knife, and they both were strong, stronger than I'd imagined.

The stairway seemed blocks long, creaky, hollow, and as I trudged farther, the heat got hotter. The light grew redder. I expected to see the biblical face of Lucifer. Instead, I only saw more red light below, more black darkness to each side. I heard a sort of roaring noise. Was it a monster? Were they going to feed me to it? Before all this happened, I would never have believed in a monster. But at this point, I had climbed a tower. I had seen a girl with healing tears. I had seen a ghost, and I was not convinced it was my imagination. If magic was real, why not monsters? Why not the gates of hell? The closer I got, the louder the roar, and I pictured a hellhound, gnashing his teeth.

I would never see Rachel again. What would become of her, alone in the tower? Would she grow old and die alone? Or would some other guy come to her rescue? And would she know what happened to me, sense it, somehow, as I had sensed her existence, had known she was there in the woods. Even now, I heard her voice crying, "Wyatt!"

It was amazing that, faced with my own death, my first, my only thought was of Rachel. Maybe not amazing. I had seen, faced death before, and it couldn't scare me. Leaving Rachel scared me.

So many steps. Would this never end? But as long as I was walking, I was alive.

Finally, though, we reached the bottom. I stumbled a bit, expecting another step, and backed into Carl. He tightened his grip on me, then pushed me around the corner.

It took a moment for my eyes to focus in the new light. It was not the mouth of hell which, I guess, was a good thing. It was a room, a cave about the size of a hockey rink. The roar came from a waterfall on one side, blue water rushing down the cave walls. But it was what it was watering that was so weird.

The light came from huge lights hanging from the ceiling, a greenhouse of some sort, artificially lit. Below the lights hung thousands of plants, suspended with no dirt, but growing. Each plant was a vine with a dozen or more bright blue flowers.

I remembered reading about hydroponics in science class once. That must be what this was. The plants got nourishment not from sun and soil, but from the artificial light and possibly, from a substance that was being sprayed on them by dozens of workers in blue jumpsuits. They all looked forward, like they didn't even see us.

The substance wasn't water. It came from a dark blue river, carved into the granite that glowed red, flowing through the hydroponics garden. At one end, it formed a waterfall to water the plants. That was the water I heard. Several rowboats were tied to a makeshift riverbank, and more workers rowed through the "field," picking the blue flowers and carefully placing them into bins on one of the boats. When the boat was filled, two boys got in and began to row.

"What . . . what is all this?"

"Nothing. Just a cave. None of your business."

But, of course, I knew. This was the green, the salad Danielle had eaten that had made her hallucinate. It was a drug, and these people, these zombies, were on it. They were growing it here, and that was what the old man's daughter, the others who'd disappeared, had been addicted to.

But why did they want me? Or Rachel? What could we do?

"We need the girl," Carl said.

You mentioned that. "For what?" I asked even though I knew it didn't matter. I wasn't giving her up no matter what. "So you can bring her here and turn her into one of them?" I gestured at the zombie workers who were carrying buckets of water from the blue waterfall to the plants. They all looked like they were staring at a television that wasn't there.

"The workers are happy," Carl said. "See, they're smiling." He gestured toward a girl with a painted-looking smile on her face. Blond and blue eyed, she could have been Rachel's sister. "Besides, we only want to talk to the girl. Zach was more than an employee. He was our nephew. Now, he's gone so, of course, we want to meet his daughter."

"You expect me to believe that you kidnapped me and are holding me at knifepoint, all for some sentimental family reunion?"

"She's been taken away from us, hidden all these years. Who knows if she's safe."

"She's safe from you." A guy my age walked by, looking straight ahead. "I'm not telling you anything."

"So you do know where she is?"

"It doesn't matter."

"Then we'll go with plan B," Carl said, "lock you up and get the information from the old lady."

"The old lady? Mrs. Greenwood? But she doesn't know anything about this, about . . ." I stopped myself before I said Rachel's name. "She's just a sweet old lady who lost her daughter. If she knew about the girl, her granddaughter, she'd be with her. She'd have taken her someplace."

"That's what we always thought, assumed for a long time. But when you showed up, came to live with her, we realized she must know." That was Henry. Carl gave him a hard look.

But I said, "Why?"

"Because of the prophecy. She had to know that the girl was the one who—"

"Would you shut up!" Carl bellowed.

"Why? You have him here. I'm the one who told you about him. Why should I shut up?" He sounded like a little kid more than an old man.

"I don't know," Carl said. "Could it be because you're stupid and always saying stupid things?"

"That's not nice."

"That's not nice," Carl imitated. He reached into his pocket and handed Henry something. "Do you think you could, for once in your life, open the door?"

"I'm not sure I'm capable," Henry said.

"Do it!" Carl bellowed.

"Okay, okay." Henry squeezed past Carl and me to a small door in the wall. "You're gonna put him in here?"

"Think so?" Carl thrust me forward and into the room. It was gray, empty like my mother's basement at home. "Let's see if he changes his mind."

Again, with surprising strength for an old guy, he pushed me to the floor. While I was struggling to get up, I heard the door slam, the key in the lock.

My arm throbbed like maybe it was broken.

46

Rachel

Wyatt did not come, did not come, did not come. He had said he had something to do before he came, but that he would be here early. I took "early" to mean perhaps ten, perhaps eleven at the latest.

But now, it was noon (by both my own clock and the strange, glowing one I had discovered on his telephone), and he had not come.

Nor at one.

Nor two.

Mama always left me breakfast and lunch, feeding me, I now realized, as if I were a pet. I had been too excited to eat breakfast, and now, I was too excited for lunch. I longed to go, to leave my tower, to find him. But, though I might shimmy down my hair rope without him, how would I pull myself back up?

Did it matter?

Did it honestly matter?

I had lived half my life, now, atop this tower, if you could call it a life, sitting here, reading, waiting for Mama. The only thing that had kept me alive, kept me sane all these years, was the thought that, someday, I would leave. Someday, I would be released or, if not, escape. I realized that that was why I had woven the rope in the first place, why I had hidden my ability to do so from Mama. I had done it not for the contingency that someone would rescue me, but for the certainty that I might wish to rescue myself.

And now was that moment.

Yet, I hesitated. Wyatt might still come. He had said he would. But if I waited too long to leave, it would be dark and colder. Then, I might never find him. I realized I had so little idea of the outside world that it was likely I would be unable to navigate it. Would the world be a pleasant place like the town of Hertfordshire in *Pride and Prejudice* or a war-torn one like the Paris in *Les Misérables*. Or, perhaps it would be like the horrific world portrayed in *The Time Machine* with predatory Morlocks seeking to eat gentle creatures like myself. Of course, Wyatt had told me no such thing but, perhaps, he did not wish to frighten me.

Still, I decided I would wait one more hour.

At three o'clock, he had still not come. I determined to try once again to call the number that was Mama's and, if he did not answer this time, I would go.

I pressed the part of the phone that would dial her number.

It was answered almost immediately.

By Mama.

"Wyatt? Wyatt, is that you? Are you all right? Where are you?"

I said nothing. She sounded worried.

"Wyatt, did you go skiing? That's fine, but I need my car back. Wyatt?"

I pressed the button to disconnect the line.

I made my decision. I would go. Yes, it was highly possible that I might die, that I might freeze to death, be eaten by animals, or captured by the same person who killed my mother. But I might as well risk it. If I could not leave, could not find Wyatt, I might as well plummet from this tower.

So, I went to the closet and took my warmest dress, a sweater, an extra pair of shoes. All my shoes were thin and unfit for snow, but I could at least have a second pair. I put on the coat Wyatt had brought, my mother's coat with the note in the pocket. Then, I took a blanket. Then all the blankets. Then, I put some back because I could not walk with all the blankets, but I took two. After all, I was leaving forever.

I remembered what she had said on the phone about needing the car. Did she need it to see me? If so, that would give me more time before I was discovered. And maybe Wyatt would still come.

I emptied the pillowcase from my bed and stuffed it with everything. I made myself eat something and took the rest of the food with me. It might be a long journey.

I walked to the window and stared down. The sun had already fallen below the trees. I couldn't see it. I couldn't see anything but trees and snow. But on the wind, I heard a voice, whispering.

"Rachel," it said.

It sounded like his voice, Wyatt's voice. He said he had sensed me in my tower, that he had known I was there. Perhaps that meant I could sense him as well.

No, I just wanted so much to hear him.

I made up my mind. I tied the rope, dropped my belongings to the ground, then slid down the rope behind them.

"Ouch!" I fell, hard, on my ankle. It twisted strangely. Had I broken it? I rose, careful as possible. I could walk, but it ached. I gathered my pillowcase and the blankets. It was cold, so cold. I had been foolish to do this.

On the wind, I heard Wyatt's voice, saying, "Rachel!"

"I can hear you. Where are you? Are you in danger?"

"Rachel?"

I wanted to run, but the snow was too high, the ground too rocky. My pretty shoes did nothing to protect my soft feet. I had no hat. I pulled up the coat's hood, wishing I had my long rope of hair. But there was no way to get it. I looked behind me, and saw it, waving good-bye, already distant. I imagined myself, leaning out the window, seeing my hair touch the ground. No time for silly rememberings!

I turned away and trudged on. Ahead was nothing but snow and evergreens. And Wyatt. Wyatt. Behind me was the whole rest of my life. Which was nothing. I looked back at the tower. I knew, somehow, I could never go back there again.

I willed myself to walk faster. I had a dim memory (not a silly one this time) of being a little girl, running in the snow and feeling warmer. Yes! Movement made one warm. Stillness, cold. So the faster I walked, ran even, the warmer I would feel.

My ankle no longer ached. I kept going. I counted my steps. One, two, ten, a hundred. Surely, if I could walk a thousand steps, I would see something. A house. A town. A person who would help me find Wyatt. But I never reached even a hundred steps, much less a thousand. I kept losing count. The sun sank lower still in the sky. Though I did feel warm from walking, with night, the air would grow colder. Say what I might about my life before—I had never been cold, never hungry. Mama had always protected me.

Mama!

If only I could talk to her. I could, I knew, on Wyatt's telephone. I had the means. But what would she do if I called her. Would she help me find him? Or would she send me back to my tower, where I would wish to die, having lost my only chance at happiness.

The sun was setting, and I looked at the red sky and begged for a sign, anything, to tell me what to do.

I heard only Wyatt's voice, the voice saying, "Rachel!"

But that was enough. I decided I would chance it. I could, after all, show Mama the letter, the one to her daughter, Danielle. My mother. It said that I was destined to do . . . something together. And was it not destiny even that I had found the letter, at this exact moment? Surely, that would persuade her.

I took the phone from my pocket. Even though I was in the wool coat, the phone was ice cold against my face. I almost dropped it with my fumbling hands. Finally, I found the place on the screen. I touched it.

Nothing happened. No ringing. I looked at the phone.

Words came up as if by magic.

"Call failed. Try again."

Yes. Yes! I wanted to try again. I did. And again. But each time, the same thing happened. I shook the phone. Why would it not work?

Then, I remembered Wyatt's surprise that it had worked in the tower. He said it must have been because of the height.

Now, I was on the ground, and my calls were failing, as was my courage. I had no way to contact Wyatt, Mama, or anyone. I had only to keep walking and hope someone would find me.

Someone who did not mean me harm.

Oh, what had I done? What had I done? Wyatt might be trying to call me at this very minute, but unable to. And I was far from my tower, so far I could never get back before darkness fell. Mama or Wyatt would find nothing of me. No, I had to try. I had to move on.

The ground was clearer here, due to the abundance of trees. I walked faster, almost ran. My hood slipped down, down my back. I adjusted it.

Again, it fell.

I pulled it back up. Then, I realized why it had fallen. My hair was in the way. I adjusted it, placing my hand around my thick locks and pulling them over my coat.

The hair spilled down to my ankles.

It was growing again, growing even faster than before. A mere hour ago, it had only reached my shoulders. Was it responding to the cold to warm me? Or something else?

The awareness of its magic strengthened me, made it possible for me to keep going. One step. Ten. One hundred. Five hundred. The sky was blue-black dusk, but I was not cold. I felt as if I could see even in the darkness.

Now, my hair touched the ground and streamed far behind me. I searched the trees around me for a bit of vine, to tie it. In so doing, I noticed something. A clearing. Holding my hair the best I could, I walked forward and peered between the trees.

A road. I remembered roads from long ago, when I was a child. Roads led to towns, to people. Suddenly, I heard a whooshing sound, then a crackling as something went by, something red.

A car.

It had to be a car, though so far away still.

There was a road up there, and cars, a town and people. But what should I do about it? If I approached the road, would good-hearted people see me and help me find Wyatt? Or would bad people, the people who had killed my mother, come and kill me?

I had to try again to call Mama.

This time, the telephone worked. Perhaps it had something to do with being closer to the road.

"Mama?" I tried three times before I was able to form the words, her name.

"Who is this?"

"Mama, it's me, it's—"

"Dani? Oh, Dani, can it be you, after all these years?"

It was darker now and so cold. In the distance, I could see the lights from the highway. I listened to Mama's voice, calling, "Dani," and for a moment, I wished I could be Dani, alive, on some roadside somewhere, calling for my mother. I longed to pretend I was her, to make Mama happy, to make Mama not angry.

But it was cold, and I was me, only me. I had to make her understand.

"It's me, Mama. Rachel."

A sharp intake of breath.

"Rachel? But how?"

I had to talk before she put it all together herself. She would be so angry. "I'm on Wyatt's phone. Wyatt has been visiting me, in my tower. He gave me his phone to make me safe. But, Mama, I am afraid something has happened to him." I began to cry, feeling, as I did, my red, wind-burned cheeks begin to heal. "Something terrible. He is missing."

When I said, missing, I wondered if it was more dire, if he was dead. But no, I had heard him. His voice. In my head. Surely, if he was gone, I would be able to sense it.

"Stay in your tower, Rachel. Do you hear me? Someone could—"

"I have already left my tower."

"What?"

"I have left my tower, Mama. I have gone to look for Wyatt. I am standing under a tree beside the road."

A wail of some wounded thing met my ears. I realized it was Mama. Mama, wailing as if learning of the death of her child. It was a horrible sound.

"Mama, please. I am fine."

"Do not move, Rachel. Do not! I will borrow a car. Wyatt has taken mine. I will come to get you, but in the meantime, hide. Oh, please hide."

I had come so far. I did not want to hide. Yet, I knew nothing about towns or roads or directions, and my hair was now more than three times the length of my body. I remembered seeing a small house, shuttered for the winter, with no car in the driveway. Perhaps I could hide there.

"Yes, Mama. I will wait for you. But come quickly, for I feel he is in grave danger."

"I will come. I will come soon."

"Thank you, Mama. We must save him."

A pause, and I could almost hear her shaking her head as she did, lately, when I expressed doubt at anything she said. The wind howled, and I gathered my still-longer hair around me. "I love him, Mama."

"I will come right away. Now, hide!"

47

Wyatt

The room had no light. Even when my eyes should have adjusted to it, nothing. I reached out with my foot, feeling to see if there was anything in either direction. With my one good arm, I checked my pockets to see if there was something, anything that would help. Nothing but Mrs. G's keys. I pulled them out and touched to see if any of them had a sharp edge, something to use as a weapon. Nothing.

I felt a slight movement and saw the flash of a light. A flashlight. On the keychain. I pressed it again, and a tiny light shone. The floors, the walls, all made of gray concrete. The room was empty, the size of a closet. I walked to the door and spent several minutes trying first one key, then the next, in the old lock. I took the flashlight off the keychain, then tried to slide the big car key into the space between the door and the wall, to jimmy the lock. But since I couldn't simultaneously see the lock and use both hands to try and open it, it was hard. I stuffed the keys back into my pocket.

In the pitch-dark room, I could hear the waterfall, people moving around. Who were they? Henry and Carl's employees? They seemed more like captives, prisoners. Should I try to get their attention? Would they help? Or would they turn on me?

I didn't know. I decided to think about it. I had time.

Then, in the darkness, I heard the sweetest voice, the only voice I wanted to hear.

"Wyatt!"

"Rachel!" Was she here? I wanted but didn't want her to be. What if she was hurt, in danger?

"Where are you?" I asked.

And, somehow, I knew she'd left her tower to come to me. In fact, I sensed her in the freezing cold, walking through the snow to find me. She was walking toward a road, a road where these guys might be looking for her.

"Rachel." I whispered it. "Be careful. God, be careful."

"Wyatt?"

"Call Mama." Could she hear me? I couldn't tell. "Rachel, call Mama."

I sensed her shivering. Then, I heard her voice. "She is coming. But where are you?"

Could she really hear me? "The Red Fox Inn. In Gatskill." I began to shiver myself. It was like I was with her, inside her. "But Rachel, be careful. Don't go with anyone but Mama."

I hoped she heard me.

Rachel

Walking had, indeed, been keeping me warm. Now, in the still dusk, I was cold, colder than I have ever been. My hair had grown still longer, and I gathered it around me, realizing as I did that it would impede me, make it impossible for me to run from anyone who wished me ill. I brought the scissors with me when I left, in case of trouble. I could cut it. Yet, I suspected it had grown for a reason, as it had grown before to enable me to escape. I remembered, also, the biblical story of Samson, whose strength had come from his long hair. Could it be that my hair would empower me? That it grew when I needed it?

I heard a sound, a car flying past. Was it Mama? Or someone else, looking for me? No, it was gone; it was nothing. But the car had created a wind, which bit into my arms, my shoulders. I gathered my

246

hair around me. I hoped Mama would come soon!

I remembered something else. When my hair first began to grow, that was when I first began to dream about Wyatt, had first sensed he was coming. That was why I had made the rope, to allow myself to escape. That was also when he had, he said, begun to hear me singing.

Did my hair do that?

Only one way to find out.

I looked around, to make certain no one was there, that no one was coming, looking for me.

Then, I opened my mouth and yelled with all my voice.

"Wyatt!"

"Rachel!" His voice. It was coming to me on the wind.

"Wyatt?" Still, I could not believe it was him.

"Call Mama," his voice said.

I answered him. "She is coming. But where are you?"

"The Red Fox Inn. In Gatskill."

The Red Fox Inn! I remembered him mentioning that. I was shivering so hard, but through my chattering teeth, I heard him say, "Rachel."

It was so soft I could barely hear it. But I whispered back, "Yes, love?"

"You have to get the key."

The key? Had he said the key? What key? "I don't understand."

But suddenly, the wind was frantic, furious, blowing snow up around me, whipping it into my face. And then, another car, a red one, big. What I thought might be called a truck. Yes, truck. It was huge, and it was slowing, stopping near me. Oh, no. Was it someone, someone come to take me? I tried to crouch as low as I could, hide behind the snow-banked bushes, but I knew that if someone were looking for me, he would find me.

49

Wyatt

The key! I remembered, now, the key in the hairbrush. Danielle had shown me. Or was it a dream? Still it might be important.

"Rachel," I said, "you have to get the key."

A pause. "I don't understand."

"The key. The key! It's in my car, outside the Red Fox. It's inside the hairbrush on the front seat. I think it opens the door or something here. You have to get it. Or, better yet, go to the police with it." Because, even as I said it, I knew I didn't want her coming here. If they'd locked me up, what would they do to her?

"Rachel?"

No answer. But even though I was inside, trapped, I heard a whistle of wind in trees. Nothing else.

"Rachel?"

I wondered if the brothers were outside, if they could hear me. But if they could, they would probably think I was some idiot, babbling to myself. Still, I lowered my voice.

"Rachel?"

No answer. And then, I sensed that the reason she wasn't answering was because her attention had turned to something else.

Rachel

The truck came closer. It was huge, and it was terrifying. I knew it would swoop down upon me, like a falcon or owl, and carry me away. I huddled under my hair, digging deeper, deeper into the snowbank.

"Rachel!"

"Mama!"

She ran toward me, slipping on the snow, arms outstretched. I rose to meet her. When she came closer, she gasped, stopped. Staring at me.

"That coat! It's . . ."

"Danielle's—my mother's. I know. I'm sorry! Wyatt gave it to me. I shouldn't have snuck out with him, but I didn't know, didn't know it would cause so much trouble!"

And part of me was sorry, but part was not because it had to happen. It had to. Everything couldn't just stay the same.

She was staring at me as if I had grown a second head. "Your hair?"

"It just started growing." I clutched it around me.

"Today?"

"No. I mean, not only. Weeks ago, when I asked you for the scissors. That was when Wyatt came. I made a rope for him to climb. And then, it stopped, but it started again today. I don't know why. It's like it grows when I need it. I wondered why I needed it today."

On the road, another car roared by. Mama and I both started and crouched down. It passed. She grabbed my hand. "No time for this now. We must go—now, before anyone finds you!"

I tried to run, even walk, to her car, but my hair was caught on something. A branch. I yelped, and reached to untangle it. Mama helped me and then, her holding my hair, we walked to the car.

It was nearly dark, and a tight squeeze with all my hair. She reached over me to push a button which, I guessed, locked the door. I sat in silence as she locked her own, then fastened herself into the car. She looked back over her shoulder, then backed out onto the road.

"Best to put the hood over your head," she whispered. "It will be dark soon, and they won't know this car—it's the neighbors', but best to be safe."

I obeyed. I felt safer—a bit—now that Mama was here. I could smell the scent of her house on the coat. Now, I knew it was her house. Yet, I knew that there was something I, and only I, would have to do to find Wyatt. I pulled my hair toward me. Perhaps I should braid it. Yes, I would do that. I began to sift through the hair, looking for the ends, so I could arrange it behind me.

I knew she wanted to ask me more questions, why I left, and how. There would be a time to answer those questions, or maybe there wouldn't. But now, I didn't want to talk about it.

I breathed in. "He said . . ." There was a car behind us, close behind, which seemed strange on such a deserted road. Its lights glowed bright in the mirror between our heads. I saw Mama's hands on the steering wheel, gripping, her knuckles white, striped red. I sunk down in my seat, still arranging my hair.

The car roared around us at incredible speed. Soon, I could only see the red lights on the back of it as it disappeared into the night.

Mama laughed, a short bark. "Crazy driver." Then, she turned to me. "I don't even know where we're going."

"Maybe . . . the police?" I wasn't sure whether this was the way to go, but in books, people called the police when there was trouble. Wyatt had mentioned that he should have called the police about his friend Tyler.

But Mama shook her head. "I'm afraid not. The police were . . . not helpful when Danielle disappeared." She pursed her lips together. "They thought she had simply run away . . . or perhaps, that I killed her. And I can't take you to my house. It's no hiding place, and we can't hide anymore anyway. No, we will have to settle this ourselves."

I had feared, or maybe anticipated that. On both sides of the car was blackness, black trees, black rocks, black space. Mama was barely a shadow beside me. "I think he is at the Red Fox Inn, in Gatskill. I heard . . ." I stopped. It sounded crazy.

"What?"

"Sometimes, I can hear his voice in my head. And he can hear mine. I know he can. That is how he found me."

Mama nodded. "I had suspected as much. That's where I was going, in any case. The Red Fox Inn was where it all began."

"Where what began?" I found the ends of my hair, and I arranged it, as best I could, into three sections. I began to braid it as close to my head as possible, though I knew it would grow.

There were no cars on the road now. It was so quiet, so dark.

"All of it," Mama said. "I suppose it is time to tell you. Perhaps I should have told you long ago."

The scary car was long past, but her knuckles were still white. I wanted to embrace her, but I feared it would distract her. "Tell me what, Mama?"

She sighed. "Once, when I was a much younger woman, I had a difficult life. I took care of my elderly parents, worked hard at a job, and didn't have much hope in my life."

"I'm sorry, Mama."

"Then, one day, a smiling stranger came along and I believed myself in love. He offered me a magical leaf. He said that, if I ate it, I would be happier, more alive. I ate it, and so I was. I saw wonderful visions, even felt like I could fly, and when I ate that leaf, which was a drug called rhapsody, I felt like I had no problems, even when the stranger left. But then, there was no more rhapsody, either, and I was miserable. I tried other drugs, but they weren't the same. I went through horrible withdrawal."

She looked at me, then away, and I realized she was embarrassed. I decided to say nothing, so she could go on.

She did. "Just at that time, I met a wonderful man, your grandfather, and we fell in love. I told him about the rhapsody, and I found that, with his help, I was able to control my urges. We were married and were very happy. Soon, I was expecting a baby, which would be the culmination of my joy. My husband's name was Daniel, so we planned to name the baby Daniel if it was a boy, Danielle if it was a girl."

I nodded. She meant my mother, Danielle. I continued to work on my hair, though it was already nearly a foot from my head now.

"And then, my husband was killed in an accident. I was all alone, frightened, no family, no friends. I only wanted to return to the one friend that had kept me company before, rhapsody. I had heard on the street of a secret place to get the drug underneath the Red Fox Inn. I went there, and I stole it. I was, of course, caught, and the owner, a man named Carl, said that he would tell the authorities, who would take my baby from me. I cried and cried, my remorse was so deep. Finally, he agreed to let me go. But he looked at the baby, who had such startling blue eyes, almost the color of rhapsody flowers themselves, and he said, 'I have one condition. When she is seventeen, she must come here to work for me.'

"I looked at the man. He was very old with wrinkles upon wrinkles. I thought that by the time my child was seventeen, he would surely have died. Besides, I had no choice. I realized my mistake, and I wanted to leave right away. I agreed to bring her back when she was seventeen."

I stared out at the sky, which had become gray with clouds, like a rain storm was coming.

"I raised my daughter, your mother, a wonderful little girl, and though it was hard, I never used rhapsody again. To do so would be to approach the place where I almost lost my daughter. That thought, alone, gave me strength. Gradually, I forgot all about it. But when Danielle was about to turn seventeen, I remembered the man's strange request. I didn't want to give her to him. I hoped he had died, but one day, when my daughter was at school, he came to my door, asking for her."

"How old must he have been then?" I asked. "A hundred?"

"That was the strangest thing. He did not seem to have aged at all in seventeen years. If anything, he seemed younger. And when I refused to open my door, he pushed it in like it was nothing. I stared and stammered, pretending I didn't know what he meant. Then, I said no. No, of course she can't come. And yet, I had nowhere to go. I tried to keep her inside the house, so he wouldn't be able to grab her. But a young girl does not want to stay inside."

I nodded. I knew this was true.

"My Danielle," Mama said. "She saw a boy in the garden, and she began to sneak off with him."

I looked down. It was just what I had done with Wyatt.

"I did not find this out until later. At first, when she was gone, I thought she had been taken from me. I looked all over for her, cursing myself for not sprinting her away, not protecting her better. But then, she came back, and I thought it was all right. The boy had left her, it seemed. I learned that she was having a baby, and I didn't care, didn't fret as any other mother would. I just wanted her to stay with me. In fact, realizing my foolishness, I made plans to move across the country, to start a new life. And then, Danielle disappeared again, this time for good."

I felt tears come into my eyes. Poor Mama! "How alone you must have been."

"I was. And the police were no help. At first, they said that Danielle must have run away. She was a teenage girl. People had seen her with this boy, and he had disappeared, so they assumed she had run off with him. However, I continued to call the police, badger them. My daughter and I may have argued, but she would never have run away. Also, I began to hear stories of other young people disappearing, including another girl from town, Suzie Mills. When I told the police this, they became annoyed. Suzie was an addict and probably dead of an overdose, they said. They had found out that Danielle was pregnant, and they accused me of killing her, because of my shame and anger. They threatened to arrest me, but I knew they had no proof because I hadn't done it. Still, I gave up on calling them. I only hoped that, someday, she would come back."

Mama slowed the car, and I knew why. The road was winding here, frightening. She was weeping and could probably barely see through her tears.

I heard her voice in the dark truck. "Then, two months after Danielle disappeared, there was a knock on my door. I opened it, hoping as I always did that it would be Danielle, returned to me. But when I looked outside, instead of Danielle, there was a blond young girl, cradling a tiny infant in a blanket."

I knew that was me.

"It was Suzie, the girl who had disappeared. She was not dead, but she told me that Danielle was. She couldn't tell me how she knew, but she knew. She thrust the baby at me and said to take it, keep it, that it was Danielle's baby, and that the people who had killed Danielle had told her to take it and put it in the incinerator at her father's veterinary office. She couldn't do it. I took the child in my trembling arms, and listened as she babbled what sounded like nonsense. 'Take the baby far away,' Suzie said. For there was a prophecy that this baby, Danielle's baby, would be the one to break a curse, to stop the rhapsody that had tainted the town for decades. She said that the baby's father, whose name was Zach, had known that Danielle would be the mother of the baby that would bring it all down. He had come to her on purpose, impregnated my daughter— because his uncles were the ones who had the rhapsody. He knew how it had harmed people.

"Suzie told me that this baby could be the one to change everything. That is why they wanted her killed. She also told me that your name was Rachel."

I shook my head. This was crazy. It was too much. And if I was the one who could do this, how was Wyatt involved? Why could I communicate with him, even when he wasn't there?

"She begged me to take the baby and hide it. They must never know she hadn't killed you as instructed. I did take the baby, you, away for eight long years, as I had planned to take Danielle. I took you all the way across the country and raised you. But even far away, I worried that someone would find you, take you away from me. So, finally, I brought you home, put you in a tower where no one would think to look, in the middle of the woods, and went back to my old house thinking that, when they saw I was all alone, they would leave me be. For eight years, they did. I wept every night because I could not have you with me, my granddaughter, the only one I had left, and I yearned to see you, yearned to have you in my house."

I touched her hand. It was good to know that she too had missed me.

She said, "But then, one day, Danielle came to me in a dream. Or maybe I just dreamed about her. She said that her friend Emily's baby, Wyatt, would be the one to break the spell with you, the one that could free them all. She made no sense, but she was my daughter, so I listened to her. She said that Wyatt must come to live here. Of course, I thought it was crazy. Emily would never agree. But the very next day, I received a call from Emily Hill. I didn't know if it was merely coincidence, or if she had seen Danielle too, but she was asking me if Wyatt could come here, and I said yes."

"That is incredible. Incredible." I was finally warm, almost too warm. My face was flushed, and when I looked into the backseat, my hair filled the entire thing.

"I knew that he would find you. I encouraged it, allowing him to take my car every day, hoping he would have some sort of contact with you."

"He did. I can hear him, in my head. I heard him a few minutes ago."

She nodded. "I was frightened, but something had to be done. Over the years, I have read the stories of other teens, other young people, who have disappeared, usually visitors, people who wouldn't be greatly missed. But I knew it was the rhapsody that had taken them, and it must be stopped. It must be stopped."

"But how?" I saw lights. We were in a town now. It was a small town, but, as I had seen that night on the train, the occasional neon sign identified the businesses: Gatskill Diner, Gatskill Repairs, Gatskill Library. Then, nothing for a long time. I had braided my hair, as best I could, but there were several unbraided feet near my head where my hair had just grown. It would have to do. I held the end of my hair in one hand. The braid streamed behind me. Then, I saw a sign far ahead.

Red Fox Inn, it said.

As we drove closer, I heard a voice. Wyatt's voice.

"The key," it said. "I found the key."

"What key?" I asked. Mama turned to me, and I gestured to my ear, so she would know it was Wyatt I heard, Wyatt to whom I spoke. His voice seemed clearer now, and I did not know if it was because we were closer now, or if it had something to do with my hair. I had first started hearing him when my hair began to grow.

"The key. In the hairbrush—your hairbrush," his voice said.

"Hairbrush?" Then, I remembered. I had told him about the hairbrush I had when I was a little girl. That must be what he meant. But it was gone. I had not seen it in years. I turned to Mama. "When I was a little girl, I had a hairbrush, a pretty silver one with a flower design. What happened to it?"

She looked surprised, then said, "How strange. It just disappeared." We were close now, and Mama slowed the car. I knew she was as reluctant to arrive as I was, more maybe.

"Wyatt found it." I said, "Wyatt, *where* did you find it?"

"In a junk shop." His voice was as clear as if he were standing before me. "It's in my car, in a bag on the seat. I think you need it."

We were not quite to the sign, but I gestured to Mama to slow down, to stop, before she got there. She had already been about to do so, it seemed, and she slowed the car and went a bit to the right, into a clump of brush by the road.

I said to her, "Wyatt says there's a key in it that I may need. It's in the car."

Mama gestured toward a green car parked in front of the place. "My car." She fumbled in her purse. "I have a spare set of keys to the door. But how did he know . . . ?"

"I told him about it, that you used to use the brush. Is the key anything special?"

"I don't know. Suzie brought the hairbrush when she brought you. She said it was very important, that we must always hold on to it. I didn't know why, though. I just thought it went with you, because you had such beautiful hair. I can go get it."

"Maybe I should," I said.

"No. You can't."

"But I must. This . . ." I gestured with my hair. "This shows that something is supposed to happen. I'm supposed to save Wyatt, maybe save . . . everyone."

It was overwhelming to think of, but it was true. For so long, I had thought my life was worthless, that no one would be affected if something happened to me, if I didn't exist. Now was the time to make my existence have worth, make it have value. And if I had to risk that existence, I had to.

I reached for the handle of the car's door.

"Wait!" Mama said. "Just . . . please, let me get the key. We can look at it, and then, I will go to the door of the place and distract them."

"But . . ." She was going to lock me in the car while she went out to look. I could not handle it.

"I know you're right, Rachel, my darling Rachel. I'm not treating you like a child. I know you have to do this, find this. But if I distract them, you can sneak around and look for a door. Or for Wyatt."

I nodded. It made sense. She opened the car's door and started to get out. I saw that she was old and bent, and it was difficult for her. Yet, she had come to me every day, all these years. I felt warm and slipped out of my coat, my mother's coat. My hair would be enough. For one second, though, I savored the scent of her. I would never see her, but she gave me life, and she left me the letter. It was enough to go on. Ahead of me, in the dim light, I could barely make out Mama, opening the car door. A light went on inside. She bent and took something out, then closed it quick. She hobbled back toward the car, holding it out to me.

It was my brush. I knew it as if I'd seen it only yesterday. I took it in my hand and touched it. I ran my finger along it. I began to brush my hair. As I did, I heard a click. Something opened, and a key fell on to the shallow snow.

I picked it up and examined it in the dim light. It was heavy and old. I didn't know what it opened, but I knew it was important.

I clutched it in my fingers and said to Mama, "Go."

Then, I wound my hair as best I could around my neck and shoulders, and I waited.

51

Wyatt

I sensed that she was close. Her voice sounded like she was in the room with me. It must have been nighttime now, and I hoped that the darkness would protect her. I could still hear the waterfall, the people working, from outside my door. Were they insane? Enslaved? Or did the rhapsody enable them to work endlessly? I wondered where Carl and Henry were, and suddenly, I didn't want Rachel to come. I wanted her to run, hide. Even if I never saw her again, it would be okay. I wanted to save her, save her as I hadn't saved Tyler.

I said, aloud, "Rachel, I changed my mind. You have to leave."

A moment later, I heard her reply. "I cannot leave. I have to do this."

"But Rachel, you can't. It's not safe."

She didn't answer.

52

Rachel

I waited until Mama had been gone awhile. I hoped she was okay, but I knew that, no matter what, I was going. I heard Wyatt's voice in my head, urging me to be safe. I knew I wouldn't. I wished I could hear Mama, know what was happening, but I could not. I worried about her. Everyone was trying to protect me, at great risk to themselves. It wasn't fair. I would rather risk my own life than be left here, worrying.

When Mama had been gone several minutes, I checked to make sure no one was outside, nor on the road. Then, I opened the car door. After making sure to pull all my hair from the car, I stepped onto the still-snowy ground.

"Rachel, please don't go," Wyatt's voice said.

"I'm coming," I said, "so it would be more helpful if you could tell me where to go, what to do."

"I'm not sure," he said. "I'm sorry. I'm underground and can't see anything."

"It's okay," I said.

"I love you."

"I love you too. I'll find you."

He seemed to know that was the end of the conversation. At least, he stopped talking. I walked, dragging my hair behind me, next to the bushes and peered around at the building. I could see Mama in the doorway, talking to someone, even arguing. What if he came out, looking for me? With my long hair, I was vulnerable. It was like a cat's tail, always hanging out, giving the cat away.

There was an opening in the bushes, a spot with several trees. I pushed through them and, gathering my hair into several loops, tried to walk closer, pushing against a tree ahead of me.

Suddenly, I heard a crack. Then, the tree I had touched disappeared from under my hand. It broke in two, the top half collapsing against the other trees.

Had I done that? Was I so strong that I had broken a tree, albeit a small one, without even thinking? Had my hair given me the strength of Samson after all?

More carefully this time, I walked through the remaining trees. I tried to avoid pushing against them, but when one proved too tight a squeeze, I shoved it. It gave way, and I stepped around it.

Finally, I was in a place where I could see the door, see Mama through the trees.

Only where was Mama?

She was gone! Had they taken her? Hurt her? I felt as if a hand was squeezing my stomach. Yet, I had to move on. I had to find her and Wyatt now.

I followed the line of trees, this time to the back of the building.

There was a light inside, but it was very dim. I had to push a few trees out of the way, and I enjoyed it, like a child with a new toy. Would I have strength to fight whatever came too? I hoped so. I also hoped I would know what to do. Mama had said it was a prophecy that I would end this all. But how?

I reached the back of the building. I wished I had a candle, so I could see. Still, I emerged from the trees and ran to it, pulling my hair behind me. Then, I started walking, trailing my left hand behind me, feeling for a doorway, a window, any way to get inside.

Suddenly, my feet hit a new surface. While, previously, I had felt only snow over soft dirt, like I had felt by my tower, now, I felt something hard, like a floor. The next moment, my hand touched a railing.

It was a staircase, and it went under the ground.

"I'm underground," Wyatt had said. I stepped forward. Perhaps there was a doorway down there, a way to find him.

As I did, I felt a tug on my hair. I reached up to pull it back, but I couldn't.

Then, I felt a hand on my shoulder.

"Gotcha," a voice said.

53

Rachel

Someone was here! Someone was touching me. My instinct was to fight against him, push him to the ground, escape. But something stopped me.

If he captured me, perhaps he would take me into the building. And that was exactly where I wanted to go.

I said, "I was just looking for Wyatt."

"I know what you're looking for. And I know who you are." His voice was thin, like an old man's. He kept hold of me, pushing me ahead of him to the very staircase I had been investigating. "Come with me. I'll take you to Wyatt, and your grandmother."

In the dim light, I saw his face. I knew he was Carl, the man Mama had spoken of.

I became the usual Rachel, the old Rachel. Sweet, gentle, compliant.

"Oh, thank you, sir."

"You're welcome, dearie." He loosened his grip upon my arm a bit, but he didn't let me go. With his shoulder, he pushed me down the steps.

The walk downstairs was long and dark. I tried to think of a way to talk, to communicate with Wyatt, without this man knowing. "You're taking me downstairs?" I said. "What's down here? Where is Wyatt?"

No answer. I was talking about him, not to him. There was obviously a difference or else I would have heard every conversation he ever had. I called, "Wyatt, where are you? I am here, on the stairway!"

"Quiet, girl!" the man said. "I told you I'll take you to him, soon enough."

This man was not helping me. I knew that. I tried as hard as I could to hold my hair around me. I couldn't imagine how long it must be now. I feared to tumble over it and down the stairs. I knew if I tried to run, he could catch me by it.

In the darkness, I heard Wyatt's voice. "I'm in a room," he said, "a closet at the bottom of the stairs."

The staircase was dark and seemed to be endless. Still, I tried to reach out my hand, to touch the wall, to find a door.

"Rachel, be careful," Wyatt's voice said.

I kept walking, and he said no more. As I plunged still lower, I heard a strange noise, a whispering or whooshing, like that long-ago train, and I saw a glowing light. But there was no door. At least, I could not feel a door. I kept walking but contemplated the possibility of flight, the possibility of making a break for it, even falling down the stairs. He could not see me in the dark. I could get ahead of him.

266

But where would I go?

One step, then another, down, down. My movements were automatic, but my mind was racing. What was down there? What would they do to me? To Wyatt? As I approached, the sound seemed less like a train, more like wind or rushing water. The glow became brighter, and I knew that, soon, my captor would be able to see me. I felt his hand tighten on my shoulder whenever I tried to move away.

I made a decision. With one swift movement, I elbowed him in the stomach then used my leg to knock him to the ground. Yes, I was stronger. I knocked him aside with less effort than it had taken to fell the little tree outside. It was nothing to do this. I felt, then heard, him fall to the ground. Then, I grabbed my hair and ran down the stairs, fast as possible. I knew he wouldn't give up that easily. I had to get ahead of him.

It was hard to see, but as I got lower, the light got brighter, the sound of water louder. Still, I could hear him behind me, struggling. I had nowhere to hide, nowhere to go but down. I trailed my hand along the wall, looking for a door, a window, anything, any way to find Wyatt. Where was Wyatt? I tried not to think about the other one I had lost. Mama. What would I do without Mama? I hoped they wouldn't hurt her.

I heard footsteps behind me, beating, beating, but below, I heard sounds too now. Some sort of drumming. Was it footsteps as well?

Finally, I reached the bottom and stopped.

It was the strangest place I had ever seen. The light all around me was bright red, and even though I was inside, underground, there were plants, so many plants, hanging, growing from the ceiling. Each plant had so many bright blue flowers, and I knew it was the rhapsody. Mama had said that the Red Fox Inn was where it had started.

Hundreds of people, also in blue, worked, tending the plants. The drumming was one man who beat a drum, perhaps to keep them going. It seemed to be working for they all marched in rhythm. Who were they? What were they doing? Would they attack me if I came closer? I heard footsteps above me, and I knew I would have to decide, and soon.

Then, suddenly, the drumming stopped. A voice yelled, "It's her! It's the girl!"

As one, they all looked up.

Then, they started toward me.

54

Rachel

There were dozens, even hundreds, of them, a mob, all wearing the same blue outfits, all crying out to the others. Their screams were like a thousand birds. Each time I thought the last had approached me, another appeared. They came closer, closer. Their movements were regular, almost robotic, their gazes fixed and glassy, as if they might be blind. Then, I remembered what Mama said about the drug, the rhapsody. They must have been drugged. This must be what it looked like. Did they mean to kill me, tear me limb from limb? Above me on the stairs was the man, who I knew meant me harm. Below were these people. I did not know what they wanted. The only protection I had was my hair, mostly unraveled, hanging behind me in a loosened braid, and the key—I knew not its purpose—which I still clutched in my hand. All around the room, I heard them murmuring, saying something about golden hair. Holding their hands up as if they would tear me to bits.

A woman approached me first. At a point about ten feet away, she stopped walking. What did she mean to do? I saw that her eyes were the same shade of blue as her clothing, an almost inhuman shade, the same color as the flowering plants that hung from the ceiling. Like the others, her eyes appeared foggy, as if she was not sure what she was seeing. I remembered my strength. I could fight her off if she tried to harm me. But I couldn't fight all of them.

Then, suddenly, she stopped walking. Her eyes focused. On me. She said, "Are you her? Are you the daughter of Danielle?"

The question surprised me, as did my answer. I had never known my mother's name before today, but now, it seemed obvious, inevitable. I had no choice but to tell the truth, whatever the consequences.

"Yes." I stood taller. "I am her. I am Rachel."

A cry came up from the woman and from a few others who were close enough to hear. "It is her!" they said. Others, farther back, heard what she said and took up the cry, and soon, the whole room was buzzing, chanting, drumming, saying, "It is her! It is the daughter!" They all came closer, and my fears melted. They did not mean me harm. If anything, they were welcoming me like a queen.

Suddenly, I felt a hand upon me, on my neck, clutching me. It was the man, the man who had pursued me. He had me. "You're not getting away that easy." He whistled to three men standing behind him. They grabbed me.

I struggled against them, but I was outnumbered. Then, more came to the aid of their friends. They grabbed my hair and pulled it hard. I was knocked to the ground, and the men were above me, tying my hair around me. I kicked and struggled against them.

And then, they were lifted away from me. The mob, women and some men, were grabbing them, holding them. Even as they struggled, more and more of them came to join them.

"We will help you," said the women who had first spoken to me. "We will try, but they are stronger."

"Why?"

"We have been here longer than they have. We are already beginning to die. What helps them kills us."

"Kills? Did she mean the Fox brothers?" But there was no time for conversation. They were helping me, that much was clear. But just holding the others at bay wasn't enough. There was something I was supposed to do. I didn't know what. Also, I had to find Wyatt.

The woman who had first approached me said, "You are the girl, the girl we have been waiting for. We had heard you were coming. We knew, when you were seventeen, you would come to save us all."

I stepped backward, shocked. "But how? How did you know about me? I didn't know about you, about anything, until today."

A woman broke from the crowd. She was slight, smaller than me or even Mama, and she had blond hair like mine. "It is foretold that the seventeen-year-old girl, daughter of Danielle Greenwood, would come to help us, would destroy the rhapsody that has enslaved us for so many years."

I had figured out that much. But I said, "How do you know this?"

"When you were a baby, you were captured. You were taken to be killed. But you were not killed. Someone brought you to your grandmother's house and told her to hide you away. That person was me."

I gasped. Many behind her gasped as well. Some who had fought against me tried to break free. Those holding them renewed their grip, but it was obvious it was difficult. Some others joined them, all holding Carl and the others at bay.

I became aware of the scent in the air. Like flowers Mama brought to me at the beginning of spring. Then, I realized it was the rhapsody. Was it hypnotic, having an effect on me? I felt almost dazed.

But I fought against the feeling. I must find out what I should do. I must save Wyatt.

"Where is Wyatt?" I asked.

The woman looked confused, then turned to the woman behind her. All stared at one another. They didn't know.

Aloud, I said, "Wyatt, where are you? I am here, in the rhapsody room. I did not see a room by the stair."

Then, I looked around. There were more staircases, three, four, five, some going nowhere, others going up to trap doors like the one I had entered through. He could be by any of them.

"Will you help me find him?" I asked the woman.

She shook her head. "You must help us first. You must. Do you not see, they have been depleting our town, this area, for decades. You were our hope, our only hope. That is why Zach made sure Danielle would have the baby, to save us. And we have waited seventeen, almost eighteen, long years."

In my head, I heard Wyatt's voice say, "I'm all right, Rachel. I'm okay."

I felt so tired. The scent of the rhapsody was having an effect on me. It made me feel first tired, then exhilarated. I touched a vine and I wondered how it would be to eat one tiny bit. But with my new-found strength, I fought against it. "What must I do?"

The yellow-haired woman, who appeared dazed as well, said, "When I brought you to your grandmother, I brought something else. Do you know what it was?"

I felt the key in my hand. "I think so." I held it up. The yellow-haired woman smiled and nodded. "But what is the meaning of it? And how did you get it?"

"I stole it, the night I took you to your grandmother. I stole it

272

from Henry, for he was softer than Carl. With this key, you, and only you, can reach the waterfall that feeds the rhapsody. You will destroy its water supply and the rhapsody will die. We will be free."

"What? Really?" It sounded far too simple. "Turn a key in a lock, and then, it will all be fixed. Let me at it. Where is the lock?"

The woman shook her head. "No, that's not all. If it were all, I would have done it myself. There is something else, something only you can do."

"But what?" I asked.

"I do not know," she said.

Of course she didn't. How would she?

"We were told that only you could destroy it."

I sighed. "And where is this, this lock?" I asked again.

Her eyes, every eye, scanned upward. I looked up too and saw that the ceiling was high above me, high as the staircase I just walked down, higher than my tower. The woman pointed to a sheer wall. At the top of it, there was a platform. Above it, a little door.

"Up there," she said.

I wanted to say it was impossible. I could not climb such a wall. I had only done so with Wyatt's help, and this wall was much higher. Only yesterday, I did not return to my tower because I knew I could not do it.

Yet, I remembered my newfound strength, and I wondered if I could. I had to.

I said, "I will try."

55

Rachel

Several of the blue-clad crowd escorted me to the wall. Some held my hair, caressing it to their cheeks as they walked. I wondered that not one of them could help me, lift me up, perhaps, so I could climb it. But as they moved about, I saw that they could not. They were weak, fragile. All who possessed any strength stayed behind to grapple with the dissenters who, even now, fought against them and sometimes broke free. Only the weakest stayed with me. With neither light nor adequate food, it was a wonder they were still alive at all. I had to help them. I had to.

The wall was made of stone, unlike my tower. At different, odd places, bits of rock stuck out. Could these be footholds? They would have to be. It was the only way. Some were very small, though, and my shoes are worn and wet. Still, I would have to try. I had lived seventeen years as a captive, a prisoner, feeling that my life had no purpose. Now, I could show that it had.

But where was Wyatt? Selfishly, I wanted to save him too. I wanted him with me. If he were here, he could help me. Yet, he had not answered. I could not find him anywhere.

There was no rope to grasp on to, to steady me. If I fell, I would be hurt, possibly killed, and all would be lost. I saw the first outcropping of rock, above my waist, nearer my shoulders. I stepped upon it, then reached up with my right arm, finding something else to hold.

I was able to pull myself up, but the next outcropping was even higher. Also, my full skirt obscured it somewhat, and my hair. Still, I stepped up on it with my other foot. A gasp went up from the crowd, then a cry.

"Can they stand below me?" I asked the woman. "In case I fall."

She looked disappointed and I thought, perhaps, this was not the right thing to say. Still, I was not their mother. I was not here to comfort them. I needed help.

The third set of rocks was a bit less of a stretch. I was able to advance a bit, then to the fourth. But on the fifth, I felt a scrape against my hand, then saw blood. Tears sprung to my eyes, but I could not wipe them, could not heal myself, at least without risking a fall. My arms ached from holding on already. I stepped on the next stone, almost slipped. Another gasp from below. I looked down to see them all moving backward. So they would be no help if I fell! I was high, nearly a quarter of the way there, and the world swam beneath me. The smell of the flowers, the rhapsody, comforted me, but it also made me tired, so tired, like Dorothy and her friends in Oz, when they fell asleep in the poppy field. I wanted to fall, simply fall down and go to sleep, immerse myself in it, forget about them.

"Eat it!" a voice in my head said, and again, I wondered if I should. But I knew that would be wrong. I had to keep climbing. I must stop this. It was the only way to buy my freedom, my real freedom to be a normal girl, not one trapped in a tower. I had been hiding all my life. Now was the time to reveal myself, or die trying. It struck me that these workers had also been trapped, like I had, only worse. How horrible not to see the sunlight for what may have been years. No, I had to help them, even the ones who fought against me.

I resolved not to look down, except just far enough to find a foothold.

With my bleeding hand, I held on. With my right foot, I stepped up, then my left, then pulled myself higher. Below, I could hear them breathing, rhythmically, all as one, the same as when they did their jobs. This spurred me to try harder, climb higher. I found a foothold, then another and another. I was doing this. I didn't need a rope, didn't need anyone. I was strong, the strength from my beautiful hair. I climbed higher, higher, more than halfway up now. I did not want to think of how I would get down. There would be time for that later.

Then, suddenly, I heard a voice.

"Rachel!"

Mama's voice.

"Rachel!" Wyatt's.

Were they both there now, both below me? I looked down again, a mistake. I could not see them. The scent of the rhapsody seemed, if anything, even stronger up here, and my head swam with it. I could not see either Mama or Wyatt below. Yet, they cried for me.

Aloud, I said, "Wyatt, where are you?"

"Down here!" a voice said below me. Strangely, I heard it not in my head as I had in the car, or on the road, but in the room. Was I hallucinating? Was it the rhapsody? "Come down and help me! They're going to kill me!"

"Wyatt?"

"No, Rachel." This time, the voice was in my head like before. "Don't come down. It's a trick, a trick to get you . . ." Suddenly, the voice became muffled, and the other voice resumed.

"Please, Rachel, come help me!"

I didn't know what to do. I decided to say it, very softly, to him alone. Meanwhile, my arms were tired, so tired. "Wyatt," I whispered, "What should I do?"

I heard his voice, something like his voice, but I couldn't understand what he said.

Then, the other voice, the Wyatt voice from the ground. "Aren't you going to help me, Rachel?"

"No," the voice in my ear said. "Keep going!"

I looked down, though I should not have. I should not have looked, not only because it made the world swim below me, my head spin, but also because I saw a man. He was one of the strong ones, one who had stood behind his master. Now he had broken free of the others and was coming toward me. He was climbing the wall to get me. He had a knife.

"Rachel, help me!" Wyatt's voice said.

But I knew it was not Wyatt. I knew it was not Wyatt because, at that moment, I finally saw him. The workers had let him in, let him through. He seemed injured, one of his arms hanging strangely at his side. He started toward the man who was after me. He was going to climb the wall too. But how, with his arm so damaged?

"Keep going!" his voice said in my ear. "Keep going, and don't look back."

I obeyed. I knew I had to. The man was gaining on me. He was within inches of my long hair. He was slower than me. The drugs, perhaps, made him weak, but I was cornered, and he would eventually catch me. I saw Wyatt start to climb up behind him. Below, I heard a commotion as several others broke from the pack. They, too, started after Wyatt, but the others tried to fight them.

I could look no more. I also could not hold on to the rocks anymore. I needed to move, to shift. My arms and shoulders ached. Still, I found another foothold and lifted myself up.

"Where are you going, Rachel?" Wyatt's voice said. "I need you to help me."

"No," I yelled to whoever it was. "You are not Wyatt. Wyatt does not want my help." My arms ached, but I took another step up.

"That may be true," the man said, "but if you don't come down, we will kill him."

My heart was racing so fast it hurt. My hands ached, my head spun, and I wanted nothing more than to go down, But would they let us go, even if I came down? Impossible.

As if hearing my thoughts, the man said, "If you come down, we will let you go. All of you. You only need to cut your hair."

In my head, I heard Wyatt's voice. "No, Rachel, don't do it! It's a trick!"

Then, a groan as he tried to climb higher.

I did not look down to see if he had his knife poised at Wyatt's neck. I did not know what he would do if I kept climbing, my aching hands being ripped by the rocks. But even as I did, I whispered, "Should I come down?"

Wyatt's real voice, the one in my head, said, "Rachel, don't. Don't you understand? We have to do this. I have to help you. If it is a choice between being a dead coward or a live hero . . ." His voice was stopped.

I remembered the story he had told me, about his friend Tyler. It was true. He regretted doing nothing there. He would not wish to do nothing again.

I looked down to see what had stopped him speaking.

Despite his broken arm, he had nearly caught up with the man. Now, they struggled below me. But not far enough below me. The man had been, it seemed, about to overtake me. He was only inches away, struggling with Wyatt. If they fell, Wyatt would surely die.

As would I, if I fell.

The rhapsody smell was so sweet, so strong in my nose, my lungs. I wanted to go back, to help Wyatt. Yet, I knew this would be the wrong thing to do.

I made my decision. I climbed higher.

And suddenly, with this resolve, my strength was greater. I could keep going, I could climb forever. From below, I heard struggling, a scream, a crash as first one, then the other, fell to the ground.

I could not look down. I felt the world go black.

I wanted nothing more than to let go, to tumble to the ground. I knew I couldn't. I found a foothold and climbed higher, even as I said, "Wyatt? I love you, Wyatt."

But he did not answer. For all I knew, he might never answer again. Was he was dead? Finally, I found a last foothold. I reached up and pulled myself up onto the balcony.

My arms and hands were throbbing now, but I looked around.

I heard Wyatt's voice, small and weak, say, "I love you too."

There was, as they had said, a keyhole. It was old and rusted. I reached into my pocket and took out the key, the key that Wyatt had found for me.

I chanced a look down at him, at my beloved.

Both had fallen. My beloved was crumpled on the ground below. He was bleeding. He did not move. The workers surged around him, and their opponents, the ones who had fought against me, surged toward the wall.

I plunged the key into the rock.

56

Rachel

At first, nothing happened. Then, I jiggled the key in the lock. The door opened to reveal . . .

A length of pipe?

Pipe? I did not understand. It was old, rusted. I released the key with my throbbing hands. At first, it stuck in the door. Then, it fell, down, down so far. It landed on the floor without a sound, right next to Wyatt.

Below, the water kept rushing, just as it had before. The rhapsody still bloomed. The dissenters came closer. Nothing had changed, nothing. Nothing except that my beloved was dead, and it was all for naught. I had done nothing. I knew that, soon, the men would have their hands upon me, and I didn't care. I didn't care.

I looked at the old, rusted pipe below me, and I began to weep,

weep for my lost love, my lost life, my lost everything.

And with that weeping, I remembered the blonde woman's words. *There is something else, something only you can do.*

And, with that, I began to weep harder. But now, I fixed my weeping eyes right over that old, rusted pipe so that the tears fell directly inside.

And then, I was crying harder, so much harder, like my tears had become a sudden rain shower, and they fell inside that pipe.

A cry went up from the mob.

I looked down below me. The men who had been climbing toward me stopped their pursuit. Indeed, everyone below me seemed silent, frozen, all staring at one thing, at the rhapsody plants.

The flowers drooped, turning from blue to brown before my eyes. The rhapsody was wilting. It was as if my healing tears had sealed up its ability to accept water. It was dying.

And so was my Wyatt. If he was not dead already.

I knew what I had to do.

Now that the job had been done, the mobs of people were moving away, streaming away to the stairs. The rhapsody dead, they were leaving. The man who had been climbing the wall stopped in his tracks, knowing now it was useless. But I could not watch what happened. I knew what I had to do. I knew they would not help. I wanted scissors, but I only had a key. A key with a sharp side. I grabbed a big section of my hair and began to saw upon it with all my might, using the key. I could see below me that it reached nearly to the ground. I sawed and sawed, and as I did, I was crying, weeping for Wyatt. Little bits, then, finally, the whole braid of hair gave way under pressure from the key. It detached itself from my head. I pulled it up beside me. Part of it was still braided, from the car. The rest was not. From where it ended, I began to braid.

Below me, I heard a voice, Mama's voice. "Rachel!"

I looked down. It was her. It was really her!

I kept braiding, but I shouted, "Is he alive?"

She heard what I said and rushed over to Wyatt. She touched his neck.

A moment later, she said, "Just barely."

It was enough. But I had to go, had to go now.

I looped the hair around the railing that held the platform in place, then knotted it. It was not completely braided, but it hung to the bottom, beginning to unravel. It would have to do.

I tested the strength of the knot. I could not help Wyatt if I fell myself. When I was certain it would hold me, I grabbed the rope, first with one hand, then the other.

Then, as I had the first day we had met, I slid down it, to Wyatt.

Once down, I rushed toward him. I felt weak, spent. I knew that my strength was gone and I hoped that my other gift, the one gift I still needed, was not. I had counted on it.

I reached Wyatt. He was bleeding in so many places. Yet, I could tell that he was barely alive, and even though I had used so many tears, I found more.

My tears touched his flesh.

57

Wyatt

I was floating, first just above my body, then high above, like the
snow angels we had made that time only real. I saw Rachel turn the
key in the lock. I saw the rhapsody wilt.

And then, I saw Rachel begin to climb down.

I was dying. And yet, it didn't matter, for I had fought. This time
I had fought. I had done the right thing, the good thing. I hadn't
let fear or even inertia stop me. I had done what I was meant to do.
I closed my eyes. Even though I was bleeding, nothing hurt. I felt
relaxed, at peace.

Then, there were hands on my body, on my face. Something wet.
Tears.

I opened my eyes.

Rachel was there.

284

"My darling," she said. "My Wyatt, it's not too late."

"You came back. I didn't expect you to. I didn't know if you'd still be able to heal me. I was willing to sacrifice, for you, for them."

She kissed me and said, "Yes, but I'm so glad you didn't have to."

The room was empty. The rushing water had stopped, and the rhapsody, just wilted, was melting away. All the workers had streamed up the stairways and out the door, the Fox brothers behind them. It was as if the rhapsody had never been there. I held out my hand to Rachel. "Hey, your hair looks cute short," I said. "And you're pretty strong. Mind giving me a hand?"

She took mine. "Gladly."

She helped me up and gestured to Mrs. Greenwood, who was standing nearby. "Mama, I think you've met Wyatt."

She nodded. "Lovely boy . . . if a bit of trouble!" She reached for my arm. "I think you're going to have to help me a bit with these stairs. The trip down was bad enough."

We rearranged ourselves, one on each side of her, and started toward one of the staircases. "This one goes outside," Rachel said.

But when we reached it, there was a girl standing halfway up. A woman, actually, about my mother's age, with light blond hair.

"I thought . . . ," she said, "I thought someone should come back to thank you . . . and to explain. You see I'm—"

"Suzie!" Mrs. Greenwood said. "Suzie Mills!"

"Suzie?" That had been the name of the old man's daughter, the one who was missing.

"Of course I remember you, Suzie. You're the one who brought my Rachel to me."

"Yes," she said. "I brought her to you, because, even though I was crazy, addicted, I knew it was wrong. They told me to kill the baby, and I couldn't kill a baby. I just couldn't. And, then, they told me this wasn't just any baby . . ."

She started to cry.

"You did the right thing," Mrs. Greenwood said. "There's nothing to cry about."

"But there is. I had a chance to escape then, but I didn't. I could have gone home, but the drug, it had such a hold over me that I went back to it, back to them, instead of going home to—"

"Your father," I said. She was so skinny, maybe eighty pounds, and she was much older. I wondered if he would even recognize her.

"Yeah," she said. "My dad. We fought all the time when I was a teenager, but I know he was right. I was doing crazy things back then, and it made me an easy target. That's what they did, chose kids who were easy targets, runaways, or kids like me who were already in trouble. And I made myself one with a lot of partying, but it was nothing like the rhapsody."

"Won't it be hard without it, even now?" I asked.

She nodded. "Yeah. It'll be hard, really hard. That's why some of the workers there fought against you. They wanted it to stay the way it was, even if they had to be prisoners."

"But you didn't?" I said.

"No. I've seen how it is. People have been getting sick, they've been dying. The younger ones don't know, but I do." She sniffed.

"It's all right," Mrs. Greenwood said.

"I know. I'll have to find the strength. We all will."

"You will." Mrs. Greenwood stroked her hair.

"I was just wondering . . . ?" Suzie said between sniffles.

"If we knew where your dad was?" I asked.

"Yeah. Is he alive still?"

"Yes," I said. "I saw him, just yesterday."

"Really?" she said. "So you can bring me there, to him?"

"I can. Or we can," I said, starting up the stairs again. I turned back to Mrs. Greenwood and put my arm around her. "And, after that, we can go home and play Battleship and watch *Star Trek*—all three of us."

All of us, Suzie first, then me and Mrs. Greenwood, with Rachel behind us, started up the stairs. It was a long walk, but considering what had been going on up until then, it wasn't that difficult. When we reached the top of the stairs, we saw that it was daylight. I escorted Mrs. Greenwood to her own car, then, after I ascertained that she was okay to drive it, I took Rachel and Suzie to Josh's old truck.

We drove east, into the sunrise.

Epilogue

Wyatt

In the week since Rachel destroyed the rhapsody and released the workers, a lot happened. That first day, we reunited Suzie and her father, with a lot of tears of happiness.

And then, the police brought charges against Carl and Henry. They weren't able to bring drug charges against them, because there was no evidence at all that the rhapsody had ever existed or that it was a drug, but they brought over a hundred kidnapping and false imprisonment charges against them, including mine.

"I don't think they'll live much longer anyway," Mrs. Greenwood said while we watched the news (which, conveniently, came right before *Star Trek*). "They were eighty if they were a day, even when I was a young girl. Obviously, they derived some sort of power from the rhapsody. It prolonged their lives."

"And strength," I said. "That old guy broke my arm."

"Now that it's gone, I suspect they will be too."

I hoped so.

"What I don't understand," I said, "is why I could communicate with Rachel. I mean, when she was in her tower. I heard her, and no one else could." I remembered New Year's Eve. Everyone else had been just as close to the tower as I was, but they were sure it was only a loon or maybe the wind. They didn't hear anything.

"I'd thought about that myself." Mrs. Greenwood paused the television just as the starry background came onscreen, before the announcer said, *Space: The final frontier.* "And the only thing I could think was that it was Danielle."

"Danielle?" I said at the same time Rachel said, "My mother?"

"Yes. Rachel, I told you I had seen Danielle in my dreams, just a few months ago. She came in a dream and spoke clear as day. She said that Wyatt should come here, that he could help Rachel to fulfill the prophecy. I brushed it off, but the next day, Emily Hill called me."

"She did?" I said.

"Out of the blue. I mean, we'd exchanged Christmas cards, and once, she came up to visit. But I hadn't heard her voice in years. But that day, she asked if Wyatt could come stay here."

"Did she know?" I asked. This was a big shock to me. I thought she'd just wanted to send me here to get me out of town.

Mrs. Greenwood nodded. "Just yesterday, I asked her, and she said she had had the same dream. She just hadn't told me about it because she thought I'd freak out."

"Good call," I said.

"And then, when you came, you saw Danielle yourself."

"Twice," I said.

"Twice?"

Oops. I hadn't told her about the second time. "So you think she, what, facilitated my communication with Rachel? Like a ghost or something?"

"A ghost or maybe a vision. I think she loved Rachel and wanted to help her, somehow."

At this point, it wouldn't be the weirdest thing that had happened. Not by a long shot. I said, "Do you think she'll be coming back again?"

Mrs. Greenwood shook her head. "I don't think so." And then, she un-paused the television, the announcer's voice, blasting: *These are the voyages of the Starship Enterprise.*

The rest of the week, the town saw more action than it had probably seen in twenty years, as the police solved numerous missing persons cases, including finding Bryce Rosen, the guy on the Missing Person flier outside Hemingway's. Dateline NBC was there and every news station in the country. Parents flocked to pick up their children, all believed dead, some for as long as thirty years. The Fox brothers had held them all this time, and now they were released, some to loving families, others to rehab centers.

And Mrs. Greenwood was right. The only one who wasn't found was Danielle.

"Suzie told the truth," Mrs. Greenwood said. "She really is gone. I never fully believed she was. I guess that's why I never cleaned out her things. I should do it now."

Rachel had been staying in Danielle's room since she came home. We looked at each other and said, "We'll do it," because we knew it would be too painful for her.

"Thank you."

One thing that hadn't changed about Rachel was her hair. It was still short, and it wasn't growing. Or, I guess, it was growing at a normal rate, not a crazy one. Her magical tears too were gone now that they had served their purpose. And if I wanted to talk to her, I had to go find her.

Which wasn't that hard, since we were both living at Mrs. Greenwood's house for now. We had both started classes at the local school, not online, so we had to wait until Saturday to clean out the room. That morning, we put Danielle's things in bags, some for the garbage, some for charity, some for Hemingway's junk shelves, "Because, really," I said, "you never know when someone might want a pair of shoe skates—some people might think in-line skates are dumb." And some things, like old yearbooks and photographs, Rachel kept for herself.

Rachel took out one of the desk drawers so she could go through it. When she tried to put it back, it wouldn't go in. "Check underneath," I said. "Sometimes, something gets stuck in the tracks." I had to tell her things like this all the time, because she'd never done normal stuff like other people did. Even the dishwasher fascinated her completely, and she kept putting dishes in so she could run it and see them come out clean.

Rachel held the drawer up and looked under it. She drew out a blue envelope.

She looked at it, then gasped.

In what I recognized as Danielle's handwriting, the letter was addressed to Rachel.

> Dear Rachel,
> I am writing this to you because I know you will be born, and I know you'll be a girl. I'm going to tell whoever takes you to name you Rachel because that's my favorite name.
> I hope that you've grown to be a beautiful

young woman when you read this. I know that I probably won't be around, and that makes me sad, but it also makes me happy that I could have you. We all have our destinies. Mine was to be your mother, and I hope that was enough. Yours is to be someone special, heroic, and I hope that, since I am your mother, that makes me a heroine as well.

About your father. I met him when I was a teenager. We fell in love, and then, he left me. But he sent me a letter not long after. He told me that you would be an incredible person. You would have healing powers and strength, and you will change everything for many people. I hope you will have enough strength for what you need to do. And I hope you will have help.

I loved your father very much. I hope that you will meet someone, someone like him, who will show you all the beauty of the wonderful world.

Your father also told me to be careful. I am trying, but I don't know if it will be enough. If it isn't, I want you to know I love you, my baby.

Your mother,
Danielle

"And did I?" I said after we had both finished reading it.

"Did you what?"

"Show you the wonderful world?"

"You did. You showed me everything, everything I've ever seen. You saved my life."

I kissed her. "And you saved mine right back. Several times now."

She looked around the room with its boxes and bags everywhere. Her eyes fell upon the window. "Oh, look, it's snowing," Rachel said.

"Then I guess there's only one thing for us to do," I said. "Make an angel!"

Author's Note

Rapunzel was one of my favorite fairy tales when I was a child (long before it was a Disney movie—people, Disney did not write these stories!), to a degree that I once tried to write a musical version of it in high school. As soon as I finished writing *Beastly*, I started on a version of *Rapunzel.* I thought that, as here, rapunzel would have to be a drug. Why else would a mother give her baby away for it?

However, it was difficult to write a book in which the heroine is trapped in a tower; more difficult still if I tried to let her out. I ended up putting it down.

Then, one day, my husband was watching the History channel, and instead of wars, they started talking about Greek mythology, specifically, the story of Danaë, mother of Perseus. Like Rapunzel, Danaë was kept in a tower. But there, it was because of a prophecy that she would bear a son who would kill her father. She had to be stopped from bearing that fateful child. However, as anyone who has read mythology knows, you can't stop a prophecy, so Zeus came to her in a shower of gold and impregnated her. (My husband says that ancient Greek girls who got pregnant must have told their parents, "Really, Dad, it wasn't Konstantine! Zeus came to me in a shower of gold!") I had read this story in high school, but now, it seemed like the History channel was talking to me. Several months later, I was driving to New York City with my kids to see the musical *Shrek* (another princess in a tower story), and my daughter, Katherine, was reading her required summer reading book aloud. It was Edith Hamilton's mythology, and it was the story of Perseus and Danaë. I knew I was meant to write this book. This does show how long these stories have been with us—Danaë was likely the original Rapunzel. Or, perhaps, there was a Rapunzel even before that.

For more information on fairy tales, visit www.surlalunefairy tales.com. It has all the classic stories and even merchandise.

Acknowledgments

Thanks to my editor, Antonia Markiet, also, Rachel Abrams, Phoebe Yeh, and my agent, George Nicholson.

Thanks to Debbie Fischer and Joyce Sweeney, for reading an earlier version of this and telling me it wasn't that bad (even though it was).

Special thanks to Heather Rivera, for allowing me to do belay training with the moms in her Girl Scout troop and writer, Elisa Carbone, for giving me rock climbing advice, so that snobby rock climbers like her (her words) wouldn't talk trash about my book.

READ ALL OF ALEX FLINN'S TEEN NOVELS!

THE MODERN FAIRY TALE RETELLINGS

TACKLING TOUGH ISSUES